ELLE HARTFORD

A Thousand and One Alibis

The Alchemical Tales #7

Contents

Welcome

Long, long ago, a coven of witches created a world just
beyond ours—a realm of fairy tales.
In Beyond, humans rub shoulders with mythical creatures,
and magic mixes with science.

There are only three rules:

Happily

accept that we share the same home

Ever

remember that what you take, you must also give

After

struggle will always lead to new beginnings

So, if you are ready . . . you are welcome here.

* * *

The Blue Desert Isles
Rebirth
Oasis
to continent
Baby Island
Kairoi
to New West Key
Island of Kairoi
estuary
Wellspring
Palace Jasmin
Shifting Sands
marina
Bessie's road
N

Cast of Characters

Top thirteen, in alphabetical order

Aly: pragmatic, avid walker; mother to Red and partner to Zady

Babagha', Lieutenant: assistant to Officer Ja'far, freshly returned to Wellspring; nickname Babs

Dean: new secretary at the Palace Jasmin; from Argen

Gene: apothecary in Wellspring with a rather short temper

Ja'far, Officer: new officer taking up post at Wellspring; nickname Jaja

Jasmin: fairy blood; mysterious owner of Palace Jasmin

Luca: bookseller and scholar, complicated past; dating Red

Morgiana: Jasmin's assistant, known to be strict

Nouronnihar: newcomer to the island; secretary at Palace Jasmin; from New West Key

Red: alchemist and child of Seers, full name Cinnabar Sunset; dating Luca

Sinbad: experienced sailor and eager storyteller; leader of a small crew staying in Wellspring

William: canine familiar, capable of protection magic and plenty of sass

Zady: letter writer, dreamer; mother to Red and partner to Aly

1

Signed, Sealed, Delivered

Dearest Cinnabar,

Everyone's so looking forward to your visit. We could use some practical alchemy around here. Turns out the island is awash with strange visitors—not that you are strange, of course, daughter, but a handful of strangers washed up on the western beach just yesterday. I'm sure you'll meet them; you're bound to get here before they're in any condition to leave. As it is, none of them seem able to talk sense yet. They've been sharing the most extraordinary stories of shipwrecks and sabotage—quite outlandish, that's what we thought, frankly. Too much seawater is never good for the imagination. Time will tell the truth.

And in any case, there's no need for that to color your trip. We have so many things to show you; too many for a mere seven days, I fear. But we'll make the best of it. You'll probably say it all looks exactly as it did when you

> *left twelve years ago!*
>
> *Now, because I know this will reach you just before you set off, let me just add . . .*

"I hate it when she does that," I sighed, as I skimmed through the rest of the letter.

"Does what?" My long-suffering boyfriend, Luca, poked his head around a precarious pile of books. In the cozy gloom of his bookstore, his green eyes shone bright.

"Pulls the divination thing on me," I said. I passed the letter to him, pointing out the sentence halfway down the page.

Luca cocked his head as he read it. I watched him in the silence. The sight of him was reassuring—the black scholars' robes he always wore, the hood thrown back to reveal dark skin and deep green tattoos disappearing under close-cropped black hair. I even loved the ghostly, twisted horn that rose from the crown of his head—a mark of an old curse, usually hidden under his hood by magic. It made him look like he'd be more at home deep in the shadowy forest rather than in his quaint bookstore, but Luca could never be considered out of place. Through mystery and life and business, he was a pillar of positive thinking.

And even though a trip home is often considered a positive thing, I needed Luca's cheer more than ever. I pulled my knees up to my chin and waited for his thoughts.

"I don't know, Red," he said, when at last he looked up. "Maybe she was just guessing what time the letter would get to you because she deals with the postal service a lot. You *do* send lots of things back and forth, and the post offices are getting better and better about predicting when things arrive."

I stuck my tongue out at him and snatched the letter back. "Who gave you permission to be so rational? I thought you were supposed to be on my side."

"Usually your side *is* the rational one," Luca replied, his wide grin warming my heart. "Are you sure this isn't just pre-trip jitters?"

"No, I'm not sure," I grumbled back. "Have you picked out which books you want to bring yet? Because if you haven't, and we miss the boat, that's probably fine . . ."

"It's not fine," Luca told me firmly. "We're going. I'm excited. I think you will be too, once we're on the road." He disappeared behind the stacks of books again, sorting and mumbling as he read the titles to himself. In the midst of this, he added offhandedly, "Did you read the rest of the letter yet? I think you'll want to see what she goes on to say. It sounds like they might need—"

Luca was cut off, unfortunately, by the chime of the bells on his shop's front door. Before the bells had finished ringing, the interloper—William, of course—was already talking.

"Just finished up with Thorn," he announced, trotting over to where we sat beside the sales counter. William, a magical creature who looked like a big black dog, was brisk and matter-of-fact. "She's going to keep an eye on Rhys and the shop for you. Because we all know how you worry, Red."

Technically I had only asked William to *remind Officer Thorn that we're going out of town for a short trip,* but I should have known that would become a gossip-about-Red session. William and our local police officer were alike enough that they often butted heads, but just as often ganged up on me.

Before I could speak up in my defense, William plopped down beside me and rattled on. "Actually, she said she'd look after the shop starting *now*, this evening. I tried telling her we don't leave until tomorrow morning, but she said she'd swing by anyway. I said she's only doing that because then she has an excuse to head in the direction of Magica's, and she said she doesn't need an excuse to do that."

"Maybe she's just feeling left out," Luca suggested, smiling. "Seeing as she has to stay behind in Belville this time."

"Too bad. Unlike the rest of us, she's *assigned* to Belville," William sniffed. "She can't just go gallivanting across Beyond. Especially when it's not to investigate a crime."

"About that—" Luca began.

But I was already talking; something William had said bothered me. "Is it not enough that Rhys will be running the shop while I'm gone? He always does just fine. Why does she feel the need to be swinging by?"

Rhys was my assistant at the shop—technically, William might count as an assistant too, but Rhys was actually interested in potions. He refused to make any without my supervision, but he knew enough to sell them and keep the books, and no doubt the store would be even cleaner when we came back than when we had left it. Plus, William adored Rhys; I found it odd that he wanted Thorn to double-check Rhys's work.

"Because if she feels like she's doing something *here*, she won't show up in Oasis," William informed me.

Luca and I exchanged a glance before breaking into laughter. Since William and I had settled in Belville, we hadn't managed to leave it without our friends tagging along in one way or another. When we'd gone to Seaside for a friend's wedding, Officer Thorn had been called there too, to solve an unusual crime. And more recently when Luca had gone to a conference in Brass, Thorn had managed to have us all brought in as consultants on a big-city murder.

"I doubt there'll be any need for her to visit the Blue Desert Islands," I said, relieved. "Luca, were you trying to say something earlier?"

"Um—I forgot, but it'll come to me." Luca was dabbing at his eye with his sleeve, still grinning at William's stubborn determination to have a vacation *without* Officer Thorn.

"Can it come to you over dinner?" William wagged his fluffy tail, ignoring our mirth. "If you take any longer, all the good seats at Lavender's will be gone."

"You mean the corner seats at the bar, from which you can spy on everyone else in town?" I winked at Luca, who was chuckling again. "I could eat, definitely. Did you finish with your books?"

"Done," Luca declared. This was slightly worrying, because both his piles of books were equally tall. Unless he had some kind of charmed luggage, he was going to be carrying around a lot of extra weight—and volume. *But,* I reminded myself, *that's his choice.* I'd only slipped one book and a journal into my own knapsack. I knew I'd be a little too nervous on the journey to read anyway.

"Then let's *go,*" William reminded us. Luca, seeing my glance at his books, was grinning at me, and I was staring back like a lovestruck ewe. Normally we managed not to be *too* cutesy, but that was mostly because William was there to bring us back to the real world.

William bounded out into the street, which was darkened in the twilight but alive with townsfolk walking to and fro in the summer heat. Some looked curiously at the bookstore, which had closed several hours ago. Before they could get any hopeful ideas, Luca pulled me out the front door and locked it.

As we stood on the front step, he handed something to me—the letter from my mother. He'd carefully refolded it. "Make sure you *do* read it," he told me kindly. "You'll be glad you did."

I sighed as we set out toward Lavender's Tavern. *You'll be glad you did* sounded more like a threat than a promise.

2

Under Way

Now, because I know this will reach you just before you set off, let me just add a warning. One of the changes around here might shock you. Do you recall the estuary preserve on the other side of the island? An heiress from the mainland bought it just six months ago. No one has met her yet, but she is making her presence felt! I need hardly tell you, her imperious ways have not made her popular in Wellspring. She outright banned the stranded sailors from her property, which has raised more than a few eyebrows, I'm sure you can imagine. And no one can quite figure out how she bought the preserve in the first place, since no one will admit to selling the land. Some believe she's committed some kind of fraud. With all your worldly experience with crime these days, don't be surprised if our neighbors ask your opinion—just mind you're careful what you say! She must have piles of money, and whenever such treasure is involved, even the smallest mistakes can lead to disaster.

But enough of my doom and gloom. Aly and I are so looking forward to your visit, dearest daughter. You need but say the word and we'll be at the marina to meet you—but, failing that, we'll be eagerly waiting at home!

Love,

Zady

I didn't really focus on the second half of my mother's letter until we were on the train, rattling toward the coast.

Our friends in Belville had ended up throwing us an impromptu farewell party at Lavender's the night before, and then—naturally—Officer Thorn had insisted on marching us down to the docks herself. (Fortunately, she'd also brought us breakfast pastries and liquid caffeine, so I could only roll my eyes and smile at her enthusiasm. I think William spent those ten minutes in terror that at the last second, she'd announce she was joining us!) From little alpine Belville, we took a ferry to Pine. Pine, right across the lake from our home town, was the Pastoria County seat and therefore "busy." It was still by no means a city, but it was a useful transportation hub. We'd had just enough time to run through town to the train station, where we managed to catch the brand new high-speed line to the eastern coast.

It may have been powered by magic and smooth as glass, but on the inside, the train felt old-timey and comfortable. Luca, William, and I had a compartment to ourselves. Luca sprawled across one padded bench with his chin in his hands and his nose pressed against the window. I leaned against the window opposite him, while William had opted to curl up on the burgundy carpet between us and go back to sleep. Our luggage was stowed safely on the racks above our heads, but I still had my knapsack at my side—and, therefore, the letter.

Luca must have felt my eyes on him when I finally lifted my head. He turned my way. "Did you just now read it?"

"I did *skim* it before," I protested vaguely. "But there were so many other things to think about, setting up the shop and cleaning the apartment and all. So . . . Yes, I just now read it."

After considering me for a moment solemnly, Luca swung his feet around and sat up, leaning back against the wood-paneled wall. "Want to talk about it?"

"No. Yes." I sighed over the word, smiling ruefully at him. We both knew I had trouble talking about my feelings, and he had been supportive as I tried to work on it. "I'm not sure what to think about it. All the 'doom and gloom' and heiresses and mysterious shipwrecked sailors. I never would've thought that estuary could be *bought.* But I also don't want to know about any of that. I don't want to get involved in local politics. This is just supposed to be about you meeting everyone, you know?"

"I know," Luca agreed, green eyes warm and understanding.

"I just—it's just a lot. And maybe it's nothing. Like I said, I don't know what to think," I admitted.

"Maybe it's not something you need to think about, Red," Luca suggested. "Sometimes we just *feel* things."

I let my eyes drift out the window, to the sunrise-kissed forests passing in a gilded green blur. There was not a cloud in the sky. Another gorgeous summer day. When I looked back at Luca with a sour face, he chuckled.

His amusement made me laugh, too, at my own stubbornness. "I get it. That's something Zady would say, by the way. You all are going to get along like a house on fire."

"Preferably with no arson involved," Luca quipped lightly. "You know I've been looking forward to this trip forever, Red."

"Yeah." Still, it made me blush. Luca told everyone that he'd liked me from the moment we met. It had taken me considerably longer to understand my own feelings for someone I thought of as a best friend.

It wasn't like I'd eschewed relationships and feelings when I'd taken up science and alchemy. I prided myself on *not* filling the stereotype of lofty, arrogant, lonely scholar. And yet . . . leaving home to become an apprentice, and then traveling for years as I honed my craft, *had* been lonely. I'd had William with me during my traveling years, of course, but he could be just as reserved as I often was. Luca's unprepossessing charm and kindness had been a blessing to us both.

Ironic, perhaps, since Luca himself had lived most of his life under a curse. But I didn't think of him as cursed at all. In fact, I felt the opposite as I said impulsively, "Luca, you don't—you don't think there's something *wrong* with me? With me being away for twelve years, I mean?"

On the floor between us, William stirred. "You mean with you studying a craft, working nonstop for nearly a decade to build up savings and a reputation, and then pouring your energy into achieving your dream of setting up a shop?" He rumbled.

Luca leaned forward over his knees. "What he said. You've been busy. And also—"

"If anything's wrong with you, it's that you never take *any* breaks. Let alone a week to cross the continent and an ocean," William added.

"I thought you were sleeping," I told him, sticking out my tongue even as I grinned. "Clearly *you* still manage to take breaks."

"Someone here has to," he grumbled.

"And also," Luca repeated firmly, amusement clear on his face, "there's nothing wrong with you, Red. You just are who you are, and we love you for it. And we all know what it's like to have a complicated past. William and I especially."

Over the past winter, we'd had a dramatic run-in with someone from William's past. Reminded of it, I bent down to ruffle his fluffy ears. He endured the affection, proving that he also felt the emotion in Luca's sentiment.

"There's nothing wrong with them," I said, meaning my family. "It's just . . . a legacy that I've never been a part of. The Seer thing, it's a big deal. And I could never do it."

"But you *can* see things others don't," Luca said very softly.

I met his gaze gratefully, and with another blush. "The odd ghost-like creature or creative solution, I will grant you. But that hardly counts as divination, and you know it."

"There's a lot of kinds of divination," William pointed out. He seemed focused on a spot on the floor.

Luca lit with a scholarly interest. "I'm familiar with the idea from books, of course. Seeing into the future—there are a lot of ways people have tried to do that, historically speaking. I've never wanted to press you on it," he added, "but seeing as we're on the subject, would you mind explaining exactly what your family does, Red?"

He'd never pressed me on it because he was literally the sweetest person I knew. The truth was, I wore all my secrets on my sleeve, and I saw now how frustratingly tempting that might be for those closest to me. Underneath my alchemical goggles and lab coats, I had the bronze skin and straight black hair of the Blue Desert Islands—hair interspersed with iridescent strands, mind you, which I avoided ever mentioning, thereby forcing my friends to do the same. They'd also tactfully avoided ever pressing the fact that, despite my claim to having no magic, I was incredibly fleet-footed. All to do with my heritage . . .

Now it was my turn to lean back and be thoughtful. "You're right, now is definitely the time. I don't want you to be caught off guard, either of you. It's just been a long time since I tried to explain it.

"It helps if you know about the islands, too," I decided. "There's a group of them, the Blue Desert Islands—obviously, that much you knew, since we're headed there. But, what I mean is, they're culturally linked, not just geographically. So, everyone who lives there is probably a Seer in one way or another—or at least, that's how it used to be, before Oasis became a popular tourist destination.

"In any case," I went on, doubling down on my effort to be concise, "on each island, there's a clan of families, and they all will practice one type of divination. So on Oasis, the big one, the clan calls itself 'Tamers of the Dragon'—"

William snuffled. I poked him with my foot, grinning. "Get used to it. They're *all* into the esoteric language and metaphors."

"Glad to know it isn't just alchemy that made you that way," Luca said cheerfully.

"*Anyway*," I said, not deigning to respond, "the Dragon folks, their big thing is fate—like telling people 'oh no, you're going to kill your father and marry your mother,' that kind of thing. Mostly they do palm reading and talk about lengths and endings of lives."

"And people go there specifically to have their fate told to them," Luca said, not quite asking—because it was common enough knowledge—but still looking for confirmation.

"Yeah, they've made a whole industry around it, more than any of the other clans have. If you remember Clare, from a few summers ago, she was from the Followers of the Sphinx, which tends to be more watching pendulums or going into trances and delivering these huge, vague prophecies. 'Cycles' and rise and fall of empires, that kind of thing. They're on one of the smaller islands. My family, and basically everyone on Kairoi, they're called the Spring of the Unicorn. It's hard to explain, but basically, they're about . . . just *wisdom*, is how they would put it. They do a lot of meditating and fire gazing and gossiping amongst themselves about how they think certain 'signs' or portents are going to play out."

"Fascinating," said Luca, unnecessarily. His whole attitude conveyed scholarly excitement over learning something new.

"And yet Red here barely has a sense of direction," William commented.

"Wow, thanks," I retorted, nudging him with my boot again.

"I'm just saying. You could hardly even cross Market Square blindfolded—"

"And that's why we have you, right?" Luca beamed down at William, who grumbled a little but seemed pleased. He *was* our resident magic expert, as he often liked to remind us. Luca looked up at me and added, "Did you know from a young age that you weren't having the same experience everyone else did? Is it an innate power, like a sixth sense, or is it more of a skill that gets honed? How would your family feel about divination aids, like tarot or runes? Did you ever try using those?"

"*Wow,*" I repeated, laughing. "Hold up. I had no idea you were so interested. Uh, let's see, *yes,* I always knew there was something everyone else knew that I just didn't get. But I really wanted to."

"That's why you went into alchemy instead," Luca smiled. "Solving scientific mysteries instead of spiritual ones."

I smiled back. "Something like that, definitely. As for it being inherited or being a skill, I think it's kind of both. Although, I'm not sure even people within my clan could say for sure. Everyone has their own approach. And I did try reading some tarot cards back when I was an apprentice in Brass, but I hadn't seen them up to that point. And as far as I was concerned, they were just pretty cards with interesting alchemical symbols on them."

"Maybe things like that just aren't needed on the islands," Luca mused. "It *is* really interesting, Red. I get that you've always been worried about people assuming you can 'tell their future' because of where you come from, or something like that. But the truth is more interesting than what people might assume."

Nail hit on head, I thought, glancing thoughtfully down at William. Somehow, despite hiding a part of me for years, I'd still ended up with friends who knew me so well.

William panted back up at us. "If you two are going to insist on talking for this entire train ride, then one of you better go buy me second breakfast."

Luca and I exchanged a glance and then burst out laughing. Luca was already on his feet, heading for the dining car. It looked like William's challenge had been accepted.

* * *

"The entire train ride" was only five hours—such was the miracle of transportation magic. Not even magic could change the fact that we lost daylight as we traveled east, though, nor make the journey any less tiring. We arrived at a bustling port city and just had time to snag a snack from a street vendor before shuffling aboard the large catamaran that would take us to Kairoi. The boat was easily as large as Lavender's Tavern back home, and we found ourselves awash with tourists: people of all shapes and sizes, dressed in their floral, beachy best, no doubt headed for Oasis. The catamaran route would drop them off first before heading to the smaller islands, so I knew we had a little time to settle in.

"Come on," I told my companions, taking hold of Luca's hand and nudging William with my leg. "Let's get off the main deck and find a bathroom."

"There's one up by the bow if you want to go so bad," William replied, rather loudly. A family of elves eyed us with interest.

"*Everyone* will be using that one," I said. Since the catamaran was boarded by a long gangplank that deposited all passengers on the main deck, it was the busiest place on the ship. "I need somewhere where I can take some time."

"Ew," said William.

I nudged him again, and tugged Luca away from his conversation with a nearby scholar on vacation. "I *meant* so that I could change. You might want to, too," I added to my boyfriend.

William focused on him, too. "Did you bring anything aside from scholar robes? Are you allowed to be seen in anything else?"

"We are," Luca said modestly. "When we're off-duty."

"You'd better be," I added. "And if you don't have anything, then we're buying you clothes at the nearest gift shop. I didn't bring you all this way so that you could get heatstroke from wearing all black in a tropical climate."

Both William and I shifted to consider Luca's duffel bag as it was buffeted by the crowd around us. No doubt we were wondering the same thing: *did he really only bring books?*

"Stop worrying," Luca told us, grinning. "I brought other clothes. And I also brought some spending money for gift shop clothes, too, just in case."

I shook my head at my alpine forest-dwelling partner. He was already sweating. He'd probably never owned a pair of shorts or even lightweight trousers in his life.

After a little navigation, we found a bathroom perfectly suited to our purposes. William was stuck as he was, of course, being simply a big furry dog. But he insisted that he didn't notice the heat, on account of "magic." I left him to guard our bags and very happily changed.

It had been a lifetime since I'd been on this coast, on a catamaran, or been trading my tights and tunics for airy, brightly patterned linen skirts. I was surprised at how easily it all came back to me. But when I rejoined my friends in the hall, they didn't seem as invigorated as I was.

Luca tilted his head to the side. William cleared his throat. "Are you sure you aren't an impostor? Red *never* wears dresses."

"She did for the ball," Luca reminded him. "And for Ostara one year. It was very pretty. You look very pretty now, too," he hastened to add.

I rolled my eyes at both of them. "Forget how it looks. The

important thing is, the large majority of me is not going to get sunburned. Plus, it has pockets." I demonstrated, sticking my hands into the yellow camellia-covered maxi dress and holding the seams out so that the hem drifted over my sandals. "Anyway," I added, demonstration over, "are we just going to let Luca get away with his new look?"

William looked up at him, then looked away with a whine. "There's nothing to say."

"I thought the effect was very dashing," Luca said, holding up his arms to investigate himself. His loose white collared shirt and billowy sleeves certainly didn't hamper his movement, though his brown trousers were quite slim down to the ankle, where they disappeared into his boots.

"You look like a pirate," I informed him.

"I didn't have any good sandals," he lamented.

William sneezed. "It's not the footwear that's the problem."

"We'll work on it," I assured Luca, linking arms with his. "Let's go back up on deck and catch some of the breeze."

"Do you like my hat?" he asked as we walked along. I considered it sideways; it wasn't all bad. Wide brim, light straw, it at least had trim edges. So he wasn't a rough-and-ragged shipwrecked pirate, just a fashionable one. As I looked it over, he said proudly, "Trent did a glamour spell on it for me, just like my hoods back home, so that it hides the curse."

"It looks good, but you didn't need to do that," I said. "Most people we meet will probably be able to sense the curse's effect on you, if I'm honest."

"I figured. But it's nice to look like just me," Luca replied.

I wasn't sure what to say about that. Sometimes I worried that Luca was ashamed of his appearance. In all other ways he had accepted his life's changes in stride, as far as I could tell. But that horn—it *did* look a bit deathly. The old curse on him had had a lot to do with "dark" unicorns, protectors of decay and shadow deep in the forest. It was the sort of thing that had been very taboo in his culture, but didn't seem so far-fetched in mine . . . as he was about to realize, for perhaps the first time.

I saw that first hint of realization dawn in his eyes when the catamaran finally slowed to dock at Kairoi. Though the island was far less developed than the popular Oasis, it still had an elaborately carved wooden gateway at the dock, welcoming visitors and family back home. And in that looming wood arch, the unicorn was a common motif.

I breathed the sea air deep as I looked up at those mythical creatures and wondered just what exactly was in store.

3

Voyagers Arrived

The catamaran deposited us at the dock and left us to fend for ourselves. Around us, the small marina was quiet: all the fishing boats were tied up for the evening, their owners swallowed up by the island itself. It rose up from the ocean abruptly, a long-dead volcano creating a deep purple backdrop. A small town of convenience had sprung up among the scrubby trees around the marina, but the bulk of the island sheltered behind the old volcano: stretches of desert running down to the waves, called the Shifting Sands.

William shook himself and glowed faintly blue in the twilight as we passed under the archway onto solid land. "Some pretty serious protection spells there," he observed, low enough that the few remaining passengers nearby couldn't hear.

"Really? I remember them only having really basic protections when I left," I said, glancing up at the arch again. It told me nothing, of course. Unlike William, I couldn't sense magic—in fact, I hadn't even felt a thing as we walked through the protective spells that would supposedly prevent anyone with ill intent from entering.

"Things may have changed in the past twelve years," Luca pointed out. When I made a face at him for reminding me how long I'd been gone, he added, "I don't mean anything by it, Red, it's just how things are. Things *do* change."

"I wonder how recently," I said, thinking of the purchase of the estuary. Was some rich recluse aiming to take over the island?

"Less wondering and more leading," William interjected. "Unless you plan for us to sleep out on the beach tonight?"

Luca shuddered. The beach on the marina side of the island was pitifully narrow and a bit rocky. It was good for the boats, because the water became deep quickly, but it was not the sun-and-sand idyll that most pictured when they thought of the Blue Desert Islands.

"Fear not," I teased, nudging Luca's shoulder. "Come on. There's a routine bus service that runs around the island. The stand is just ahead."

I'd forgotten how long and light the evenings were on Kairoi. We could pick our way through the soft shadows easily, walking over the planks of the dock to a gravel road. A breeze had picked up, and Luca sighed in relief beside me. Even I had to admit it felt good after the bright sun.

The bus stand was a little thatch-roofed structure huddled up against a dark rocky cliff. We crossed the road to get to it and found ourselves in good company. Two police officers in their tan tropical uniforms sat on the lone bench.

Maybe my exposure to Officer Thorn had made me a bit soft on police officers. I nodded at them warmly and asked, "Any idea when the next bus will be?"

There was a brief shuffle as they each looked at the other.

One was tall and thin, the other short and muscular, but both appeared brown-skinned and mostly human—just like me. It was impossible to grow up on Kairoi and not be a *little* touched by all the magic and divination in the blood, hence the "mostly."

Between the police officers, an unspoken power dynamic was playing out. Judging by the patches on their shirtsleeves, the taller one was the actual officer, and the shorter one was perhaps a trainee or assistant. That clearly didn't mean that they followed every order, though. Much as the taller one glowered, the shorter one did not volunteer to speak. Apparently, dealing with public inquiries was the leader's burden.

"It should already be here," the tall officer said at last, his voice tight and unpleasant. He tugged his guild-issue brimmed hat up, revealing a smooth bald head.

"What a day," Luca exclaimed, impervious to the officers' discomfort. He dropped down onto the bench beside them and beamed. "How far did you both come? We've been all the way from Belville, way up in Pastoria, today. You wouldn't believe how fast the new train goes!"

"We arrived at the catamaran by airship," the tall officer said stiffly, as though train travel was for criminals.

"We just graduated our training program at the main Guild office," said the shorter one, peering around his leader to look at Luca. The tall one jabbed him with his elbow, perhaps displeased at this admission.

"Oh, congratulations!" Luca, too, leaned forward to focus on the slightly friendlier face. "Are you here for vacation? Or is this your new post?"

"New post," said the assistant. Now that the ice had been

broken, he seemed to be the more talkative of the two. "It's been the plan all along. We grew up here and—"

His words were drowned out by the crunch of gravel as the bus approached.

The officers stood, and William and I shifted in anticipation of where the bus's door would be. But at the last moment, mayhem intervened.

What had been a low hum of brakes and gravel became a screech that pierced the evening calm. The front of the bus wavered for a moment in sudden shadow. And then Luca, who had just been rising to his feet, fell back against the bench with a stranger in his lap.

"*Luca!*" It wasn't me, but William who barked. The glow at the edges of his fur flared in a bright blue warning.

"I'm fine! I'm fine!" But Luca's voice was muffled and breathless.

The police officers and I exchanged looks, our mouths hanging open. The bus had stopped a yard away, and somehow seemed reproachful.

"What just happened?" I asked anyone who might know.

"*Dreadfully* sorry." The shadowy stranger finally disentangled from Luca and stood. "I thought I might miss the bus!"

William was still shining fiercely, and his growl was not pleasant. "So you decided to run over and get hit by it instead?"

"No one got hurt," the tall police officer said, stepping in at last.

Luca accepted my hand up and smiled at me. "Not hurt," he confirmed. To the newcomer, he added, "You sure gave me a scare, though."

"Yes, well, sorry about that, and all. I couldn't see you," our unfortunate intruder said.

I distinctly heard the shorter officer whisper to the other, "I'm colorblind and *I* see him just fine," and I had to admit, I agreed. Luca in his white vacation shirt was nowhere near as incognito as Luca in his black scholar's uniform had been. I frowned at the stranger.

In the glare of the bus's headlights, it *was* difficult to see details. But as the dust settled and I focused, I got a clearer picture of the stranger. He was a young man, his button-down shirt open at the collar and a dressy jacket flung over one shoulder, its lapels crushed in one hand as he held it in place. He wasn't dressed as a tourist, certainly, but his short black hair went every which way atop his head, so he didn't look professional, either. In his other hand he held a briefcase that was so full that its profile was trapezoidal instead of square.

"Right, so, are we boarding now or what?" he asked. His voice was a little high and self-conscious. His nose was crooked, like it had been broken—perhaps more than once.

"One moment," the tall officer said, his angular face not friendly in the least. "Your name, please?"

"I say, you aren't going to write me up or something, are you?" the young man shifted anxiously over the gravel. "It's Dean. Unless you need my full name? I'm going up to the Palace. I've just been hired on for a job there."

William snorted audibly. I leaned my knee into him.

"That's enough for now," said the officer, as his assistant wrote everything down.

Enough for the police, perhaps, but it certainly left *me* wondering. *Is he going to get written up? He didn't actually do anything illegal,* I thought. *Maybe reckless, though. But do these officers even have jurisdiction yet? They sure are starting early, aren't they?*

Also—"palace"?

Dean wavered, too, perhaps as uncertain as I was. But in another moment, the hesitation broke and we all streamed toward the bus.

It was probably the exact same bus that had run round the island when I was born. In its previous life, it had most likely been a trolley or train car in some big city: its faded panel sides and hard bench seats spoke of mass transportation. But it had been retrofitted with wide rubber wheels to navigate the sandy island roads, and the pockmarked glass of its front windshield had been melted down and replaced many times over the years. For all the storms it had likely weathered, it still looked exactly as it always had. I was certain that in the daylight, I'd see it was still painted the same neon orange and white.

The bus itself was affectionately known as "Bessie" on the island. Thanks to an old spell from some visiting, grateful sorcerer, Bessie could drive herself—as long as she only ran on the one road that circled the island. She'd never needed to do anything more. She did, however, carry an attendant— a small gnome in sun-bleached overalls who nodded at us individually as we boarded. The gnome introduced herself as Suzy and informed us that if we made any more trouble, she'd throw us out the window in the middle of the route.

And then, most strangely—to me, at least—the bus lurched back into action, heading west.

"Suzy," I called, poking my head into the aisle, "did the route change?"

"Yep," came the answer from the conductor's seat. She didn't even turn around. "Six months ago."

Luca rustled in his seat beside me. I turned back to him

with a wrinkled nose. "I love you, but if you make another comment about things changing over time—"

"I wasn't going to," he interrupted, with a playful smile that added, *but if I did say that, I'd be right.* "I was going to ask if you're worried. Will the new route still take us to Wellspring?"

"I'm positive it will," I assured him. "It's literally the only town on the island. I just thought the route was weird because Wellspring is only about fifteen minutes away if we go east. But by going west, we have to go around the whole estuary and desert first, which I think will take us an hour."

At this point, Dean poked his head over our seat. "Six months ago's when Jasmin founded her settlement here and built the Palace," he said helpfully. "Are you saying my stop's first? Brilliant. I'm late as it is. I really don't have an hour to wait."

Something about this young man made me want to hit my head on the seat in front of me. *Maybe it's just because it's been a long day, like Luca said,* I reminded myself. I skipped over comments I *wanted* to make, things like *I wasn't talking to you* and *what a surprise to hear that you're running late.* But I couldn't resist pointing out, "This island has been settled for generations."

"But not by Jasmin," Dean replied. His dark eyes shone. Clearly, this mattered a whole lot more to him than it did to me.

Luca saved me with his usual tact and curiosity. "Is Jasmin the one who bought the estuary?" he asked Dean.

"I think it was just a bunch of wilderness before," Dean said dismissively. "But what Jasmin's managed to accomplish already is a miracle. At least, that's what I've heard. I haven't been there yet, myself."

"And what," asked William, who was sprawled across a full bench on the other side of the aisle, "are *you* going to do, when you go there?"

"I'm her new secretary," Dean said with pride.

I could practically hear the wheels turning in Luca's head. "She needs a new one after being here six months?" he asked, concern in his voice.

"Actually I think I'm the third," said Dean, totally unconcerned. "None of the others could cut it. Maybe the heat did them in, ha ha! But I'm going to be better. Third time's the charm, and all that, you know."

"Off to a great start so far," William rumbled.

Fortunately, Dean didn't seem to catch the sarcasm.

Instead, he turned his attention back to me. "You said you used to live here a long time ago?"

I wondered desperately when the police officers would consider themselves invited into the conversation. They were sitting up front, oblivious, but I was dying for a distraction. "It's been a little while," I admitted through gritted teeth. "I've never heard of Jasmin."

"Oh, she's wonderful," Dean said reverently. I gave myself a mental pat on the back: at least Dean was distracted! He continued rapturously, "They say she might be part angel, you know. I've never met one myself. I've never met *her* either, not in person, not yet. Her previous secretary did all my interviews via magic mirrors. She has *all* the latest magitech and most complex spells at her Palace. She even has—"

The bus screeched to halt again, a strangely familiar moment even though we were now inside instead of out on the road. Dean stopped talking abruptly as his head whipped forward and back.

The tall police officer rose. "What's happened now?"

Suzy, too, was standing on her seat to peer out the windshield. "Somebody in the road," she informed us.

"The bus actually hit someone this time?" Dean asked, as though this was a homicidal vehicle from which he had been saved by divine intervention.

"Bessie never hit nobody," Suzy said with vim. "This's someone already *in* the road. And they ain't moving."

My stomach plummeted.

Maybe I shouldn't have said to myself that I was dying *for distraction . . .*

4

Wellspring

Of course, for as much as I knew at that moment, the body could have been entirely alive. It could have even been a puppet or a prop, for all I knew. And yet . . .

When you've been roped into enough police investigations, you do start to get a little pessimistic at times.

Behind us, Dean fainted. His body hit the bench like a sack of pretentious potatoes.

"Oh, what is it *now*?" Suzy demanded, turning on her chair.

The two officers turned, too. Both shouted orders, but it was no use. William was glowing, yelling about incompetence, and Luca was halfway over the back of our seat, calling back to me for assistance, and I was venting my frustration at the officers themselves. For several moments, no one was heard.

"Enough!" Suzy finally bellowed.

In the abrupt silence, the tall officer stepped into his role. "Babs, see to the young man. I will investigate the person in the road. The rest of you, remain here. You," he said, singling out Suzy, "see that they stay put!"

The little gnome turned to us with her arms crossed.

William and I plopped ourselves down onto our seats again. Luca was still struggling to right Dean. As the tall officer disappeared down the steps and out the bus door, the short one—Babs, apparently—came down the aisle toward us.

He'd removed his hat, revealing a round face and straight black hair in a bowl cut that tended to fall over one eye. Underneath his other eye, I caught sight of a long scar. It seemed out of place: Babs' general air was one of geniality, like he was more inclined to gossip than to fight. He took a seat beside the unfortunate secretary and spent a few moments getting Dean into position before administering a small bottle of something pungent—old-fashioned smelling salts, unless my alchemist's nose deceived me. While Dean coughed and flopped around, regaining consciousness, Babs grinned at us, his audience.

"They teach us all about it at the Guild," he said. I'd heard much about the Police Guild from Officer Thorn back home, all of it glowing. I was not surprised they offered a class on how to deal with victims of fainting.

"Do you need us to do anything?" Luca asked.

"Nah, we'll just let him settle in for a moment," Babs said, glancing at Dean. Dean said nothing, but he looked a bit like he *had* at last been hit by a bus. I had to wonder what was in those salts.

"Your name is Babs?" William said pointedly in the meantime.

"Yeah. Lieutenant Babagha', Babs for short. I'll need all your names, probably, for the report," he affirmed, taking out his notebook once more. "Dean's I have . . . but the rest of you?"

Lieutenant was a title I hadn't heard in a while. Usually it was an assistant position reserved for larger police stations, where many officers were working. The lieutenant would act as the chief's second-in-command. I was a little surprised that the Police Guild had decided to send a chief *and* a lieutenant to what was essentially an island backwater, but it did explain the officers' relationship.

"That's William, an arcane familiar," I said, since my companions seemed to suddenly be shy. "And Luca, a scholar. They're both with me. You can call me Red, but if you need my full family name in order to find us again, it's Cinnabar Sunset. We'll be staying in Wellspring."

"I'm sure we'll be able to track you down," Babs said cheerfully as he made note. "Say, are you *the* Cinnabar?"

"Uh." I slid a reluctant glance at Luca, who was silently chuckling at me. "Maybe?"

"Left the island to be an alchemist," Babs told William, as though my friends wouldn't know my history. "It was legendary. No one had left in years. You're the reason Ja'ja and I decided to go to the Guild!" He added, beaming at me.

If only Officer Thorn could hear that, I thought. It made me grin. "Really? I'm not sure I remember you, I'm sorry."

"We were only little when you left," Babs explained. Luca was now fully laughing at me and my chagrin.

"That's great," I said weakly, trying not to think about the fact that both officers must have gone through at least ten years of Guild training. They'd seemed too old to have started training *after* I began my apprenticeship. Now I was the one who felt old.

Fortunately, William broke in. "What's the other one of you called? Ja-ja?"

"That's just what *I* call him," Babs said, still brimming over with satisfaction. "He'll hate that I told you. His actual name is Ja'far."

The name rung a bell, but I didn't have time to remember why. Just then, Officer Ja'far himself appeared back on the bus.

But this time, he was nowhere near as composed as he'd been when he'd walked away moments ago. He'd lost his hat and he was breathing hard.

"The body," he panted. "Whatever it was. It's gone!"

* * *

There *had* been a body in the road . . . But that was the only thing we could be sure of.

All of us, even Dean, poured off the bus and paced around in the darkness, as though we could prove Officer Ja'far wrong. As we bumbled around on the road in Bessie's headlights, we went over it again and again.

Bessie never stops for nothing, Suzy said on repeat.

Someone has been here, William insisted at every moment.

But nothing, none of the clues on the checklist, no footprints or drag marks, the two officers said in a round.

But we all saw it, was Luca's refrain. He was calm in his insistence that we should trust our senses. And since he probably had the best vision in the dark of all of us, I trusted him.

Acting on that trust, I bent down to examine the road itself. We may have been on vacation, but I still had at least *some* of my alchemical tools—not least my goggles. I tugged them down over my eyes and let the magicked lenses do their work.

With my goggles on, I could see through the shadows much

more easily. I could also magnify my vision and detect traces of light or substances that normally I wouldn't be able to see. As I scrutinized the gravel, a red stain caught my attention. It hadn't been visible before in the low light. But as soon as I noticed it, I saw that it spread under Bessie's front wheels.

* * *

"Bessie's *never* hit someone," said Zady.

"Besides," Aly said, "you all would have felt the jolt. Did you feel it?"

Arrayed on the plush cushions of my mothers' sitting room, we all agreed that we had not. William was polite; Luca was ecstatic. Seeing their reactions made me smile, no matter what the subject—or the context.

Truthfully, the mystery on the road had taken a back seat to my feelings about coming home. Those were complicated to say the least. But when the police officers had eventually deposited us on my mothers' front door step, it had felt totally natural to collapse onto the nearest comfy surface and start gossiping.

As a town, Wellspring was bigger than Belville, its homes sprawling among the sand dunes. My mothers' house was no exception: it stood two stories tall, blocky and white, just like the neighboring homes. Outside its thick walls, a dusty path wound its way to the town center, a ten minutes' walk away. The general feeling had always been one of timelessness and spaciousness—or perhaps that was my own nostalgia; so far, it seemed to hold true.

And neither of my mothers had changed a bit. They insisted we use their nicknames, as everyone else in Wellspring did.

Zady, letter writer extraordinaire, still wore her long black hair in many braids down to her waist, and still favored dreamy colors, as evidenced by her lavender tunic. Her dark eyes were serene, her face as open and unlined as ever. Aly had always been more proactive, with her golden eyes and dark hair cut to frame her sharp chin, and her insistence on wearing thick leather sandals and cuffed pants, like at any moment she might have to trek across the desert and anything too flowy would just weigh her down.

Both knew a good story when they caught wind of one.

"No doubt the police will tell us tomorrow it's something to do with Jasmin and her Palace," Aly said wryly.

"I had a feeling nothing good would come of that. You should have seen how the bonfire flickered when she arrived," Zady added, looking significantly at me.

"I *would* have been much more confused if you hadn't mentioned something in your letter," I admitted. I ignored the mention of "the bonfire," which was a large fire maintained in the center of town where everyone—aside from me—had always practiced their divination.

"I want to hear all about it," Luca added, "but I'm also so curious about Red. Did you know the new police officers knew her?"

"Of course, did you remember them, Cinnabar?" Aly looked amused. "They would have been, oh, maybe ten the last time you were here."

"Or eight," Zady chimed in. "Such nice boys. Poor Officer Brooks has been waiting for a replacement for such a long time."

"They'll have quite a case on their hands now," William observed, his tail wagging. "A disappearing body—like something out of an old ghost story."

"True, but when you look close, that kind of story always has a basis in something," I put in. "Even if it isn't actually ghosts."

Zady beamed benevolently at me. I'd been a little concerned that she might be upset that we hadn't arranged to meet them at the marina, or even opted to teleport to town—a very efficient, but also very expensive and frighteningly experimental mode of travel. But I needn't have worried. Both my parents had been enthusiastic hosts from the moment we'd arrived. Lightly, Zady said, "That's our girl. We do have so many stories for you, Luca."

"That said," Aly added, naturally, "it's a bit late for reminiscing tonight."

"Of course!" said Zady. "Cinnabar, love, I know you said you already ate on the road, but what about rest? Aren't you and your friends tired? Don't let us keep you up too late."

It *was* late, and I was tired. But I knew that if he was given the chance, William would be practically nocturnal. I glanced at him, but he seemed preoccupied.

"Maybe we *should* get some sleep," Luca decided for us. "We'll have lots of time tomorrow for catching up."

"That we will," Zady agreed, returning his smile. "And, Hestia willing, we will make the most of it."

5

Apothecary Blues

I woke the next morning in a decidedly anti-story mood. Luca and I shared the house's sole guestroom. It was on the second floor, with plentiful windows set high into the walls. They were spelled to keep out bugs, but not light. Despite having finally gone to bed around midnight, I woke at dawn.

It took me a moment to make sense of where I was. Luca was a reassuring presence, of course, but I didn't recognize the colorful wall hangings and woven blankets at first. The white walls seemed to stare back at me. It was at once nostalgic and strange. For the first time, I missed my cluttered studio in Belville.

I also missed having a potions lab at my disposal. With too much energy and no experiments to check or chores to do, I decided to go for a walk.

After slipping out of bed and hastily donning a blouse and long golden skirt, I picked my way over William, who had apparently elected to sleep in the tiled hallway outside our door. If he thought he was keeping an eye on me, he was going to wake up sorely disappointed: his own snoring was far louder than my footsteps as I made my way down the stairs. After a few years of accidental investigations, I'd become pretty sneaky.

"Oh, Cinnabar, you're up," said my mother, Zady, as I passed the sitting room.

I had to laugh at myself. *I guess I'm not that sneaky.* I paused and poked my head through the wide, arched doorway. "Hey, Mom. I thought I'd go for a walk before breakfast."

"You always have had restless feet," she said, contented. I resisted the urge to point out that *everyone* in our extended family had restless feet: it was a product of the supposedly unicorn-related divination magic in our blood. My strengths may not have extended to actual divination, but I did still share a few characteristics with everyone else. That said, Zady looked quite content on the couch, as usual. She had a portable desk in her lap and was clearly writing letters. For someone who often came across as dreamy, she'd once said she preferred day dreams and gossip to night dreams. She went on, "Aly's planning a nice big breakfast, so mind you don't run into anything too distracting while you're out."

"Got it. No more potential death discoveries," I said dryly.

She looked up and smiled at me. "Good luck."

As I continued down the hall and out the front door, I shook my head and chuckled to myself. Categorically, when a diviner tells you *good luck*, it means things are about to get messy. That was about the sum total of what I'd learned from my attempts at divination as a kid. But Wellspring almost never suffered any kind of crime. The community was so tight-knit that most arguments and resentments were worked out with words rather than actions. And most of the residents, when faced with stress, opted to meditate rather than reach for the nearest weapon.

Meditation, or their gardens. My mothers' was carefully arranged in patterns of colored rocks and succulent plants that enjoyed the desert climate. It stretched out from the front of the house on either side of the path as I made my way to the road, thinking. There had been *one* incident, back when I was in my early teens—a series of vandalisms. I hadn't thought about those in years. *Come to think of it, wasn't it a pair of younger kids who were caught? A particularly short one, and his more scrawny friend?*

While I was straining my memory, feet pounded the stepping stones behind me. I turned, looking back toward the house, just as Luca came up on my other side and slung his arm around my shoulders.

"Good, you didn't make it very far," he said, panting. "Zady said I only just missed you."

"I guess you must've. I thought you'd want to get some more rest," I said, grinning. All thoughts of past crimes were forgotten.

"Are you kidding?" Luca paused as we reached the road. "I don't want to miss a thing. I can't wait to see the town in daylight. Is that where you're headed? Or did you want to go to the beach?"

I laughed, shaking off his arm and steering him to look first right, then left. "We'd have to go that way, east, down to the beach. There's a side track that's probably still there that would go right to it. But the only people there at this hour will be the serious beachcombers. If we go this way, west, we'll get to town. Things'll probably be closed still, but we can look around. You can see the bonfire, if you want."

"Excellent," Luca said as we started off. "Not to take over your solitary walk or anything. Were you hoping to be alone?"

"Too late now," I said, grinning as I bumped his shoulder. "It's fine. I should probably get out of my head anyway, so I can be better company."

"It's so cool to see everything properly now," Luca mused, looking around us. The sunlight on the dunes was peachy and calm. The sand stretched out to our left, behind the house, up to the old volcano, which was painted in shades of purple by the light. Farther down the road ahead of us, the tops of houses were visible between the hills. Unlike in Belville, most of the homes in Wellspring were spread out.

"It's funny how different things look at night," I agreed absently, thinking of how many times I'd run to and from town as a kid. And trying *not* to think of the mystery we'd encountered on the bus.

"And we're heading kind of north now—north-west, I guess?" Luca clapped his hands as he looked at me, invigorated. "I'll get it eventually. Even if there *is* only one mountain and no trees to navigate by. Why do you think you need to be better company, Red? I'm sure your family knows you just as well as William and I do, if not better."

This was a habit of Luca's. He'd let something slide, only for a moment, just long enough for me to think I'd gotten away with it, and then come back to it as though it was totally natural—*neutral,* even. I glanced sideways at him. He knew that I saw what he was doing. And I was certain he felt no remorse about it, since it usually worked to get me talking.

"All the old stories," I admitted, with a sigh. "I'm not sure how I should feel about them."

Luca's gaze was on the sandy road beneath our sandals. "Are

you sure there *is* a 'should' way to feel about them?"

"Life here has obviously changed," I added without thinking or responding to his question. "The 'Palace.' The police. Even simple things like the bus going a different direction."

"Do those things matter?"

I sighed again as I tipped my head up to the blue sky, searching for answers. All I saw was a lone seafaring bird. "Not really. It's just the way they add up. Together, it all sort of makes a pervasive fish-out-of-water feeling, you know?"

"I can see that." Luca nodded thoughtfully. "I wonder if it would help to learn about Jasmin, since she's the source of two out of three things, at least?"

"You sound like Saki," I said, as the rooftops of town came into view. "'Know thy enemy,' and all."

"We don't know she's an enemy," Luca was quick to say.

"True. But still, it's hard not to feel like there is *something* going on," I said. "And the whole town will probably be in on it—or want to be in on it. Just you wait and see."

"Well, whatever it is, that 'something' doesn't have to affect your visit home, you know?" Luca's eyes were kind. "You haven't really been yourself since the night before we left."

"I have so too," I said, recognizing how petulant I sounded and turning it into a joke. "Who else could I be?"

Luca ticked off examples on his fingers. "Not planning our travel down to the last moment, not knowing the bus schedule by heart, not worrying about everyone having proper clothes before we left—"

"Okay, okay, I get it," I interrupted, laughing. "I'm not *that* uptight normally, am I?"

"William and I think of it as 'organized,'" Luca said loyally. Then, in a lower tone, he added truthfully, "Well, William mostly says *annoying,* but you know he means well. And we know you do, too."

"Yeah, well, some things—like remote island bus schedules and catamaran arrival times—are unknowable ahead of time," I informed him. *And rather than try to guess, or let Aly and Zady guess, I let us all just play it by ear.* It *was,* I had to admit, a little out of character. "I guess when I think about life here on Kairoi I just sort of give into the unknowableness of it all."

"Doesn't that include new developments, too?"

Luca was missing town landmarks to make his point. I nudged him. "I know. You're right. Unless we get pulled in to all the new drama somehow," I added, mostly to myself, before launching into tour-guide mode. "We're coming up to the town center now—got your sunscreen on?"

Ahead of us, the road ran up to a small raised plaza and the bonfire, ever-burning flames in a cauldron as big as a bathtub. I'd never understood it. You'd think a mystical clan called "*Spring* of the Unicorn" would be focused around a gurgling water feature or pristine pool, or something. Instead, these flames were the center of town life. Many evenings, people would sit on the benches around the little plaza and watch the fire. Every significant town event I could recall had been there. It was literally at the center of town, right in the middle of the main intersection. The cauldron itself was covered with carvings of symbols and different deities. Rather than choose a specific god or goddess, most Springers, as they called themselves, were open to whatever divine influence wanted to step in and help. Zady favored Hestia, for instance, while I'd only ever known Aly to call upon or swear by elemental forces. It was another of the intricacies of Seer life that I had never fully understood.

"It's truly a marvel," Luca said, watching the flames spark up to the sky.

"It's something," I agreed. "And here's the town, basically."

Wellspring proper was just four blocks around that plaza. An open-air market for groceries, crafts, and imported goods took up the block to our right, while the post office stood like a little sentry on our left. Beside it, a string of shops started, going down to the corner and stretching down the other block. Across the corner from us stood an old building that served as the basis of operations for town government—and the police station. Down the road behind it was a low-slung old schoolhouse building. And on the remaining block, what had once been a community center of sorts was now clearly a boutique hotel.

"Maybe Wellspring isn't such a backwater any more," Luca teased as we walked down the road toward the hotel.

"I guess fortune-seekers need somewhere to stay," I agreed wryly. "To be honest, we never really did use the community center for much. Usually, if there was a meeting it was out here on the plaza, or at somebody's house."

"That's neat," Luca commented. "No wonder your parents have such a nice sitting room. And a big garden."

"Wait til you see their kitchen," I agreed, smiling. "Need the post office, while we're here?"

"There won't have been time yet for any letters from Belville," Luca said, though he did peek across me at the dusty building. "How about we walk down the street and see the shops?"

"Sure, but don't hold your breath for a bookstore," I warned him lightly. "I was always told that scholars were afraid to come to Kairoi because they didn't want their fortunes told."

"I can see why. Some things are better found out on your own," Luca quipped by way of agreement. "But I'm still excited."

We passed a few new businesses—a hair salon I didn't recognize, and a fancy dress store clearly aiming to attract customers from the hotel. But right next door was an old shells-and-gems shop I remembered fondly. I lingered, staring at the window displays, while Luca went up to the corner.

"Red," he called back. "Look at this. Did they always have an apothecary?"

Definitely not. I picked up my pace and joined him in staring at a roadside sign that read, "Cures for all that ails you!" in bright red script on a white background.

Behind the sign, the shop itself was decorated in red and white, too. A thin striped awning stretched over the door, which stood open. The windows were shaded, but it was clear that the place was open, even as early as it was.

And Luca, of course, was already going in.

I followed him with butterflies in my stomach. *Apothecary* referred to both the store and the person who prepared the medicines sold there. Technically, "apothecary" and "alchemy" were not the same thing—one sold vitamins and first aid supplies, while the other was a scientific discipline. But they were related—far more so than alchemy and divination. Would this be someone in town who spoke my language? Someone who could make me regret leaving? Or would it be a disappointment, some kind of snake-oil store?

At first glance, it was difficult to decide. The store was filled with freestanding shelves, shelves that reached nearly to the ceiling, and were arranged not in rows but in a sort of maze. One sweeping glance and I saw fingernail clippers, magical amulets, cauldrons, and a small potted mandrake. Behind the sales counter at the back of the store, the wall was packed full of jars and vials. Those were more familiar, many containing powdered minerals or dried spices and flowers. The place smelled right, too: an earthy musk with sharp-edged herbal overtones.

But the *sound* was strange.

"Did you order the pill casings? You know they take a while to get here!"

"We got the indigo and wolfsmallow by the early morning post!"

"But I need pill casings for the prescriptions today."

"Should I change out these mouth-wash potions from last winter?"

"I can put in an order for those!"

Curious, Luca and I made our way further into the store. The sales counter formed a bank along the entire back wall, punctuated by several antique cash registers. Behind this fortification, we found one white-coated apothecary and two assistants in aprons.

The apothecary looked tired already, so early in the day. One assistant bustled back and forth along one end of the counter, while the other messed about with boxes stacked on a shelf and created a small avalanche.

The apothecary saw us first, but remained behind their chest-high island of bottles and pills. After a few helpless gestures, they caught the attention of the bustling assistant, who turned and spotted us with a little jump.

"Oh!" she said, scooting over to the counter. "Are you here to pick up Jasmin's order?"

Luca shifted, stepping on my foot—most likely on purpose.

"We're just visiting. But Red here's a—"

"Big fan," I interrupted, before he could out me as an alchemist. I wasn't sure I wanted to be drawn into the mayhem of the shop's operations. "Of Jasmin, I mean. I hear she's done great things."

The assistant leaned her elbows on the counter, obviously pleased for a bit of gossip. "They say she's going to put this island on the map," she said happily. "Won't *that* be good for business!"

"We certainly hope so," Luca said politely, before I could think of anything.

"Do come in if you need anything," the assistant continued without blinking. "We have *everything*!"

"I can see that," I said, my gaze wandering back to the apothecary.

"But for now, we won't take up your time," Luca decided. With a cheerful wave to the assistant, he steered me out of the store.

"*On the map,*" I whispered as we hit the street. "On the map! Like it wasn't before!"

Luca chuckled. "I thought you'd be more horrified that they weren't on top of their routine stock orders."

"That's why I have Rhys," I said airily, before returning to what had bothered me. "Can you believe the nerve?"

"Yes. And I bet they'd be happy to sell you a nerve-soother, if you like," Luca joked.

"Don't you start. You sound like Officer Thorn."

"Well, there's one thing she's right about," Luca said. He paused, and for a moment I was terrified he'd say something about investigations and murder. Instead, with a wide grin, he said, "I could really go for some baked goods right now."

6

Interrupted Tales

Fortunately, we made it back to the house before Luca fainted away of hunger. We found Aly and Zady both in the kitchen, coordinating tasks over the obsidian kitchen island. It was a much more cohesive scene than the apothecary had been.

"This is amazing," Luca said, announcing us both. The main hallway deposited us directly in the combined kitchen and dining room, which took up the back half of the house. On one side, black counter tops, a blue tiled sink, and a fancy new icebox reigned; on the other, a round table was already set with colorful dishware and napkins. And beyond them both, the screen door to the back patio was open, letting in what remained of the early morning breeze.

"We like entertaining," Aly told Luca from her spot at the stove, her dark eyes sparkling.

"And *you* are very special guests," Zady added, her arms full of baskets piled high with precisely the baked goods Luca had been hoping for. "I hope you're hungry!"

"Why didn't anyone wake me?" William's yawning voice

came from the hall behind us. "You didn't already eat, did you?"

As the others laughed, I assured him that he hadn't missed a thing. By that time, the air was full of the scent of vegetable frittata, and my stomach was rumbling.

We took our places at the table and eventually dug in, the conversation dominated by compliments to the chef and requests for more. All my misgivings and worries had taken a backseat, and it finally hit me that my two best friends were now meeting my parents—and how amazing that was.

So, naturally, just as we were finishing up and considering what to do with the day, a knock came at the door.

Luca and I were at the sink, me washing dishes and him drying them. Zady led our two newest police friends into the kitchen, too.

"We need official statements," Officer Ja'far informed us, hat in hand. He must have agreed upon the plan of action with his fellow officer beforehand. Babs was nodding, notebook already in hand.

"Did you find out new information?" Luca asked, his towel drifting down.

Ja'far looked hesitantly around at the five of us, but apparently decided that there was no use for it. "More than that," he admitted. "We found the body."

* * *

While Aly and Zady finished up the cleaning, Luca, William, and I took turns giving our statements. We sat out on the back patio, as the day was only warm so far—not yet sweltering. William took a while with his, the blue glow tinging his fur making me worry as I watched through the screen door. It looked like he was arguing with them. Luca, of course, was quick and friendly. I went last. I did my best to be helpful, but the truth was I had seen so little—only the blood on the road.

As I sat with the two officers at the patio table, straining to remember anything else, the rest of the company must have decided it had been long enough. Aly came out with a tray of iced teas and three curious faces streaming along behind her.

"You *are* done, aren't you?" she asked the officers, as everyone pulled wicker chairs over to make themselves comfortable.

"I suppose," Officer Ja'far admitted begrudgingly.

"And how is Officer Brooks?" Zady asked pleasantly as she took a seat.

"He's having us handle this investigation," Babs volunteered.

"Quite a show of faith," Aly observed. "And—should we be addressing you as 'Chief,' Ja'ja?"

Luca and I exchanged an amused glance around the pole that held up the patio umbrella. I'd often seen the Aly-and-Zady tag team at work as a child, and it was fun to see it in action on someone else.

"Just 'officer' is fine," Ja'far said, looking distinctly uncomfortable in his starched collar. "After all, Wellspring Station is small."

"And informal," Babs said, with strange emphasis.

"You seem to be doing very well to me," Luca said encouragingly.

Ja'far turned on him. "*Informal* is a professional designation," he said crisply.

"It means the station has two or fewer officers present, and a low rate of local crime," Babs explained. His eye was on me, and my stomach plummeted. I had a feeling I knew where this was going. "Therefore when a major crime *does* occur, it is an unusual strain on the officers—and the community. During such times, all hands are allowed—and expected—to be 'on deck,' so to speak."

"I thought 'all hands on deck' was just something Officer Thorn says," I protested weakly.

"And I don't see how the Police Guild can expect everyone who's *not* police to follow their rules, too," William pointed out from his spot at my side. I wondered how long he'd been holding on to that quibble.

"If we didn't all follow the rules, there'd be no justice," Officer Ja'far reminded him primly.

I got the feeling that this conversation had created an opening that Officer Babagha' had been campaigning for. He turned fully to me. "You're the one who found the blood. You analyzed it with your goggles. It would take us days to do that kind of test—"

"I identified it, not analyzed it," I protested.

But it was no use. "—and think of how much farther we can get with the skills of a great alchemist on the team," Babs concluded, his brown eyes shimmering.

I shuffled in my seat. "I'm not a—"

"Of course you are," Zady interrupted. "Paracelsus said so."

"You've been writing letters to my *mentor,* too?" I could have hidden my face in my hands.

"Of course," said my mother, with placid satisfaction. "You didn't expect me to *not* ask for news, did you?"

"It's up to me to make the final decision," Officer Ja'far interjected. Truthfully, I was grateful to him in that moment. The entire conversation, I felt, was getting out of hand.

"And what *is* your final decision?" Aly challenged, when he fell silent.

The two police officers exchanged a look.

Definitely it was them who were the vandals way back when, I decided as we all looked on. And seeing their dynamic now, I could tell how Babs influenced his friend. Fortunately, the influence in this case seemed to be well-meant rather than criminal.

"We *could* use the extra help," Ja'far admitted at last. The sharp angles of his face softened, just for a moment, into a relatable expression of overwhelm. "Especially from someone who can be a neutral third party in the community. We've already had offers from the town to hold a special divination session tonight, of course, but something more . . . scientific might also be helpful."

"I brought the paperwork for you to sign on," Babs informed me, breathless with victory.

"There's *paperwork?*" I asked, half amused. Officer Thorn had never made me sign a thing. But just like Babs, she never stopped to think I might refuse to help.

"While you straighten that out," Aly broke in, "don't you think you had better tell us everything that happened?"

Officer Ja'far sighed—but for just a moment, I thought he seemed relieved. "Oh, go on then, Babs. You may as well tell them."

"It was like this," Babs began, without another hint of provocation. He stowed his notebook and any thought of paperwork, and turned to address the group, self-importance in his voice. "Since it was dark last night, and we didn't have any equipment, we eventually had to give up our search. Even though Bessie and Suzy did see something—as much as Bessie can 'see' things—"

"I wouldn't say doubtful things like that too loud, if I was you," Zady murmured over her tea, as though Bessie might crash through the garden and exact revenge.

"Right, so, they were *certain* they saw someone," Babs said. "Plus, we have William's testimony that some kind of magic was nearby. And then of course Red found the blood. It was a lot of blood. It was hard to tell with the gravel, and hard to see in the dark. The stain was several feet—"

"Enough detail," Officer Ja'far said irritably. "Just give them the broad idea. That should be enough."

"So, there was blood," Babs said, indefatigably. "But no body, at least, not any more. And no traces of magic that we could tell. There wasn't anything we could really do, we thought. So we took the new secretary up to the Palace, and we took these three home—that much you all already know. After that we went back into Wellspring, to the station. It was really late, but Officer Brooks had waited up for us—"

"How nice," said Zady.

"Remind me why *he* isn't here," William rumbled, low.

"And then Officer Brooks said, why didn't you look in the rest of the estuary when you passed it on the bus—"

Aly startled, setting her drink aside. "The estuary?"

"What's special about it?" Luca asked, leaning in.

"The pull of the tide there is very strong," Officer Ja'far informed him.

"It's where the shipwrecked sailors were found," Zady said, more spine-tinglingly.

"But didn't Jasmin buy it?" I asked.

"Her new so-called Palace is up on the cliffs just above the estuary," Aly explained. "No one actually knows how much of the rest of the estuary she owns, but she hasn't tried to fence it off yet, at least."

"So we were supposed to go look there," Babs continued. "But we couldn't hardly go in the dark. But then, Officer Brooks said, someone was probably murdered and you have to catch who did it so you have to act fast, so we turned around and—"

This time, the interruption was more permanent. From the dunes behind the garden wall, a strange voice shouted for help.

7

A Sailor's Life

Aly and I were on our feet, our iced teas forgotten. William, Luca, and Officer Ja'far weren't far behind. I led the way along one of the rocky garden paths to the back gate, overgrown with flowering vines. It wouldn't open—it was locked. I hadn't expected *that* development. I stepped back and let Aly open it with a key drawn from a long chain around her neck.

The strange voice shouted again. As soon as Aly got the gate open, we poured out.

Because my mothers' house was at the edge of Wellspring, their back gate opened directly onto desert that rolled all the way up to the slopes of the volcano. Sand is no fun to run on—for normal, unfortunate chumps like William and Luca, perhaps. Aly, Ja'ja, and I had our island heritage to thank. Light- and swift-footed, much more so than the average human (or magical familiar or forest elf, as the case may be), we practically flew up the first dune.

At its crest, I paused and searched for the source of the voice. It was easily found: in the little valley just beyond us, a man

52

in sun-bleached clothing leaned over a comrade half-buried in the sand.

I reached the pair of them first, skidding to a halt beside the upright man. "You called for help?"

"I did," he said. "Thank the jinn!"

I wasn't sure what spirit beings had to do with it, but I didn't argue the point. Instead, I dropped down to take a look at his companion. Behind me, Aly pulled up, with the police officer close behind.

"What happened?" Aly asked, just barely breathless.

"He got out again," the first man said. "I found him just as he collapsed!"

The collapsed man was breathing, if raggedly. He didn't look at all prepared for a desert hike. His trousers were cut off at the shins, revealing ancient straw sandals, and he wore no hat. He was shaded by the dune at the moment, but his deeply tanned skin was flushed.

"Looks like sun exposure to me," I said, straightening up. "But you might know better, Officer?"

Ja'far straightened, and the disapproving look on his face eased a little. He came over to stand at the fallen man's side.

"How long has he been out?" he asked.

"Might've been up to an hour," said the first man, sheepishly.

"Did he have any water with him?"

"He might not've. He just gets these ideas in his head," was the answer.

I glanced at Aly, vaguely surprised. *Who gets ideas about hiking without water?* Her face was impassive, though. Behind her, Luca and William slid down to join the party.

"Who *are* you?" Officer Ja'far asked, meanwhile. From the sound of his voice, he was thinking along the lines I had been.

"Officer, perhaps Brooks told you about the sailors who washed ashore recently?" Aly cut in. "These are two of them. They've been staying in Wellspring as they recuperate."

"This poor fellow's Jason. Call me Sinbad," the first one said, introducing his fallen crew mate before giving his own name with a little pride. I watched him, interested by the mix of chagrin and self-respect. Sinbad was maybe an inch or two shorter than me, but he stood straight and lightly upon the sand. He wore cut-off canvas trousers, like Jason, but his striped blue shirt was much more intact, and he sported a tan and a straw hat not unlike Luca's. *Of course* he was a sailor. How had I missed it?

He also had a short, curved sword stuck into his belt. It was old, its blade clearly nicked, but nonetheless it was dangerous . . .

. . . I wondered again about the locked garden gate. And the blood on the road.

Meanwhile, Officer Ja'far was squinting at Sinbad too. "You don't look like you need recuperating."

Sinbad was saved from answering this bit of suspicion by the arrival of Babs and Zady. "Do you need help moving the patient?" Babs called.

If Ja'far was embarrassed at having to be reminded of the actual priority at hand, he didn't show it. He knelt beside Jason and soon had the man sitting up. In what was probably a practiced Guild move, Ja'far and Babs supported Jason between them. Zady followed close behind, holding aloft a sunshade she'd thought to bring.

The trio and their over-exposed patient slowly climbed back toward the house. Sinbad lingered, addressing Aly. "Sorry for the trouble, ma'am."

"I've told you before, you don't have to ma'am me," she responded, her eyes crinkling in amusement. "You might as well go on back to the house too. Jason'll want a friendly face, and we just made plenty of iced tea."

"Thank you kindly." Sinbad surprised me with an archaic little bow before setting off. Luca fell into step beside him, plying him with questions about shipwrecks and sailing.

That left my mother, William, and me. I grinned at Aly. "I guess you don't go for daily runs in the dunes any more, huh?"

"Don't tease your mother for being out of breath," she reprimanded, smiling as we, too, made our way back to the garden gate. "I still made good time. Ja'ja could use some brushing up, don't you think?"

"I think he's just nervous," I told her.

She chuckled. "That's kind of you. I always thought he was an arrogant boy, and I'm not sure ten years at the Guild has much improved him. Anyway, ever since the injury last year, I've been ordered to limit myself to walking—except in emergencies."

"By the doctor, or by Zady?" William asked. I grinned, knowing the answer. It had been Zady who wrote to me about Aly's broken ankle. She'd fallen while running through the estuary—back when it was a wildlife preserve. Zady had been furious, because it had taken a while for Aly to be found. Recovery had been difficult, but they'd made it through, together.

"My darling wife," said Aly dryly. "So I dare not push it."

"We all need someone to look after us," I said, smiling down at William.

He shook himself. "And don't you forget it."

Aly laughed as we trudged back into the garden.

* * *

After even a short trip out onto the sand, coming back into the house was a startling relief. We found everyone in the sitting room, clustered around the couch where Jason sat. A pitcher of water and cups stood on the side table beside him. His color already looked much better.

"But what were you doing out there?" Officer Ja'far was asking as we walked in.

"Had something to look into," Jason muttered. His voice was deep and raspy. Now that he wasn't half-buried in sand, I could see that his hair was shoulder-length and gray, pulled back in a low ponytail. The wrinkles on his broad face, too, spoke to age. No wonder Sinbad was so worried about him.

Ja'far ignored us as we quietly took seats on the cushions and couch nearby. He stood focused on Jason. "What did you have to look into in the desert?"

"Just something." Jason looked away. His breathing was still labored.

"Officer, please, let the man recover before you interrogate him," Zady interrupted. She sat on the couch beside Jason as though they were at a tea party. Like a caring hostess, she offered him another glass of water and said, "How are you feeling? Do you need anything? We can run down to the apothecary."

"Petra will certainly get you fixed up," Aly added from her seat next to me. I didn't get it, but Jason did seem to brighten at the idea. Aly leaned over to me and whispered, "Remember Aunt Petra? She's one of the assistants there."

We must have spoken to her this morning, I realized, ashamed I hadn't recognized her. But then again, Aly had about a million relatives, not just on Kairoi but on the neighboring islands, too, and she called all of them "aunts" or "uncles" or "cousins," even the ones who were really distant relations or just family friends. I'd never been able to keep track of them all—it was a family joke.

"We ought to be getting back to the hotel anyway," Sinbad put in. "We're getting sand all over your nice home. Sorry, Zady, ma'am."

"Stop that," Zady said, in much the same tone that Aly had earlier.

"Maybe we should leave them to it," Babs was saying to Ja'far. "We do have an investigation to get on with . . ."

Aly saw her chance, and she took it. "It's settled, then. Zady and I will take Jason and Sinbad into town, while the rest of you get to work."

Officer Ja'far looked torn. He hadn't agreed to anything being *settled*—and yet, as was often the case, Aly had outlined a very reasonable plan. I had to hide a smile as I watched him. I wondered how difficult it must be to be a police officer in a town full of Seers.

Not that Aly relied on divination—she'd always been action-oriented. But sometimes I did wonder how much she knew beforehand . . .

It was Zady who disagreed, to my surprise. "But Jason will still need help walking, and you, Aly, are not allowed to support anyone else's weight."

While Aly rolled her eyes at me—a look that clearly said *I'm recovered, and yet will always be injured as far as she's concerned,* which was not wrong at all—Luca spoke up. "I'll come along and help if you like, Zady. As long as that's okay with you, Red?"

"Sure," I said, smiling at him. *He sure seems interested in the sailors,* I thought. The thought of that sword twinged at the back of my mind, but I set it aside. Luca would be in good company.

"Perfect!" Babs declared.

And so it was decided—with, or without, Officer Ja'far's help. I almost felt sorry for him.

William and I hung back with the officers, letting the patient and his entourage leave first. I know I at least was curious if he was ready for the walk back to town yet. Fortunately, though, Jason was much more upright between Luca and Sinbad than he had been before. The thought of visiting the apothecary— or perhaps the fancy hotel—had been a good motivator.

As Zady traipsed out the door behind them, still holding up the sunshade like a royal attendant, she tossed a house key to me. "We should have given it to you last night!" she called, before they all disappeared out the front door.

I glanced at the key in my hand and wondered. It wasn't that we'd had *no* security when I was a kid, but we'd definitely been more lax. I'd have to ask them about their new safety measures later.

"Very well, then," Officer Ja'far said—perhaps a bit belatedly. He looked around at our little crew of four. "We can finally get back to business."

"First things first," said Babs, pouring himself a glass of water and settling on the sofa Jason had vacated. "You never got to hear the end of our story."

"It's not a *story,*" Ja'far said impatiently. "Just get to the—"

"We went out to the estuary last night," Babs told William and me, ignoring his superior officer. "Or really, it was early this morning. We had to use the old police cart, since Bessie was off to her next stop, the marina. It was good we went to the station, though, because we had a chance to pick up better torches and some water-proof boots. The Guild has torches that can light up everything within a twelve-foot radius," he added, proudly.

I decided not to tell him about Officer Thorn's club, which the local Witch had enchanted to burn like a torch without consuming any fuel.

"So we went out there, just the two of us," Babs continued. "And it only took us about an hour. But then we found her!"

William and I were leaning forward, left puzzling over this sudden dearth of detail.

"Found *who?*" he demanded irritably.

"The dead lady," said Babs, rather cheerfully. "We found her among the reeds. And guess what? Red was right about the blood."

It was hard to be wrong about something I'd literally seen with my own two eyes—and my goggles—but again, I kept my mouth shut.

"The victim's throat was cut," Officer Ja'far said at last, his voice tight and scratchy.

"And not only that," said Babs. "That's not the strangest part."

"What *is* the strangest part?" William asked. At any moment, I felt sure his patience would give out and he'd snap.

"The strangest thing," Babs said solemnly, "is that we don't know her. Not at *all.*"

8

In a Strange Land

"Of course, it has been a long time since we lived here," Babs added.

For as much as I'd hated the reminders of my own absence yesterday, I had to agree with him in this case. "Yes, and it sounds like there've been some changes lately, things that might have attracted a lot of people to the island."

"Are you saying the victim must be related to Jasmin?" Officer Ja'far asked sharply.

I faltered. "No, not exactly. There have been changes that have nothing to do with her, right? And anyway, it could be pure coincidence. Or it could be that you don't recognize the victim even though she *was* living here before you left."

Officer Ja'far nodded, once, as though I'd passed his test. I didn't necessarily enjoy being treated like a trainee, but at least he was taking this seriously and carefully.

"Just like you didn't recognize us at first, and we didn't recognize you," Babs was saying, agreeing with me. He reached out to William and me, holding out his notebook for us to see. "Do *you* recognize her?"

He'd drawn several images of the victim on the blank sheet of paper. Once I'd gotten over the initial surprise—*talk about burying the lead: he goes over every detail, and never mentions he has pictures until the last moment?*—I took a good look. William glowed beside me.

I doubted either one of us would have any luck, though. Babs had drawn a portrait of the woman which showed her as young, with dark hair in a tight bun, dangling earrings, and a buttoned collar. That was enough to tell me that she probably wasn't anyone I knew on the island: everyone I remembered was as easy-going and informal as Aly and Zady were. Wellspring wasn't much of a hot spot for expensive jewelry and formal attire—or at least, it hadn't been twelve years ago.

Below the portrait, Babs had drawn a sketchy snapshot of how they'd found her. This one showed her whole body, tailored trousers and high-heeled sandals included, but she was face down in a clump of reeds. Her hands floated gently at her sides, dark markings around her wrists.

"These are good drawings, Officer," I said, "but I don't recognize anything here. Do you, William?"

"No. It's not much use having not been there in person," he said.

"Exactly," said Officer Ja'far. "It's no use lingering here. I told you, Babs."

"That was step two on our plan," Babs informed us with a wide smile. "Take you out to the crime scene."

* * *

Ten minutes later, after having carefully locked up my mothers' house, William and I found ourselves defying death on the island road.

It turned out that the Wellspring Police Station's "cart" was in fact an old farmer's cart, the sort of thing that might have been used to transport vegetables. Its old wooden sides barely held together, and though its spacious bed had been spiffed up with a colorful carpet, that was it. There were no other safety features or insulation to speak of. The entire thing operated on what seemed to be a budget-version of the spell that operated Bessie. But Bessie at least had a roof and headlights and shock-absorbing suspension. The police cart had only the reckless wind in our hair and the partial cushion of a thread-bare carpet with every bump in the road to recommend it.

Officer Ja'far sat on the front bench seat, presumably steering the thing, though it felt like he was *aiming* for every pothole. William, Babs, and I bounced around in the back like balls in an arcade toy.

"It's not that far!" Babs yelled to be heard over the rumble of old wooden wheels over hard-packed sand.

Liar, I almost said. I knew how far it was from Wellspring to the estuary.

The volcano formed the southern tip of the island, along with the marina cuddled into its cliffs. The preserved land, now mysteriously Jasmin's "Palace," was the western side, while Wellspring perched on the northeastern coast, at the edge of the desert. The estuary, a landmark all its own, was presumably at the edge of Jasmin's domain. Its meandering streams marked the distinction between land preserve and desert proper. To add to that, the estuary was huge, far larger than Wellspring itself. As spring water flowed down from the volcano's heights, it hit the sand and spread, sinking partially into the earth. The result was acres of marshy wetlands fanning out along the coast. It was a brilliant place if you were a shorebird or shellfish, but rather *less* exciting for an investigator looking for a body.

Or just a civilian waiting for a cart ride to end.

Officer Ja'far must have had great faith in his cart, however. A few minutes after the main road began taking us through the marsh, he abruptly pulled off, rattling onto a side road with ferocity. I might have tumbled right out of the cart had not William's magic caught me by the arm.

Soon after that, we lurched to a halt. As we hopped out, our boots—and the cart's wheels—squelched down into the wet sand, among the reeds. I couldn't help but be grateful, though. Besides, surrounded as we were by waist-high grasses, there wasn't much danger of quicksand. The plants' roots would help keep us stable.

Officer Babs led the way. He stomped fearlessly through the growth, while Ja'far ushered William and me in front.

"It was right here," Babs said, momentarily. He held his notebook in his left hand for comparison. "Or maybe it was just over there . . ."

I pulled up next to him and looked around. He'd taken us to a spot where the water moved with more purpose. The road, just a few yards away, passed closely over a wide stream, which then rippled past our feet. The current had cleared a pathway free of reeds and grasses, at least a few feet wide. But soon after it passed us, the stream seemed to lose steam, filtering out amid clumps of grasses that created islands and dams. I could see why Babs was confused: each reedy island looked very much like the next.

He looked up at me as I surveyed the area. "Do you see

anything?"

Next to me, William snorted. "Where's she supposed to look?"

"A clue could be anywhere in this area, if it got separated from the body and floated away," Officer Ja'far pointed out crisply.

He did have a point there.

I pulled my goggles down over my face. Too bad I hadn't brought tall boots. Gathering the hem of my skirt in one hand and carefully threading my sandaled feet between the plant life, I began to take a closer look.

"I'm sure I don't have to tell you two how difficult it is to find anything out here," I said as I went along, walking on the stream's edge.

"We looked for ages!" Babs agreed. He, too, was scanning the water's bottom.

"How *did* you find the body?" William asked. I glanced back to see that he'd decided to stay on relatively dry land. That was just as well: if nothing else, he'd help me remember the way I'd come.

Officer Ja'far also seemed hesitant to join the search. But he did explain, loudly enough so that I could hear, too. "It was Babs who found it. We stuck to the main road at first."

"Guild procedure," Babs enthused. "But I didn't do anything special, really. I just saw a big shadow. Thought it was a crocodile at first. *You* can see lots of stuff though, right, Red?"

My mind was stuck on *crocodile*. I'd never encountered one as a kid—I was pretty sure they didn't live on the island—but if they did, this would be a good place for one, I couldn't help but think. I shook my head. "My goggles do help, yes, Babs. But it's not like I have magical vision. They just expand—"

I paused. I'd seen a strange flash in the water.

Babs was talking in the distance, but it didn't sound like questions. I bent down, fishing in the toolbelt that I'd had the good sense to bring along. Goggles were one thing, but it turned out my truly useful tool was a waterproof magnet. I used it to fish a set of gilded keys out of the sandy stream bed.

I gave them a cursory glance, noting that they weren't pitted by the sand or rusted by the water yet—so they'd probably recently been abandoned. Reassured, I shouted to the others about my find.

"I was worried an alligator had got you!" Babs yelled back.

"What else is there?" Ja'far demanded.

"Leave it to Red to find something already," was William's take. I couldn't tell if he was chagrined or proud.

Either way, all three agreed to search the nearby area more thoroughly. They converged on the stream I'd chosen, walking up and down its banks and bushwhacking through the miniature islands, faces intent. There were a few yelps as we startled nesting birds, but otherwise we were silent. Only the estuary made noise, its gentle waters seeming to laugh softly. I realized that the water level was affected by the tide, and chastised myself for not checking tide charts before we'd come out here. Of course, I'd had very little warning . . . and so far, luck had been on our side.

Despite another half hour of searching, though, we found nothing more.

"The water must've washed everything away," Babs commented as we gathered back near the cart.

"I did wonder about the tides. A receding high tide might have taken everything light along with it. Everything but these," I said, holding out the keys I'd found.

Officer Ja'far picked them up with gloved hands, separating the little cluster carefully. On one thick ring, two keys and a little rectangle hung together. As I watched him examine them, I was reminded again of the keys back home. *So my mothers aren't the only ones who are more worried these days,* I thought.

"They must've been hers," Babs said, looking on. "The victim's. I'm sure that was the island where we found her."

"We don't know that," Officer Ja'far insisted.

"William can scan them," returned Babs. Turning to William, he added, "You're magic, right?"

"Of course I am," William grumbled. Blue energy crackled around his head briefly, just for show. "But that won't do much good when I don't know what I'm looking for. Besides, magical signatures don't last very long, not in a place like this. Especially if the tide's come and gone, like Red said. Water cleans things off."

"And we can't say how long the keys have been out here," Ja'far agreed.

"But we can say one thing," I said suddenly. A detail had caught my eye as the officer twisted the keys around. I pulled my goggles back down over my eyes, although to be honest, I didn't need them.

When Ja'far reluctantly handed the keys back to me, all I had to do was turn the golden rectangle around. One side of it was emblazoned with a sun and palm trees—a picture of beachy paradise, like the kind of vision one might find on a souvenir. In thin, curling script, it read, *Palace Jasmin.*

I pointed it out to the others with a triumphant grin, even as my stomach twisted. It looked like we would be learning more about Jasmin after all. Luca had been right.

9

Palatial Spaces

When the police cart again turned off the main road and trundled up the driveway to the new "Palace Jasmin," my insides were in knots. I wondered if just Babs, Ja'ja, William, and I would be enough.

It wasn't that it looked *scary*, exactly. The driveway was hard-packed, fine gravel, a much smoother ride than the main road had been. It cut straight through the reeds and then began to climb, making switchbacks up the side of the volcano. Palm trees had been planted at even intervals on either side of the road. Every once in a while, between palm fronds and outcroppings of rock, the golden walls of our destination were visible. It was *opulent*.

The arched gateway was festooned with blooming vines of jasmine flower. The scent was powerful, almost overwhelming. As a sentry armed with a gleaming, sharp scimitar waved us through, we found ourselves in a different world.

Jasmin's domain was perched on the side of the mountain. I could hardly believe that in six months, architects and work crews had managed to level the entire area—it was easily as big

67

as Belville. The golden walls that encircled it disappeared as they stretched around verdant gardens, fountains, and stands of imported trees. Here and there, the glint of water peeked through, creating an impression of lush pools surrounding the main buildings. Those rose in front of us with curved, pillowy roofs of deep blue tile and golden edging, with windows taller than my mothers' entire house, with silk awnings stretching to meet us and plush carpets of crimson running out to the driveway.

There was no doubt about it. This *was* a palace.

But what, I couldn't help but wonder, *does Jasmin think she is ruler of?*

The police cart lurched to a halt at the top of the circled driveway, and we spilled out, each one of us looking to the other. No one wanted to be first to track silt and sand all over the red carpet that led the way to the grand, double front doors.

Fortunately, we weren't given much opportunity to debate. A pair of attendants dressed head to toe in emerald livery immediately retrieved our little party and swept us inside. I would have felt sorry for them—their clothes looked very hot—but even outside, under the awnings the air was cool. *Magic.* Out of the corner of my eye, I saw William sparkling with it as he encountered the palace's spells. They must have been powerful: despite the growing midday heat, the palace air was the perfect temperature.

We were ushered away from the central hall, which seemed to be a grand ballroom. Instead, we scurried down a side hallway, struggling to keep up with our guides.

The far end of the hall dumped us into an office, of sorts. It was no less grand than the ballroom had been, though it was narrower, running partway down the back of the main building. Through arched windows and open doorways framed by the most delicate silk, we could see a courtyard full of blooming flowers. The sound of running water drifted in on the breeze. The room itself featured a tiled floor with an inlaid floral pattern and walls so decorated with draped fabric it was difficult to see the actual *wall*. In the corner in front of us, a gilded desk stood, much more like a showpiece than an actual place of business.

And yet, behind that polished expanse, there was a familiar face.

"Oh, I say," said Dean, starting up. "This isn't about the bus yesterday, is it? I really didn't mean to cause a scene. There's no need to involve—"

Officer Ja'far cleared his throat and held up a hand. The attendants respectfully vanished—though not so fast that they didn't see Dean's embarrassment, I noticed.

"This is about another matter," Ja'far said, in his most official voice. Babs caught my eye and winked. "Can you identify this set of keys?"

At first, this seemed like a roundabout way to introduce the main topic, *murder of a potential Palace Jasmin resident.* But I realized that perhaps Officer Ja'far hoped to get Dean to confess a little extra information, if his guard stayed down. It was much more circumspect than the investigation I was used to from Officer Thorn. My esteem for the young officer rose.

Meanwhile, Dean was leaning comically far over his too-wide desk, trying to see the keys, which Ja'far was not about to let go of. Finally, with a little exasperated sigh, Dean gave up and walked around the desk to meet us.

"Are those mine?" he asked, squinting at the key ring. "How

in Beyond did you get a hold of my set? I could have sworn I—" he began patting down his clothes. Much like yesterday, he was wearing a collared shirt and dark trousers, though now he'd enhanced the outfit with a purple vest and paisley pocket square. His black hair was just as disheveled as ever, though.

In his waist pocket, he found what he was looking for. Dean withdrew a set of identical keys, letting them dangle from his fingertips. Over the tinkle of delicate metal, he breathed a sigh of relief. "Phew! I tell you, I did not want to lose those. Morgiana was very strict. Of course, I may not have made the *best* first impression, but still, I do think I can be counted on to keep track of—"

"Yes," interrupted Ja'far, impatient already. "That's all very well, but I'm interested in *these* keys. Is there any way to identify whose they are?"

"Let's take a look," Dean said affably. Once more, he leaned into the officer's space. "I say, they really seem to be the same as mine. Remarkable. *I* couldn't tell the difference, I'll tell you that. Did you take a look at them?"

"Me?" I startled as he looked in my direction.

"I just thought, you have that air about you, you know," Dean said hastily, metaphorically walking his question back. "Police expert, and all."

"*She* does?" Officer Ja'far ground his teeth.

"It's the goggles," William commented. "I *told* you you should have left them at home."

"I never leave them behind," I protested, my hand automatically reaching up to the goggles, which were perched atop my hair. They'd become a safety blanket as well as a tool. But on Kairoi, of course, *everyone* had hair like mine—there wasn't any need to hide it. My mothers, Babs, even Ja'far would consider sparkly iridescent strands of hair to be entirely commonplace. Like everyone in the clan, they were used to these marks of divination magic.

Everyone except newcomers and transplants, of course. Dean was still looking at me with cheerful expectancy, like a schoolkid who's managed to get someone else on the hook for answering a question directed at him. It seemed to me we'd ventured too far into the weeds, so to speak. "Never mind. Dean, is there some way to keep track of all the keys that have been issued? Surely Jasmin wants you to keep track of that kind of thing, what with all the security."

I'd said the magic phrase, it seemed. Dean jumped a little, like a doe that's noticed the hunter, and scuttled back around his desk. He began rifling through its heavy drawers, pulling them out one by one while he said, "There is, of course there is! There's a register. I just signed it myself, last night. One of those big beastly things that you'd never think you could lose, and it has everything but a person's firstborn child in it, not that I mind, of course, but no doubt it'd be just the thing you're looking for—"

"This?" An assistant walked up on our right, holding a thick black binder in both hands.

"*There* it is," Dean said, beaming. "Let's let the nice police officers take a look, shall we?"

* * *

Regardless of what Jasmin's privacy policies might be, Dean seemed more than happy to let us all examine the binder. Perhaps he was simply glad that *he* wasn't the focus of the investigation. And he had yet to hear that a murder was involved . . .

Still, such cooperation worked in our favor. We all shuffled out into the courtyard, where a shaded patio held a bench big enough for us all to sit on. Like a group of relatives ready to look at a picture album, we settled in. The assistant, whose name turned out to be Morgiana, maintained her tight grip on the binder. Officers Ja'far and Babs sat on her left, while William and I peered over her right. Dean opted to sit beside William. Maybe he thought William's was the friendliest face.

Without Dean's direction, Officer Babs made his way through the binder, skimming each page and moving on when Ja'far nodded he was ready. Many detailed the sentries, gardeners, and attendants who lived within the Palace walls. *Somewhere, there must be a serious suite of rooms—even houses,* I thought, lifting my head briefly to scan the area. It was no use: all I could see was the fruit trees, statues, and fish pond of the courtyard. I made a note to bring up getting a tour of the place later.

But then again—did we need a tour? Or was I just morbidly curious? I found myself missing Luca's grounding influence. William was a dear friend, but he was just as likely to egg on a bad habit as he was to reprimand, depending on his mood. I glanced down at him: he, too, was staring at the binder, his dark eyes occasionally flashing blue.

I wondered if Morgiana or Dean could tell that William was using magic. *Where* are *Jasmin's magic-workers?* I wondered. *She must have some on staff. Dean does not seem esoteric enough in the least. As for his assistant . . .*

While the others paged through the book of employees, I shifted my gaze to Morgiana herself. Like most others on the island, she looked at first glance like an average human, but her skin was pale. And her hair was so long, thick, and stark white that I wondered if she had some other kind of magical blood. It fell straight down her back, unhindered by a headband or barrette of any kind. It completely hid her ears and even overshadowed her face. By contrast, her dress was practical and understated, the kind of light cotton pink sundress that might have been purchased at the dress shop in Wellspring. Her hands and face were carefully made up, her gaze constantly on her work. Her eyes, wide set and deep, deep blue, had the same professional distance that the other attendants' had. On a white lanyard she wore her own set of keys and an identification card—the sort of thing that screamed, *I never lose anything and I am always prepared.*

I wonder what she thinks of Dean, I couldn't help but think.

"And *all* of these people are accounted for?" Officer Ja'far asked. He was clearly getting frustrated. There weren't many pages left in the binder.

"As of this morning, yes," Morgiana said, her voice wispy.

"They do a sort of roll call, you know," Dean added helpfully from his end of the bench.

The officer's gloved hand flipped over a divider, entering into a new section of employees. *Secretaries,* the little label said, as it curved past. I did my best not to raise an eyebrow. There were clearly four sheets of paper in this section.

Any more than one might have seemed a little strange, or at least, decadent. But hadn't Dean said last night that he was the third?

When I asked him about this, his bronzed skin went beet red, and he started stammering.

Officer Babs was not to be distracted from his reading, but the noise did attract Ja'far's attention. He sat up to say, "Don't tell me you've already been replaced?"

"I gather it's rather the other way 'round," Dean admitted, lapsing back into speech. "*I* am a sort of replacement, don't you know. It's very lucky actually. You see, there was a mishap and I—well, to be frank, I wasn't really *supposed* to show up yesterday, you see. They'd already offered the job to someone else. But she never showed, and so it worked out for all us, sort of like fate, you know—"

Babs' hand paused over the third secretary's information. I took a look, interested. *Nouronnihar,* presumably their first name, titled the page. Beneath that was a picture, and some orderly information—including, at first glance, a starting day that read yesterday's date.

"She never showed up?" Officer Ja'far repeated, pointedly.

"Oh—well—*I* never saw her, anyway, and that's what everyone said. Jasmin was in a frightful state about it, of course," said Dean.

"We'd sent her keys and contract on ahead to her," Morgiana explained in her wispy voice. "That's the procedure . . . when we know a new high-ranking employee is coming."

Doubtless along with some serious anti-theft spells, I thought. I noted the assistant's shade thrown at Dean with some amusement.

"So the keys could be hers," Babs suggested brightly, looking up.

"They could be!" Dean enthused. "Maybe?"

Morgiana looked less certain.

But it was a promising thought. I leaned in, giving the portrait another look. "Babs, is this the woman you saw?"

"You saw her?" Dean asked hurriedly. "When? Where? What?"

"I think it *is* her," Babs said. He looked up at his superior officer. "If you think what she'd look like without all the water and sand . . ."

. . . *and without all the spilled blood,* I thought morbidly, before shaking the thought away.

Officer Ja'far flicked to the last page, Dean's page, just to be certain, then came back to Nouronnihar's. "I believe we have found our victim. We will proceed as if this is the case."

"V-v-victim?" Dean gasped. "Morgiana, what? Did we know anything about this?" Victim of what?"

Morgiana closed the binder. "I think," she murmured, "that it might be time for you to meet Jasmin."

10

Delicacies

J asmin, it turned out, was lingering over her lunch.

Not that I could blame her. We were ushered into her presence in a separate courtyard, this one featuring a large gazebo rising out of a crystal-clear pond. Red and yellow fish swam languidly over a mosaic of tiles in the shallow water. Curling vines with orange trumpet flowers poured down from every side, perfuming the air. After crossing a set of stepping stones that rose above the pool, we found Jasmin lounging on a velvet couch beneath the gazebo's ceiling fan. A long, low table—large enough to rival my mothers' dining table—stretched out before her, laden with tiny portions of food on stark white dishware. A finely made pitcher stood in the middle. Just looking at it made me thirsty.

And hungry, too. It had been a lot of investigating since breakfast.

Jasmin listened with polite impassivity to Morgiana's and Dean's explanations of these strangers in her home. Then with a wave of one hand, she summoned glasses and dining ware for us to join her. Everything about her was graceful. Though

76

she lay propped up on one elbow, it was evident that she was small-boned and short—had she been standing, I doubt she'd have reached my shoulder. Her skin was pale, almost startlingly so, but rosy undertones were brought out by her hair, which was a deep pink. It had been braided into a silken waterfall that fell over her shoulder, the kind of style that spent hours to look effortless. My own ponytail definitely felt scruffy by comparison. Her coloring, stature, and large dark eyes made me think that Jasmin might have fairy heritage. *Maybe* she's *the one who magicked the palace,* I thought. But her clothing, strapless folds of loose white muslin cascading down to strappy gold sandals, screamed *fashion icon* rather than *person who does menial work.*

Overall, the first thing that one could think upon seeing her was *ah, so that's how she got her name. She lives up to it.* To be honest, I wondered if that ever bothered her. Did it start to feel like a cage, after a while?

"Sit, and eat," she commanded us, her voice deep and precise.

At that very moment, competent attendants arrived with everything we could need. William and I, along with our two new officer friends, dutifully arranged ourselves on the cushions across the table from Jasmin's couch. Dean stood, fidgeting, at Jasmin's feet.

"Thank you," Babs said, breaking our silence.

At my side, William shimmered. "Nice spread."

Jasmin smiled, just barely. "You are welcome."

As I reached for the pitcher first, I risked a raised eyebrow at William. *A woman of few words, but clearly a lot of power.* Her surroundings spoke for her.

William was already putting something of everything onto his fine luncheon plate, levitating dishes of honey and prunes and glazed pecans one after another with his distinctive magic. I decided to help myself to some flatbread and a little white cheese. Babs, at the far end, was enthusiastically digging into a platter of exotic fruits.

But Officer Ja'far was not to be distracted so easily. "Jasmin," he said, sitting stiffly on his plush blue pillow, "we've come on very serious business."

Jasmin flicked a glance at Dean. I couldn't quite read it. The assistant Morgiana had long since faded into the background, but she'd helpfully left the binder to Officer Ja'far's care.

"We will need your assistance in identifying a potential employee of yours," Ja'far continued.

"I will try," said Jasmin, her gaze level on his, "but I do not deal with everyone personally."

"Surely you take an interest in what happens in your palace," he returned, a faint note of challenge in his voice.

"Surely I do," she agreed archly, and left it at that.

Babs swallowed noisily and pulled his notebook from his pocket. "What do you think of—"

"One moment, first," Ja'far interrupted, pressing the notebook back before it reached Jasmin and Dean. "Tell us about your hiring process."

"It varies," Jasmin said with a beautifully straight face.

"Tell us about your hiring process for secretaries," Ja'far insisted. I could hear his teeth grinding near my ear.

"Dean can tell you," Jasmin said. She rolled her shoulder, making her hair ripple down to the sofa.

The secretary gulped. "I, uh, it was a bally thorough process, you know. Very professional and above-board and all that."

William rumbled next to me. I wondered if he was restraining a laugh, or perhaps the impulse to say, *if you have to tell the police it's above-board, it sounds anything but.*

"Take me through it," Officer Ja'far demanded. "Step by step."

"Ah, so, I was back in the city when it all started—in Argen, you see," Dean said, attempting to stuff his hands in his vest pockets and failing. "There I was, with the morning cup of liquid courage, perusing the latest *Bulletin*—that's a sort of newsletter, don't you know, a weekly post for secretary types, like I am. Chock full of the helpful dos-and-don'ts, and the occasional cry for help—"

"Cry for help?" Ja'far interrupted, his nostrils flaring.

"Oh, I mean job postings, don't you know," said Dean.

I hid my amusement behind another sip of what was, no doubt, double-filtered extra-super-hydrating fancy water. Officer Ja'far and Babs clearly did *not* know anything this young man was talking about, and to be honest, I didn't either. I had at least been through Argen during my traveling alchemist days: it was a gorgeous city, often considered a twin to Brass, and it was near the eastern coast where we'd caught the catamaran. But I had not lingered there enough to rub elbows with the city's inhabitants and learn all their turns of phrase. I watched Jasmin, wondering if *she* found Dean's mannerisms more understandable. Her face was blank, as if she was a sculpture freshly painted.

"Anyway, that's where I saw the call—for secretaries," Dean added, veering into unnecessary detail in order to make sure we were following him now. "Jasmin had written up a fetching little description."

"Did you?" Ja'far's gaze was intent on Jasmin.

She waved her hand once more, gold bangles clanking lazily across her skin. "A secretary did it."

"Of course, of course," Dean agreed. "So I popped a response in the mail, waited the customary three days, you know, and then got my reply. And I was pretty pleased, if I do say so myself. After that it was just a few long-distance interviews and then—"

"Who conducted the interviews?" Officer Ja'far asked, still focused on Jasmin. "Did you?"

She yawned.

"Oh, she's far too busy, I'm sure," said Dean. "I mostly talked to Morgiana. And the head of security, Raja."

"We'll need that contact," said Officer Ja'far.

As Dean rattled off the location of the security office and Babs obediently scribbled it down, pomegranate juice on his fingers, I snuck a look at Ja'far. Was it just me, or was he being strangely antagonistic?

Maybe that's how new police officers are taught to act, and Officer Thorn just skipped that day, I told myself.

Birds called in the idyllic courtyard around us. I glanced around, and still didn't see anyone else. Not even a wandering minstrel to entertain the (albeit troublesome) guests. Jasmin really seemed to prefer quiet seclusion to anything else.

"So anyway, now I'm here," Dean concluded, with a forced sort of cheer. "Is that—is that everything you wanted to know?"

Officer Ja'far ignored him. "Tell me about Nouronnihar," he said to Jasmin. "Your previous secretary."

"Well, she was hardly really a secretary, was she?" Dean protested.

Jasmin looked up at him, and for just a moment, I could have sworn there was a smile on her lips. Then she looked back at the officer, her face cool once more. "I did not meet her."

"But did you approve the final decision to hire her?" Babs asked helpfully.

"I did." Jasmin inclined her head.

"And what information was presented to you when you approved?" Ja'far pressed.

"Nouronnihar va Atargatis," Jasmin said, rousing herself ever so slightly, smiling like she knew this was what Ja'far had been waiting for all along. "Merfolk, but preferred a quiet life on land. Needed somewhere to settle. She came to us from New West Key, with excellent references . . . and every kind of experience we could ask for."

Merfolk. I thought back to the pictures I'd seen of her. Babs had drawn little markings on the victim's wrists—I had assumed they might be injuries from the murder, but I realized now that they could also have been scales. Merfolk often came on land to deal with other races, and when they did so, they shed their scaly tails for scaled legs instead. Some types of merfolk, especially the kinds who had extra fins or webbed fingers, often ended up with scales on their arms, too.

That meant the markings on her arms could have been entirely natural. It was also a timely reminder that I really did not know as much about this case as I assumed.

"What kind of experience?" Ja'far asked. Babs was hastily writing everything down.

Jasmin tilted her head. The message was clear: she had so many other matters of import on her mind that she had instantly forgotten her secretary's work experience. "You'd have to ask Morgiana for that."

"But she came highly recommended?" Babs confirmed.

"Oh, yes. Very." Jasmin's eyes flickered sideways for a

moment. I got the impression that Dean had come rather *less* recommended, perhaps.

Ja'far finally unbent enough to take a drink of water. "And when was she due to arrive?"

"Yesterday." This time, the look on Jasmin's face was clearly annoyance. But like the others, it vanished quickly.

"But you never saw her," Babs added.

"Just so." Jasmin's voice was abrupt for the first time. "So you see, there is nothing else I can tell you."

"What were you doing yesterday?" Officer Ja'far asked, as though she'd said nothing.

Jasmin stared at him. At last, she said, "I conduct my business in the mornings. The afternoon, I spent in the library reading. I did not have my dinner until late."

"I saw that," Dean put in helpfully. "Interrupted her at dinner myself, when I came in."

Ja'far pivoted. "Has anyone reported a set of keys missing?"

Briefly, Jasmin's lips parted. Then she collected herself. "Not to my knowledge."

"And did you ever get Nouronnihar's keys returned to you?"

"Returned?" asked Jasmin.

"Her bags did arrive, but she didn't," Dean interjected. "Maybe they're in there?"

I could all but hear Officer Ja'far groan. "We will take a look. Add it to the list," he directed Babs.

"Is this what you needed my help to identify?" Jasmin asked, more directly.

"Not quite. Show her," Officer Ja'far told Babs begrudgingly.

Full of importance, Babs got up from his side of the table and brought his notebook around to Jasmin, holding out his sketches for her to see. I nudged William as we both watched

Jasmin blanch.

"I did not see her," she repeated.

"Does that look like *anyone* you know?" Officer Ja'far asked, peering at her for more reactions.

"No." Jasmin turned her head away. "Compare it with the picture in her file, if you like."

"We already did," Ja'far said, a bit smugly. "Is there anyone here who knew her? Anyone else we might ask?"

"You know who did the interviews," Jasmin reminded him. "Aside from them, Nouronnihar knew no one here."

"And why would they suggest hiring her if they didn't want her to come?" Dean added, as though struck suddenly by the thought.

The question hung in the air. I couldn't help but feel bad for him once more.

Maybe he'd stumbled into more than an uncooperative boss.

11

Lamps, And Other Instruments

Nouronnihar's belongings had been left, waiting for her, in one of the palace rooms. It turned out that there were many such suites—so many that Nouronnihar's quarters stood untouched: Dean had been able to get his own deluxe apartment farther down the hall.

I glanced at William. We were both panting. We'd climbed several sets of stairs to get here, led by always-impassive attendants. Officers Ja'far and Babs had taken one look at the battered traveling-cases and had announced that their time was better spent interviewing the head of security. We were on our own to go through everything, looking for a set of keys.

Jasmin's unfortunate third secretary had not been a light packer.

"I guess she really did think she was moving here, hopefully permanently," I said to William. As we watched, a tube—presumably of posters, though we'd find out soon—rolled off the tower of three trunks, a wooden crate, and two large fabric bundles.

"It's another point in favor of thinking that she *is* the victim they have down at the station," William agreed. "Why else would she leave all this behind?"

"And at the same time, no wonder she had it sent on ahead," I added, chuckling despite myself. "Alright, I guess we'd better get to it. Time to prove our worth."

"You already found *one* set of keys," William grumbled. "I'd rather not look for another. We ought to be visiting with your family."

"You can get the hot gossip later," I assured him, tugging the fabric bundles onto the luxurious king-size bed that stood in the corner. The room, naturally, was airy, expensive, and had ceilings for days. The vanity beside the window was probably worth more than my shop in Belville. Everything was done up tastefully in shades of green, white, and blue.

"Some paradise hotel," William grumped. Nonetheless, he began using magic to unlock the trunks. "What'd you think she's *doing* here?"

"Jasmin, you mean? I don't get the impression she actually wants to host anyone but her employees," I said, tugging at the ties around the bundles. "Did you notice how quiet it is?"

"Maintaining all those gardens just for *her* is a lot of work," William said doubtfully. "Not to mention all the spells on this place."

"William," I said, a thought occurring to me, "do the spells here remind you of the spells on the town gate? Back at the marina, I mean. Or even the magic you sensed last night. Is it all the same work?"

"Could be," he told me. I noticed that he'd opened the trunks, but couldn't lift the top one down with just his magic.

I left the bed to help him lower it to the floor, still thinking.

"So Jasmin is behind all this security?"

"Looks like it to me. I don't smell anyone else's magic here," he said as he began scanning the trunk's contents.

"I wonder what she's so worried about," I mused. *Her, and everyone else on the island too, all of a sudden.* It was strange—since leaving, I'd always thought of Kairoi as safe and sleepy, the kind of place where nothing would actually happen. But now, even the police officers carried blades. Officer Babs had used a large pocket knife to cut up his fruit. It wasn't much, of course, and yet it was thought-provoking.

But now was the time to work, and efficiently, I reminded myself. I pulled my own small pen knife from my belt and opened up the bundles of fabric. They were, predictably, bedding and pillows, with no trace of metal or keys to be found.

"I wonder if she didn't realize that this place was already set up?" I said idly as I moved on to the wooden crate.

"I think she had her own taste," William informed me. I glanced over to see him wrinkling his nose at a trunk *full* of brass lamps and antique sailing instruments.

"So cool! That's an astrolabe," I said, distracted. As I went over to take a look, my eye caught more details—miniature lanterns, a paperweight shaped like a masthead, even a stained-glass porthole tucked against one end of the trunk.

"Name a ship's accessory she *didn't* have," William challenged me. "This is like the Little Mermaid's storehouse."

"I think it's neat. She did have her own taste," I said, nudging him playfully before returning to my own work. "A lot of merfolk tend to like nautical fashion—that's what Taiwo says, at least. They think it's cute."

"Well, at least it's not keys," said William. From the corner of my eye, I could see that he was glowing blue—using magic to scan the trunk for something he knew to look for, rather than unpacking each item.

"You'd really think she'd carry those on her," I agreed. "But still, someone has to look through all this."

"*Someone* like the local police."

The crate turned out to be full of seaweed snacks and cookies. Put off by the sweet and salty smells, I had to admit, I could relate to William's attitude. I ruffled his ears as I returned the crate to the pile, and got started on the second trunk.

William, meanwhile, turned his attention to the third. For a few moments we worked in silence. William's trunk was full of clothing, whereas mine was stacked to the brim with books. Sorting through them with my magnet, I couldn't help but miss Luca. *Where is he now? I bet he's having a blast with Aly and Zady. He'd definitely have something to say about these . . .*

Something caught my eye. Most of the books were romances and mysteries, but there was one non-fiction reference book stuffed in the corner: *A History of Lost Nautical Treasures*, with many pages dog-eared or bookmarked. It wasn't light bedtime reading, for sure, but it did fit in with the trunk of ship-themed knick knacks. It also, like all the other books before it, contained no metal.

"You ought to put Luca into an outfit like this," William said, magically holding aloft a blue striped romper.

"Please. Did you see how interested he *already* is in the sailors?" I chuckled as I reached for the poster tube. "Let's not encourage him too much."

"Yeah, we wouldn't want him to stay here," William agreed.

I hesitated. Lose Luca? I'd never considered it. His home

was so clearly in Belville.

William slammed his trunk shut and turned his attention to the poster tube too. "So?" he prompted.

"Right." Using my little knife, I cut through the tape and pried the end of the tube up. When I upended it, a pile of papers fell into my lap, most curved to fit in the shipping container. I inventoried them aloud as I sorted through them. "A poster map of New West Key, another map of the oceans of Beyond . . . Oh, that's a pretty picture of West Reef . . . A poster advertisement for a play. And then a few notebooks. Why would she pack those in here, and not put them flat into the trunk with the books?"

I passed the posters to William and, curiously, leafed through the two notebooks. One seemed to be a diary, and instinctively I set it aside. Being nosy for the police and outright prying were two different things, as far as I was concerned. The other notebook was much more official-looking, with lined pages divided into columns, like a ledger.

A shipping ledger, I realized suddenly. One where a lot of the lines didn't seem to be adding up.

"Oh dear," I said, showing William. "Maybe Nouronnihar didn't run into trouble here after all. Maybe it followed her from somewhere else."

* * *

We reconvened with the police officers under a silken canopy in the front gardens. A trellis jam-packed with bright pink flowers and broad leaves sheltered us from curious eyes—not that anyone in Jasmin's palatial complex was uncouth enough to show actual curiosity. Except, perhaps, Dean.

But seeing as the four of us were suitably unattended, I showed Ja'far and Babs the contents of the poster tube William and I had investigated. Babs cooed over the play poster, an old run of *The Adventures of Sindbad the Sailor.* Ja'far was more focused. He thumbed through the ledger carefully.

"It seems to me," he said finally, "that our victim did indeed have 'skills.'"

William sneezed. "Did you just make a joke?" His tone clearly conveyed, *maybe you aren't so bad after all.*

But Officer Ja'far was immune to praise. "I made a wry comment," he corrected. "This bears further investigation."

"New West Key," Babs mused, as he handed the tube of posters to his superior. "Isn't that where the sailors are from?"

"The shipwrecked crew?" I clarified. Somehow, I was surprised—and I also wasn't. New West Key was a large shipping port due south of the Blue Desert Islands; a lot of imported goods did come from there, because it was a hub for trade and marine study. In this sea, to encounter sailors from New West Key was like encountering mountain goats while on an alpine hike. And yet . . . both a shipwreck and a murder seemed like too many catastrophes to befall citizens of New West Key way out here on Kairoi.

"Yes, them," Officer Ja'far answered absently as he packed away Nouronnihar's documents. "Add them to the list, Babs. For now, we need to get back to the station."

"Was the head of security able to identify Nouronnihar?" I asked, unable to help myself. I knew from my investigations with Officer Thorn that it was proper Guild procedure to notify the family of a victim as soon as identification was made—and to get permission from the family before performing any kind of in-depth autopsy.

Ja'far, however, was not impressed by my familiarity with police work. The look he gave me was withering. "Like everyone else in the Sanctuary, they insist that Nouronnihar never even showed up at the gates. Meanwhile, the sentry on guard yesterday evening insists no one from the Palace left."

"It's not *Red's* fault no one's cooperating," William said, his tone now distinctly adding, *back off.*

"You'll have to forgive him," Babs said, patting Officer Ja'far on the shoulder. "He's had a tough day."

I resisted the urge to raise an eyebrow. Sure, a person had been murdered and that was very stressful and sad, but at the same time, our day had mostly consisted of walking around a marsh and sitting in unbelievable gardens eating *very* expensive food.

Ja'far shrugged off Babs' hand and collected himself. "We know enough that we should be able to complete identification on our own. The potential victim provided professional references, and surely *they* will have seen her before."

"Unless she was a ghost," Babs said helpfully.

William snorted. "Not sure how you'd end up with a body in your police station, in that case."

"I'm just saying, vision isn't everything," Babs returned, blithe and unworried. "So, we're headed back to the station, then? Should we bring Red along?"

"We haven't been authorized to investigate the body yet," Ja'far said through gritted teeth.

"And *Red* should really get home to her family," I added, laying emphasis on the third person to point out that *I* got a say in the matter, too. "I do appreciate you coming to me for help, but I think William and I have done all we can for now."

"You've been a really big help," Babs assured us. "We'll give you a ride back. And we'll call on you as soon as we have new developments, right, Ja'ja?"

"Of course." Officer Ja'far looked about as excited about that as I was about the prospect of another ride in the back of the police cart.

I exchanged a glance with William and shrugged one shoulder. *We can't all have our wishes granted,* I thought.

12

New for Old

Officer Ja'far barely rolled to a stop on the road in front of my mothers' house. He gladly left William and me in his dust.

"If I'd've known he was practically going to throw us from the cart, I would've opted to walk," said William, sneezing.

"Or we could have just walked from town," I agreed, watching the cart rattle off toward Wellspring. "But, we're here now, at least . . ."

William and I walked up the front path only to find the door locked. I used my key to let us in, but it was clear that Luca and my parents were up to trouble somewhere else. After a cursory glance around the front hall, I found a note taped to an ornamental mirror nearby. It was on the same teal paper I remembered Zady using for notes when I was a kid, and it bore her distinctive handwriting.

"Looks like they went down to the beach," I called to William, reading the note. "They say to bring along an umbrella for ourselves and whatever drinks we want."

At the mention of the beach, William stopped sniffing

around curiously and turned into a black and blue-sparkles blur. As he raced past me to the kitchen, presumably to raid the ice box for drinks, I heard him grumble, "I can't *believe* Luca went to the beach without me!"

I laughed. Knowing Aly and her love of getting "out and about," I figured Luca had had little choice. I hurried up to our guestroom to change into a swimsuit as fast as I could, lest William get it into his mind to leave me behind.

Mere moments later, laden with all our beach gear, William and I hit the street again. William was so excited that he had actually deigned to wear a doggy knapsack, sort of a small pair of saddlebags, filled with drinks. He assured me he'd keep them cold with magic. This left me free to carry some extra towels and a portable umbrella, so I didn't protest. It was fun to see William more cheerful.

For just a moment, though, as we crossed over the tracks left by the police cart, William paused. He glanced over his shoulder, back in the direction of town. "Red," he said, thoughtfully, "*do* you think it's normal, the way Ja'far has been treating us? Even from the first night at the marina?"

"After living with Officer Thorn's rules for years, I have no idea what's normal," I admitted lightly. "I'll admit he's not friendly, but do you think there's something more there?"

"I wonder," was all William said. Then he shook himself and turned his nose toward the beach.

We cut off the main road onto a sandy path that led between several of the neighbors' houses. Like my mothers' house, most of these had walled back yards, so there wasn't much to see from the road. But the salty ocean air was invigorating nonetheless, and the possibility of ocean waves seemed to peek around every corner and dune. By the time we crested a hill and the beach lay flat before us, murder seemed a very long way away.

We paused at the top, scanning the beach. It was long and wide, dotted with picnickers and walkers. Fortunately, Zady still used the same umbrella she'd favored when I was a kid. I pointed out the fringed red and purple contraption to William, who let out a *woof* of recognition and took off at a run.

I followed a little more carefully, opting to walk. The added weight on my sandals bogged me down in the fine sand. By the time I reached the umbrella, William had shed his pack and gone to fetch Luca from the waves. It turned out that Luca *was* enjoying the beach, very much. He greeted me with a wide grin and a rather wet hug.

"Oh, sorry," he added, when he pulled back and it was clear my thin bathing suit cover-up was now wet.

"I was going swimming sooner or later anyway," I assured him, grinning back. I chucked the umbrella and the useless cover-up down on a towel next to Zady before facing Luca again. "Race you?"

"No fair!" he called, but he was already running after me, William by his side.

It was a while later that we all returned to Zady's little outpost, laughing and managing to get water and sand over everything as we got out drinks and towels. I set up my umbrella and hid beneath it—I'd had enough sun exposure as a child to last me a lifetime. Luca was less timid, though. He lay his towel out in the sunshine in front of our umbrellas and proceeded to stretch out.

William and Zady, meanwhile, looked very regal in the shade of her old fringed umbrella. Zady smiled at me as we finally settled down. "Just what the doctor ordered, I take it?"

"Or the apothecary," Luca chimed in. He lay on his towel like a kid at a sleepover, with his feet kicking in the air behind him.

"Or the alchemist," William added, panting in the shade.

"Seawater's good for anyone, in moderation," I concluded jokingly. "Although I notice a distinct lack of sailors on the beach?"

"They have a sort of headquarters at the hotel where they're staying," Luca said. "They showed it to us. Apparently they spend most of their time trying to think how to get another ship and trying to raise money."

"Couldn't they just take the catamaran back to the mainland?" William asked.

"Wellspring residents have offered them tickets many times," Zady told him. "But they insist that would be a step backwards, somehow. They seem to prefer to do things the hard way."

"Sailor's pride, and all," Luca said, his white teeth flashing against his skin in a lopsided grin.

William focused in on him with a shake of the ears. "You aren't planning to run away and become a pirate, are you?"

"Who said anything about piracy?" Luca replied, laughing. "But Aly did say we could maybe do a boat trip while we're here, Red. Would you want to do that?"

I noticed that Luca had not directly answered William's question, of course, but I laughed it off. "Sure. Where is Aly, by the way?"

"Out for one of her excessive walks," said Zady, airily. "Now that she's been banned from running, she's become fanatical about walking instead."

"One door closes and a window is opened," Luca said. "I wonder why that behavior sounds so familiar . . ."

He was now staring at me. I flushed. "I'm not like that!"

"You are," William confirmed.

"They've always been peas in a pod," Zady said, her expression fond. "The trouble they used to get into!"

"I want to hear all about it," Luca vowed, looking even more like a sleepover teen angling for spilled secrets.

William rumbled in agreement. "We never get to hear *any* juicy stories about Red."

"That's because there aren't any," I said hastily. "Wouldn't you rather hear about what William and I were up to today?"

"We all know what you're up to," my mother informed me, "but truthfully, yes, I'm dying to know what you found so far in your investigation. And it serves Aly right for missing the gossip because she went out so long!" she added conspiratorially to William, who chuckled in agreement.

I caught Luca and Zady up on our adventure through the estuary—and the sanctuary. Zady clucked her tongue when Jasmin and her palace came up, of course, but she was just as wide-eyed over the opulent details as Luca was.

"We've all heard stories, of course," she remarked, "but practically no one from town has ever been invited up there. Especially not since construction finished."

"We were wondering about that," William said. "We were wondering, why here? What's she doing here? She doesn't ever consult with anyone from Wellspring?"

"You mean she might have come here for divination?" Zady confirmed, and thought through it. "It'd be a flattering thought, in a way, but as far as I know, she's never asked anyone here for a consultation. And believe me, news like that would be all over the island in a flash."

"I think they can tell that that's the case," I put in dryly. Luca chuckled at me.

"Personally, I think it's more a case of running away," Zady continued. As she leaned forward in her old wooden beach chair, we all leaned in, too. "Rumor has it that she picked Kairoi because she wanted somewhere as quiet as possible."

"Then she could have just bought Baby," I protested. A little petulantly, I admit.

"That's another of the islands," Zady told William and Luca, who were clearly confused. "It's the littlest of the set, so everyone just calls it Baby Island. No one lives there—not since the ifrit sightings."

"A real live ifrit?" Luca's eyes shone.

"One story at a time," William insisted. "What about Jasmin? What's she running away from?"

"I couldn't say exactly," Zady said, and immediately went on: "but we're all certain it's some kind of *great* personal tragedy. A terrible betrayal—something to do with her business or inheritance, perhaps. I'm sure you've gathered by now that she trusts absolutely no one."

I hesitated as I thought this over. Was that the impression I'd gotten? It *could* fit . . . there had been a strange feeling at the Palace, underneath the glamour and beauty: maybe it had been sadness.

Meanwhile, Zady was really getting into the tale. "The secretary you said you met coming in, who was going to be the third? To tell you the truth, I'm surprised he's *only* the third. I suppose it takes a while to bring them in."

"You mean she keeps firing them because she thinks they're betraying her?" Luca asked.

"Or worse?" William suggested.

"The first one left so fast no one'd even learned her name,"

Zady said mysteriously. "And we didn't see her go, either."

I had to roll my eyes at that. "And what were you doing? Camping out in front of the Palace gates for all the details?"

"Of course not," said my mother, with dignity. "But in those early days she did order things up from Wellspring, and Aly's friends the Burtons—you remember them, Cinnabar?—they would do the deliveries. They said one day that the first secretary was just *gone.* And they wouldn't be surprised if it happened more than once."

I exchanged a glance with William. We hadn't yet told Zady and Luca who the victim was supposed to be. The unlucky third secretary. But she'd not had any chance to do her job. Even for the imperious Jasmin of local gossip, wasn't that moving pretty fast?

"Random as it is, that might be something to tell the police," I admitted.

William snorted. "That's only *if* they stop to listen."

"There'll be opportunity," Zady assured us. "There's been a clan-wide call for a divination session tonight. By using reeds, they hope to learn more about the unfortunate victim."

"Reeds?" Luca leaned in, curious. "As a focus, since the body was found in the marsh?"

"Precisely." Zady smiled at him. "We Springers find that, while fire-gazing can always yield interesting results, it is most useful to offer something to the fire—an herb or, in this case, a plant that is related to what we hope to see."

"And the police will really trust it?" asked William, interested as well.

"Well . . ." Zady's voice trailed off expressively. "Wellspring's been known to have its issues with the Police Guild. I myself will be the first to tell you that sometimes, some Seers are prone to taking their own visions too seriously. But if we provide anything, even the barest hint, it is worth trying."

I tugged at my hair thoughtfully. "I wonder how much store Babs and Ja'far will put by it. I guess we'll find out soon enough."

* * *

Eventually, Aly returned to interrupt our gossiping. To be fair, the conversation had turned more generally to island life, with Zady explaining certain rituals to Luca and William— things like "initiation," in which a young Springer accepted their destiny as a Seer and often took on a new name. What had once seemed commonplace (and unattainable) to me was enough to make Luca and William lose track of time. Fortunately, Aly reminded us that the sun was setting. Despite our late and fancy lunch, I found that I was starving. Motivated by the thought of dinner, we packed up and headed for home.

Luca, William, and I stopped at the front door, using fresh water from a nearby pump to rinse sand and salt from ourselves. I shook out our towels and carried them around the house, to hang them on a clothesline to dry. Luca followed, arms full of cover-ups and even his hat, which had been blown into the waves at one point.

"You sure are embracing beach life," I teased as I helped him pin the straw brim to the line.

"We came a long way to be here," he reminded me, smiling. "And your parents are really, really sweet, Red."

"Yeah. I'm glad you think so," I told him absently. It wasn't that I disagreed—it was the distance that he'd reminded me of.

It was a strange thought, how far we'd traveled just a few days before. And how far poor Nouronnihar had traveled, just to meet a sad fate; and how far might Jasmin have come, looking for solitude?

After cleaning ourselves up, we joined the others in the kitchen to find dinner preparations already underway. William was attentively helping Aly set the table, so Luca and I lingered around the kitchen to see what assignments we'd get.

We didn't have to wait long. I was tasked with making a salad, while Luca helped heat up flatbreads on the stove. In no time at all, we were all seated around the table, enjoying a spicy stew over rice. It reminded me, just for a moment, of that morning at breakfast—the last time we'd all been able to sit down together. Fortunately, no police visit interrupted this meal.

Once we'd washed up the dishes and put away the leftovers, we walked into town for the divination session. Zady and Aly would participate, of course, and Luca and William were excited to be spectators. I had my own doubts. To add to that, it was awkward—because most of the town had gathered, congregating on the benches surrounding the bonfire as the night deepened, I did a lot of waving and head-nodding and *yes, it's me again*-ing before everyone else settled in to stare at the flames.

I had to wonder if perhaps what Jasmin hoped to rule was simply her own space and reputation. In that moment, I could relate.

Traditionally, divination sessions would be "opened," or introduced, with a few words from someone integrally involved in the goal for the night's divination. For a session involving crime, a police officer might have made a good choice to lead the ceremony, but none were in evidence. Instead, my old school teacher stood up—a nice lady we all called "Persia," though I'd never known why. She asked everyone to *see what you can about the victim,* and then she faded back into the crowd.

Nouronnihar. I was curious what they would find. I kept thinking of her much-loved reference book on buried treasure. My eyes strayed toward the apothecary on the corner, and I couldn't help but muse on the ways our passions can sometimes get us into trouble.

Eventually, once the ceremony was done, townsfolk shared what they had seen with each other. At this, I paid more attention. There were some interesting calls from the Seers:

"An important blade, nearly lost!"

"A watery grave!"

"An old secret to be maintained!"

. . . Interesting, all of them, but not exactly *concrete.* I listened to the conversation without chipping in. *Were the divination signs always this vague?* I wondered.

Eventually, the rumors and guesses dried up. My shoulders untensed as we walked back home under the stars. Luca and William were happily chatting to Aly and Zady, too energetic to go to bed, so instead we went out to the patio in the cool twilight, carrying glasses of wine and a whole platter of truffles. As we settled in, Aly pointed out exactly what had been bothering me.

"With crime, you need clear motive and opportunity," she said, leaning back in her wicker chair, "but we really only have conjecture and rumors based on fire visions so far. That, and whatever stories everyone's been telling you about themselves."

"And the ledger," William reminded her. "But that and the keys are really the only physical evidence."

"And the blood, the first night," Luca added faithfully.

"You mean what got us mixed up in this in the first place," I added, smiling wryly at him across the little patio table. "It's odd . . . like we came into a crime that had been halfway committed."

"Or an alibi only halfway created, if you think about it from the other perspective," Zady said contemplatively. "Many tales are told in parts. If you pay attention, you'll find out the rest."

"As usual, you make it sound so easy to figure out." I sipped at my drink. Maybe it was the wine—or maybe the exhaustion—or maybe the habit of investigating, but either way, it was harder and harder to remind myself that I'd come here to make peace with *my* past, not with yet another crime.

Luca, too, was gazing off into the distance. "Some people are clever thinkers on their feet."

"Even so," said Zady, "an alibi is really only a story . . . when you think about it."

I turned to see if William had any thoughts on this, but he was staring up at the clear stars above us. I let my head settle back, looking up too. In the face of so many questions, it was somehow comforting to watch the night sky and gain a little perspective. We were only little pieces in a much larger picture—one that, I hoped, would become clearer in time.

13

Powder Keg

The next morning, our second on the island, William and Luca were wise to my tricks. I'd half expected them to sleep in after playing on the beach—and investigating, of course. But they were both up before I'd had a chance to slip downstairs.

We lingered over breakfast with Aly and Zady. When we'd managed to get through another meal without interruption, the others clearly took it as a positive sign. With a sparkle in her eye, Aly suggested heading into Wellspring, where she intended to ask around about hiring a boat for a day trip—and to let Luca loose in the market.

Luca, naturally, was all for this plan. William, too, seemed excited to see the town. He hadn't been able to visit it yesterday, and declared that he had to make up for lost time. Once everyone was ready, the two of them hit the road ahead of us, leading the way.

Zady gave Aly a pointed look and then swept past us to join them. I rose an eyebrow at Aly and waited as she turned to lock the front door.

"What was that all about?" I asked suspiciously.

"We have a bet on," she admitted, winking at me.

I had to laugh as I fell in beside her, walking down the front path. "I've never understood that. How can you place bets when you're both probably going to cheat and use divination to know the outcome anyway?"

"Hey, I resent that," Aly said, laughing because she didn't actually resent it at all. She and Zady had a history of trying to predict outcomes, and neither was above a little meddling—or divination, of course. "Sweet Cinnabar. The game isn't figuring out *what* will happen, the game is figuring out *how* it will happen. And we never know either for sure. You've always given divination too much credit."

"Sour grapes, and all that," I said. It came out more easily, more lightly, than I had expected it to. And as I recalled the night before, I realized she might be right.

"Magic grapes, in your case." Aly draped an arm around my shoulder as we meandered down the road. "I hope you've realized that you were never really missing out on much."

My mouth was dry, but still, it didn't hurt like I'd thought it might. "How would I have realized that?"

"Your studies. Traveling. Meeting William. Freeing your partner from what was clearly a strong curse. Coming back here and seeing the effect you've had, and can have, on others in the clan," Aly said. Her voice wasn't gentle or teasing—it was *proud*, I realized.

"You knew all about Babs and Ja'far," I accused. "About them becoming police officers because they saw me go off to be an apprentice."

"Sure I knew," Aly chuckled. "But I'm not the one who showed them that it was possible to dream a different dream, am I?"

I hesitated. I watched Luca up ahead, laughing at something William had said, and Zady smiling at them both. Suddenly, my heart was in my throat.

"I hope you know you never have to apologize for being yourself." Aly squeezed my shoulder before straightening up. She'd always known when I had too much on my mind to say aloud. "In any case, that's not what the bet was about. Not quite."

I shook my head, letting the big questions settle back to the bottom. "Oh? What's the bet about this time?"

"You'll see. Is there anything you'd like to do in town?" Aly asked carelessly.

"Well," I admitted, "I do want to stop by the hotel and check on the sailors. I'd like to hear their story from *them*." The ship's ledger and New West Key maps swam in my mind's eye, and with them, I was reminded of William's point that this was supposed to be a family trip. Struck by guilt, I added, "Not that I'm trying to avoid you—"

Aly laughed aloud again. "Don't worry, neither of us will be offended. I'm pretty pleased, myself."

"Why—" I paused. Despite years away, I knew my mothers well. Everything became crystal clear. "Your bet was about *me*? About the investigation?"

"About what your next step would be," Aly admitted, a victorious lilt to her voice. "Zady thought you'd want to go to the Palace again. But I figured you hadn't heard enough from the sailors, and—"

"And you cheated," I accused her, though I was laughing too now, partly in exasperation. "You manufactured the trip into town to make the sailors the easier choice!"

"I did not. If you'd wanted to go to see Jasmin again, you would have," Aly said, with total confidence. "Besides—I really *am* looking forward to hiring a boat for tomorrow. Your Luca will probably faint away from excitement."

"You can bet about me, but no bets about Luca," I warned her. At the same time I smiled, acknowledging inwardly that she was probably right.

We'd reached the outskirts of town, and the others pooled at the edge of the road, waiting for us. The sight of the post office was a convenient reminder. Leaving Aly to crow about her success to Zady, I ducked in to collect mail from Belville. There was a letter from Rhys, of course—it was his habit to write once a day when left in charge of the shop. At the bottom of his note he'd thoughtfully taken down a short message from Frank, a wizened old mink who worked in the bookstore with Luca. Frank was one of those creatures who'd lived for so long that he'd developed a little magic, including the power of speech—not that he used that power, if he could avoid it. Still, he was handling Luca's standing orders and most persistent customers in Luca's absence. Apparently, all was well on the home front.

Intriguingly, there was also a note from Maggie, Officer Thorn's sweetheart. While Luca and William perused Rhys's detailed report, I started reading:

Hi Red, Mina wanted me to write to you. I told her I'm not her secretary, but you know how she is when she gets an idea. Plus she said she doesn't want her name on the envelope. It'll make sense in a minute. I hope. The thing is, after you all left this morning, she went back to the station and she looked up the station in Wellspring. That's where you are, right? (It must be, since that's where this letter is supposed to go!) I think she just wanted to see if she knew the officers there. It turns out she kind of does, by reputation, anyway. She really thinks you ought to know that—

"You know," the post office employee sniffed, "this really isn't the place to *read* your mail."

They had a point. Wellspring's post office was quite small, and pretty busy. I stuffed Maggie's letter into the pocket of my dress and hustled Luca and William outside.

"There you are," said Zady, before I could return to reading the letter. "I have a feeling you'll want to go across the street."

"To the market already? Why?" I asked, distracted.

The expression on Zady's face was amused, and yet also a little long-suffering. "Because Aly just went after the sailors, who are somewhere by the garden stall."

Luca took my hand, already headed into the road. "Come on. I knew you'd want to talk to them eventually."

"Everyone knows what I'm all about, huh?" I remarked to William ruefully.

"*I* want to know why sailors are interested in gardening," he retorted.

The three of us ducked into the rows of market stalls, leaving Zady waiting like a sentry by the street. Though she loved her gossip and writing letters, she wasn't comfortable in crowds. Usually she'd let me or Aly do all the shopping. I was familiar with the market, which seemed not to have changed very much.

Despite the early hour, it was already bustling. We passed one canvas canopy after another, each decorated with silks and signs and piles of whatever ware the merchants were selling: painted shells, deity statues, cooking pots, edible cacti, cotton tunics, knives. Toward the end of one block up ahead, I knew, was the garden stall. It was right next to a stall that had *always* sold coffee, coffee so strong it had probably been brewing since before I was born. It perfumed the air throughout this row of stalls.

I was half expecting that the sailors were headed there, for caffeine, rather than to the garden stall. But instead we found Aly and Sinbad standing at the corner, along with another sailor I didn't recognize. Her outfit, a striped tank top and weather-beaten white trousers, was obviously nautical. In one arm, she held the handles of three new shovels, their heads resting on the ground beside her bow-legged feet.

"Maybe they're starting a landscaping business to get the money for a new boat," I whispered to William before we came up to the group.

"There you are," Aly said, with her signature crooked smile. "I'll let you take over."

"You were looking for us, ma'am?" Sinbad asked me.

"Just call me Red," I told him, though I had low hopes that he'd follow the suggestion. Thinking fast on my feet, I said, "Luca told me a little about you all yesterday, and I'm really curious to hear your story . . ."

Okay, maybe I wasn't quite thinking fast *enough* on my feet. But I must have somehow hit Sinbad's speed exactly. His face opened up in a grin. "We're always happy to tell a story!"

"You'll get more than you bargained for," his companion agreed with a similarly toothy grin.

"Great," I said, both relieved and suddenly wondering what I'd gotten myself into. "How about we get some coffee and chat for a bit?"

14

Stormy Seas

> *. . . She really thinks you ought to know that the officer there, in Wellspring, has "two strikes against him." That seems to be police talk for he's done some things wrong and is on thin ice? She said she's surprised he hasn't already been replaced. And she was worried that if you ran into Officer Brooks, he might . . .*

"So," Sinbad said loudly, startling me from my reading. "Where do you want us to start, ma'am?"

I tucked away Maggie's letter once more, with a sigh. We'd opted to get drinks from a new cafe stand, on Aly's recommendation. This one was at the far end of the market stalls, and it had a small seating section. I thought that by claiming a set of tables and an umbrella for us, I'd get a quiet moment. I'd only been partially right—it had been more like *half* a moment, it seemed.

Sinbad and his companion—who had introduced herself as

Archer—sat across the tiled table from me. William flopped underneath us, no doubt grateful for the shade. Luca pushed a huge iced chai in front of me and then he pulled up a nearby chair.

"Aly took some iced tea back to Zady, and said they'd start looking into boats," he told me.

No doubt they'll both expect a full report later, I thought wryly. But it was a weight off my mind to know that they didn't mind us investigating. I focused on Sinbad. "Where would you like to begin? You know best."

"That he does," said Archer loyally. She looked to me to be a dwarf: her appearance screamed *weathered rock.* Her skin was wrinkled and the light gray of granite, and it was hard to tell if her thick multitude of braids was white or perhaps a mossy green. Over a squashed nose, her eyes were dark and prone to squint, but she spoke and moved lightly.

Sinbad set his drink down on the table, his chest swelling. Both sailors had opted for fruity smoothies topped off with paper umbrellas. "I've been a sailor since I was a lad," he said, rather grandly. "My fortunes have risen and fallen with the sea!

"When I was young," he went on, settling into his tale, "I went to New West Key to see if I could make myself an apprentice to a great captain. They have every ship there that you could imagine. Tall-masted ships with great white billowing sails, slow-moving barges run with the cooperation of the merfolk, even modern magitech catamarans. Small outfits running back and forth every few days, larger ones that make a journey out of it, taking sugar and spices from West Key up to the coast, exchanging them for new tech and crafted goods, then taking those to the Blue Desert Islands and even the Golden Isles up north, then stopping at the coast, at Argen, before coming back down again. What a life!"

So far, Sinbad sounded like a talking version of Nouronnihar's maps. I glanced at Luca as I sipped my drink. He was looking at me with an expression that I couldn't read.

"Back then, I was all on my lonesome," Sinbad continued. "I picked the biggest boat in the marina, a wooden beauty with five masts and the crew to match. Nothing but luxury goods for them! Ah, it was grand. I saw things on that ship I'd never known existed. I started off by scrubbing the kitchen floors. I'd worked my way up to serving grub when the ship was set upon by pirates off the Golden Isles."

From beneath the table, William snorted. "Pirates? Actual pirates?"

"Aye, pirates!" cackled Sinbad, his maritime nature distinctly showing. He brandished his drink like a baton, his eyes far away as he relived his past. "There we were, in a calm sea, no breeze. We never had any chance of outrunning them. And the captain of the ship wouldn't let guns aboard, and our mage was seasick. It wasn't much of a fight, let me tell you! But as a lad, when I saw those pirates come up over the side in their crimson sashes . . ."

I had a feeling I could see where this was going. Sinbad's story was very like that of his namesake, Sindbad, an adventurous—and dubiously lucky—sailor of fairy tales. I cleared my throat. "You worked for the pirates after that, then?"

"I never had a heart for piracy," Sinbad insisted, one hand dramatically to his chest. "My real love was always the sea. But my years with the crew of the *Drowned Pirate* were some of the best adventures I'd ever dreamed of. Everyone in the

Golden Isles knew our flag!"

"So what happened?" Luca asked. "Did you get caught?"

"By the *kraken*," Sinbad said solemnly.

I frowned. "Is that the name of a police ship?"

"It's a mythical ship-eatin' creature," Archer told me kindly.

"The pirate ship was attacked by a kraken and you survived?" Luca had clearly been reading up on his sea-faring adventure stories.

"Just so!" said Sinbad. "I avoided the creature's rage by stowing myself away in an old trunk. It floated ashore on an island I'd never visited before. Just when I thought I'd live there for the rest of my life, *that's* when the police ship came by and saw the smoke from my fires!"

"And they weren't upset that you'd been a pirate?" I pointed out.

"They were coming ashore anyway because they'd all got food poisoning," Sinbad went on as though I'd said nothing. "I told them I knew a little about cooking, from my days as an apprentice, and right then and there, they marooned their old cook and they took me on."

"Wait," Luca protested, getting into the swing of things now. "They *left* their cook? The police?"

"That was some exciting sailing," Sinbad recollected. "Up and down the coastline, a new battle every week!"

"Who were the police fighting?" William rumbled in disbelief. I thought of the letter in my pocket, and wondered.

"But of course, no one can win *every* battle," said Sinbad, philosophically. "The day came when the ship's hull got split clean in two, and she sank straight down to the depths. It all happened so quick, most of the sailors didn't even know it'd happened until it was too late. But I had lashed myself to a barrel of ale—"

"Did you join the people who had taken down the ship?" Luca asked. "Was it more pirates?"

"—ah me, no! I floated ashore and I settled down in Argen for a bit, had a family. Made my way as a humble bartender. But I always heard the call of the sea. So when a captain who frequented my bar asked me if I knew a good cook . . ."

I watched Sinbad as I sipped my drink again. By now, I'd seen the pattern, as I'm sure everyone had. I wondered if he'd changed his name to Sinbad on purpose. Or perhaps he had grown up with the name and decided to embrace all its connotations? It was common for fairy tales to repeat themselves in Beyond, but they weren't often *so* on the nose, in my experience.

"And what a grand voyage that was!" Sinbad declared. "The captain's goal was to sail all the way around the continent."

"Did he make it?" I couldn't help but ask.

"The boat capsized in the northern reaches, leaving us stranded on the ice. I survived on the meat of one seal for a month. A local on a hunting expedition found me and took me back to civilization in his rowboat, but before we could get there, we were set upon by an entire pod of whales. Fins and flukes were everywhere! I saw my life flash before my eyes. But right at that moment, a civilian cruise ship floated up."

"Oh dear," I murmured, wondering what dreadful fate was in store for the tourists.

"They rescued us and I took on work as a waiter to pay for my passage. But their cook was dishonest, and I couldn't stand to see it. I got in a massive row with her, and the captain chose to believe her side over mine, so they left me stranded outside of Seaside."

"That's across the continent from here," Luca commented. "How did you get back?"

I, for one, was just glad a kraken hadn't eaten the cruise.

"A special trade run from Seaside to New West Key," Sinbad said simply. "Too bad I didn't realize at the time that they were going all that way to avoid any import fees or customs, and they were in such a hurry because their 'trade' was illegal booze. Soon as we got to port, I felt it was my duty to turn them in.

"I was back where I started," he added, "and I was able to take on work as a sailor of all trades, very handy on a ship. For a while I sailed with *The Portress* in these very isles."

William stirred again. "Is that the name of a ship or another mythical creature?"

"A fine ship," Sinbad confirmed, "captained by a husband and his wife, both fearsome banshees, and whatever friends they'd collected on the way. Said the water called to their blood. Everyone used to joke that the ship ought to be unsinkable— that the banshees would just spirit it away, like ghosts."

"But many banshees aren't actual ghosts," Luca protested. "They can sometimes *look* ghostly, but really they're a sort of magic lake guardian, similar to naiads or even dryads and elves. I just saw a paper at the scholars' conference about—"

"Trouble is, even ghosts argue," Sinbad said, again rolling right over his audience's concerns. "It all fell apart in the end."

For a moment, the sailor was uncharacteristically quiet. I sipped my chai contemplatively, resisting the urge to count the stories up on my fingers. Sinbad had had his ships boarded by pirates, eaten by a kraken, sunk in battle, capsized in ice, attacked by whales, and subject to marooning, law-breaking, and feuds. That had to make at least six maritime disasters so far. "If you don't mind," I ventured, "how did you end up here?"

"Oh, that," said Archer, speaking up for her friend. "That was all of us."

"I appreciate that, Archer, but the fault is mostly mine," said Sinbad. He smiled ruefully at us. "There's nothing like a good first mate, eh?"

I exchanged a look with Luca, who winked at me. I had a feeling we both were thinking the same thing: *which of us is the captain, and which the first mate?*

"After parting ways with *The Portress*, I found myself in New West Key again," said Sinbad. "Back where I had started. I thought, why not take charge of my destiny this time? Take fate into my own hands? So I took all my money and I poured it into a ship and a crew. *Sinbad the Trader*, that's what I called my business."

"It was a grand business," said Archer. "It still is, cap'n."

"Yes," said Sinbad, sadly. "A gilded dream. We made three round trips in all, between the Blue Isles, New West Key, and the continent, spending time to buy and sell the best wares at each port. We were on the home leg of our third trip when—"

"What was it?" I prompted. It had to be something in the nearby waters, so I hesitated to suggest a kraken. "A battle? A run-in with some kind of spell?"

"It was a storm," said Archer, looking quite downcast.

Really? Pods of attacking whales and sea battles and rum runners and then weather? I pressed my lips together, hard. I knew well how dangerous the storms blowing in from open water could be, but I also knew that most ships were equipped to handle them.

Just then, two more sailors came up, breathless. One I recognized—Jason, the older man who'd collapsed outside my mothers' backyard. He looked, once again, faint. Luca and I hastened him into the shade.

"We've been looking for you. The nice ladies said to check here," said the other sailor, in a curiously high-pitched, bleating voice. I squinted up to see very curly blond hair and brown eyes. As he came closer, standing behind Jason, I could see he was shorter than the other sailors and considerably rounder, his old white tunic straining a bit around the belly. I couldn't help but wonder if perhaps he was sheep-kin. All kinds of -kin were possible in Beyond: usually, it was a matter of heritage—say, an ancestor had made a pact with a magical wolf, and now their descendants had ears or tails and were called wolfkin. I'd never seen sheepkin myself, but it wouldn't be any more outlandish than any of Sinbad's tales.

"This is Fleece," Jason told me gallantly. "And Jason. You know Jason?"

"I do, and I'm a little worried about him," I admitted, looking at the subject with some bafflement.

"He doesn't like it when we're apart too long," said Sinbad. "Jason, it's alright, fellow. Fleece, go and get you both something to drink, won't you?"

The fourth sailor trotted off among the patio furniture. I watched him from the corner of my eye, musing. None of the sailors seemed exactly competent enough to get away with murder.

However—they did seem odd enough to get interrupted halfway *through* a murder, and then to need to clean up afterwards . . .

"Are you all together pretty much all the time?" I asked

pleasantly.

"All the time," Archer confirmed.

"Except sometimes," Jason rasped.

"Basically all the time," Sinbad corrected.

William nudged my foot. We both could see exactly where this was headed. No doubt the sailors had an excellent—if somewhat fantastic, and perhaps not quite airtight—alibi.

15

A Shine in the Dark

And she was worried that if you ran into Officer Brooks, he might drag you into it. "You know how she is," she said to me. I get the feeling maybe you don't mean to, Red, but I do think Mina has a point. The two strikes so far are, one: he didn't go out to a local island (is it really called Baby Island?) to perform a rescue, even though Mina says he should have since I guess Baby Island is under Wellspring's jurisdiction, and then two: he put in an unsubstantiated report that the island is inhabited by an ifrit. I guess that's considered pretty serious in the Police Guild, since Ifrits can be dangerous. And Mina says everyone in the upper levels was really worried Officer Brooks was too emotional about it. I'm not quite sure what she means by that, but she still refuses to write you herself. I hope this was helpful? Anyway I bet you are having a great time! Just try not to get mixed up with the police, maybe?

> *Your friends,*
> *Maggie (and Mina)*

I finally managed to finish Maggie's letter as I slurped up the rest of my chai. The sailors had all toddled off to their hotel headquarters. Admittedly, I *was* curious about that, but I'd had my fill of Sinbad's stories for the moment.

So instead, I showed the letter to Luca, who read it aloud for William's benefit.

"She always confuses me when she calls Thorn 'Mina,'" he grumped from his spot under the table.

"Mina *is* technically her first name. Or part of it," I reminded him. Our illustrious Belville police officer's full name was Wilhelmina Thorn, but almost everyone just called her "Officer Thorn" or "Thorn" or, honestly, just "Officer," because until Maggie showed up, she had been devoted wholly and solely to her job.

"I think it's cute," Luca agreed. "Just like the fact that she wasn't sure whether or not to capitalize 'ifrit.' And the fact that they were both so worried about us."

"For all the good it did," William commented. "Could you *be* any more involved with police affairs, Red?"

"You hush. I never did sign their papers. And honestly, I haven't seen Officer Brooks," I said, thinking. "I barely even remember him. All this ifrit stuff must have happened before my time, or while I was gone."

"Do you think it's still relevant?" Luca asked, looking over the letter as though there might be a hidden message.

"That depends on you," I told him. "I know *stories* about ifrits, but just the scary ones we used to tell each other as kids.

What's the actual truth?"

"Yeah," William said, lifting his head and panting amenably. "Was there a paper on ifrits at your scholar conference, too?"

"Ha ha," Luca said, grinning at him. "No, Red, to answer your question, I'm honestly not sure. I don't know a lot about them, but I think they are a type of jinn—a sort of magical, liminal creature. They tend to only live in hot climates, I think, so I never really had a reason to research them before—aside from general curiosity. I do think they're considered more like minor deities than everyday people or magical creatures. But that's about it. Maybe Aly and Zady would know more?"

"They'd *definitely* know about whatever police drama Thorn's worried about," William added.

"Right on both counts," I agreed, smiling. "Okay, if everyone's done here, how about we go find them? They're probably done with their boat business by now anyway."

We disentangled ourselves from the cafe table and made our way to the street, rather than walking back through the market. I knew that Zady, at least, was much more likely to be on the main road. We walked slowly, heading toward the main intersection and fire plaza. As we passed the hotel, I glanced at the windows. I was still processing everything Sinbad had told us. It had been entertaining—but was any of it useful? Was any of it *true?*

I half expected the sailors to pile out of one of the windows, shouting at us, or perhaps to pop up on the roof, brandishing their new garden tools. In fact, there *was* a clamor, loud voices breaking through the midday heat. But it wasn't coming from the hotel . . . it was coming from farther down the street.

* * *

"I *need* to get those shipments up to her in time!"

As we came up to the corner, we had full view of the drama. It was the apothecary I'd seen yesterday. I somehow was not surprised to find her still stressed about shipments. But this time, she was yelling at Officers Babs and Ja'far, who'd parked their rickety cart outside her shop. Babs was huffing and puffing as he hoisted a wooden box into the back.

I took a moment to be glad it was a box going back there, and not me. And to say a silent prayer for the poor apothecary's glass bottles.

"We will take over them from here," Officer Ja'far was saying, in his coldest and most officious voice.

"But you don't understand," the apothecary cried. Her short, dyed-purple hair waved with each desperate gesture. "I *have* to get them to her! They're scheduled to arrive today!"

"But they've been confiscated," Babs pointed out.

Luca and William both visibly pricked up their ears. I'll admit, I was curious too. *What could this be about?*

"You aren't allowed to interfere with my business," the shopkeeper insisted. Behind her, under the shadow of the awning, her two assistants huddled with wide eyes.

"Based upon the agreement the Guild makes with every individual town and county, we *are*," said Officer Ja'far.

"It's for the greater good," added Babs. As he turned, he noticed us. "Oh, hey, Red! We have something for you to look at!"

The white-jacketed apothecary was now furious. "You *what?*"

For as much as I hoped her fervor was due to Guild policy, I had a feeling it was about me and my involvement. I winced. Babs' timing was unfortunate.

"It is also within our purview to hire an outside consultant. In this case, an alchemist," said Officer Ja'far, as stiff as ever.

"*Her?* What about *me?*" The apothecary looked ready to burst into flame.

"But you're the one who made them," Babs said, his tone clearly adding, *so of course we can't trust* you.

"But I'm the one who *lives* here! If there's police business to consult on, you should have come to me!" the apothecary wailed.

"We have come to you for all we need, at the moment," said Officer Ja'far. He glanced my way and I got the briefest feeling that he was relieved to find me quiet and calm. "We'll be leaving now."

"Do you intend to be leaving with my daughter?" Zady appeared from the cross street and walked over to stand beside me, her presence kindly but authoritative.

At the same time, Aly went over to the apothecary. "It'll be alright, Gene. We have time to sort everything out."

"But we don't. The shipment is already behind," Gene lamented. "And why would they go to *her?* Is there some rule that a police assistant has to be a local? This isn't fair!"

I hardly *felt* like a local, so the accusation threw me for a moment. But I could see why Gene had made it. I did look a lot more like most of Wellsprings' residents than she did. In fact, she seemed to be a dark elf, with deep gray skin and pointed ears more common in mountain climates.

"The *rule* is that the consultant must be *unbiased,*" Officer Ja'far said. It was a miracle he didn't crack a tooth. "Now really, we must be on our way."

"Sorry about your shipment," Babs said unhelpfully. "That's just the way it goes sometimes."

"I'm sure your client will understand," Aly assured Gene, rather more effectively.

"You don't know her," Gene said, her shoulders slumping.

I could practically feel William vibrating with the desire to ask, *who is the shipment for?*

But it seemed best to diffuse and get away as soon as possible. "How about we meet you at the station, officers?" I suggested, avoiding looking at Gene.

"I'll come along too," Zady said decisively.

Ja'far clearly knew when to admit he was beaten. "We expect you to head there now, then."

"Some attitude for someone who needs your help," William observed, as the police cart clattered slowly down the road.

I risked a glance at Gene, who had collapsed into Aly's arms. Over the apothecary's shoulder, Aly waved a hand at us as if to say *go, go.*

She didn't have to suggest it twice. "Attitude or no, I think it's a good idea to clear out. I don't think our presence here is helping."

"Poor Gene," Luca agreed.

"Yes. She's had a difficult time since setting up her shop here, I believe," Zady mused. "But there's no sense worrying over it just yet. Shall we follow the officers' request?"

"You go on," William said. "I'll stay with Aly."

Zady thanked him, and I ruffled his ears as we turned to go. I knew he was at least partly motivated by a desire to snoop, but I also appreciated his determination to leave no one in our group alone. William was good at thinking of things like that.

Luca, Zady, and I turned to head down to the police station. It was in the old town government building, technically just across from the apothecary, but the actual entrance to the police lobby was down at the far end of the building. The officers' cart was visible, tucked into a driveway at the far corner.

We had less than a block to walk, but the street was eerily quiet. *Everyone was probably watching that exchange like hawks, and now they're trying to pretend they weren't,* I thought. Shop windows showed no sign of life, and neither did the windows of the old town hall on our right. It felt disconcerting and a little embarrassing after all the yelling. My stomach rumbled, and the sound seemed to echo over the sand, rolling between the dusty buildings.

I was relieved at first when we pulled up to the stairs that led up to the police station. But as I looked up at the glass doors and the sign, *Wellspring Police Station,* a shiver ran down my spine.

Exactly where Thorn said I shouldn't go. It was silly; she was so far away; and this errand had nothing to do with ifrits . . .

. . . Still, I had to admit, nothing good had ever come of ignoring a warning from Officer Thorn.

16

Chosen

Wellspring's police station was just barely bigger than Belville's. I was far less familiar with this one, though—I'd managed to avoid the place as a kid. The front door let us into a small lobby with a desk and chairs lining the walls. A hallway extended back through the building. The floor was tiled and the walls were white plaster, just like the vast majority of homes in Wellspring, but it didn't feel homey in the slightest; in fact, there was a vaguely downcast air that pervaded the space. Maybe it was the fact that all the pictures were dusty or slightly off-kilter, or the shuttered windows. Or maybe it was the decidedly abandoned look of the front desk, its one little potted succulent slowly drying out.

As the door closed behind us, Babs bustled out from a room down the hallway, a small glass of water in his hand. For one brief moment, I got the impression that he and Ja'far had raided the apothecary just to have something to drink. It was a fantastical idea, of course, but I *did* wonder why they'd targeted Gene.

126

And my wondering only grew as Babs greeted us briefly and then began using his water glass to soak the succulent on the front desk.

"I've been nursing it back to health," he told us.

"Uh huh," I said, watching water splash and bead off the plant's puffy leaves. I tried to be a good guest, but the alchemist and amateur botanist in me won out. "Actually, if you really want it to flourish, you should—"

"It's very well-meaning of you," Luca interrupted brightly.

"Yes, the station's been needing a bit of care," Zady added.

They both knew me—and what would inspire me to get lost in a tangential lecture—too well.

Probably better not to lecture the people who had commandeered our help, I admitted to myself. With a sigh, I refocused on the situation at hand.

Babs had finished his watering and stood cheerfully behind the desk. Looking at him more closely, I realized that he had shed his coat and was just wearing a white tunic over his uniform pants. He was sweating. *How long have they been working today already? Did they take any break at all?*

"So," said Babs, his hands on his hips, "you're probably wondering why we asked you here so early this morning."

"It's nearly lunchtime, dear," Zady cut in with amusement.

"Let me catch you up on what we've done so far," Babs continued, undeterred.

Like a siren call, this promise to share information drew Officer Ja'far out of the back. He, too, had shed his coat and hat, his bald head shining under the office lights. "There's no need for that!"

"But it could help us understand how to help," Luca pointed out reasonably.

"We only need an alchemical survey," Ja'far insisted, gruff.

"Oh, Ja'ja, we need more than that," Babs informed his superior officer. To us, he added, "We've been at it all night. We took shifts, like we used to do at the Guild when studying."

I was a little confused as to how it was possible to study in shifts, but I let the point lie.

"We positively identified Nouronnihar," Babs went on. "Now, the chest has been opened."

"Not of the victim, surely?" Zady looked horrified.

"Or do you mean 'can'?" Luca asked quickly. "Like, you've opened a can of worms?"

"It's a mess is what it is," Ja'far declared. He sat on the edge of Babs' desk, running a hand over his head. "We haven't heard back from the victim's family yet, so we can't do any kind of autopsy. But we may not need to. It's clear she was killed by a blade of some kind."

"That fits with the blood," I said, thinking fast, "and what they were saying at the divination session. But still, I wouldn't jump to conclusions. It *is* possible that some kind of poison is involved, or—"

"That's what *I* said!" Babs said loudly.

"*Shhh!* I only just now got him to *stop!*" hissed Officer Ja'far.

I glanced from Luca to Zady, confused, waiting to see what they made of this. Ja'far seemed to be talking to Babs, not about him. But there was no one else in the room he could be referring to.

"He's gone home for his mid-day break," Babs said. But he, too, spoke quietly, like there was suddenly a chance we'd be overheard.

"Who are you talking about?" Luca asked.

Neither officer looked willing to share. In fact, they looked like guilty children in school, and I was reminded how young they were to be running an investigation.

It was Zady who broke the silence, her voice at its most motherly. "It's Officer Brooks, isn't it?"

Ja'far nodded wearily.

Babs watched his friend nodding, then seemed unable to hold in his opinion any longer. "Officer Brooks says this is the second-biggest case ever on Wellspring. He says it's too much for us to handle alone, so he won't retire yet. But he also doesn't want to do an actual investigation, like we were trained to do! He wants to go—he wants to ask—he wants to use *magic* to find out about the crime!"

"The Police Guild does use magic for some things," I said, trying to understand. "Back in Belville, Officer Thorn often gets the local Witch to help out. Aren't there guidelines for how to do it safely and fairly?"

"That's the thing," Officer Ja'far said, his voice grating. "There are *rules*. Magic to scan a scene or trace something specific, yes. Magic to divine every single thing about a crime, no. *Divination* is not foolproof enough to stake justice on."

"No offense," Babs added quickly, looking at Zady.

"Why would I be offended? That is exactly what I have been trying to tell *all* you children for years," she answered calmly. "And from what I recall, you had a talent for it, Babs. And you, too, Ja'far—though do I remember correctly that you stopped wanting to study it even before you'd left?"

My ears pricked up. I didn't know anything about Babs' or Ja'far's divination skills—I had nearly assumed that, like me, they didn't have a talent for it at all. If they *had*, then why leave to become officers?

But that was a very limiting assumption—I realized my

mistake at once. Just because they had a talent for it didn't mean they had to pin all their dreams and ambitions on one single thing.

"That's true," Babs said, answering for both of them. He seemed more on edge than ever, though. "But we didn't practice at all while we were at the Guild. We didn't want to."

"That's perfectly alright," Zady said. "My thought was, if one of you has the skills, perhaps you could set Officer Brooks' mind to rest on the subject of using divination."

"Oh—it's not a bad thought." For a moment, Babs looked visibly relieved. "But he doesn't want to consult *us*, or anyone on the island. He didn't even go last night, and we were too busy. He wants something more *powerful*, he said."

Powerful, and not on Kairoi. I caught Luca's glance and asked, cautiously, "An ifrit?"

Ja'far startled like a wild horse. "How did you hear about that?"

"These things get around," Luca said vaguely. "But I take it you're against the idea?"

"*Of course* we are!" Ja'far burst. "The whole point of us being assigned here was to *keep* him from a third—"

"And to serve our community," Babs interjected hastily.

"And in the meantime," Ja'far continued, pivoting, "we have *actual* police work to do. There's too many leads from New West Key and none from the crime scene, unless you count keys that we can't trace—"

"I thought the keys were Nouronnihar's," I pointed out.

"What have you heard from New West Key?" Luca asked at the same time, curious.

"Is that why you were at Gene's?" Zady added.

I glanced at her questioningly. "Gene set up here just a year ago," she told me, "and all we know is she studied in New West Key."

In the meantime, Babs nudged Ja'far. After a moment, the senior officer nodded. So, with a deep breath, Babs turned back to us. "First, we *found* a set of keys on Nouronnihar. They were in her pocket. They look exactly the same as the ones you found, Red. And second, when we traced Nouronnihar back to New West Key and asked the police station there if they knew anything, they sent back all kinds of information. We just got it this morning. There's a lot of stuff about shipping companies, but we can't make heads or tails of it yet. And for some reason they gave us everything they had about Wellspring just in general."

"Glad to make contact with someone who wasn't Officer Brooks," Ja'far commented darkly. In the moment, I couldn't blame him. He did seem to have quite a mess on his hands to clean up.

"So it's not just stuff about Nouronnihar," Babs continued. "There was also stuff in there about everyone who's come from New West Key to live here, that they know of. Jasmin, Gene, even a few things about Sinbad."

"You're drowning in information," Luca murmured, thinking through the implications. Wellspring had very little history of dealing with paper records—and it sounded like Babs and Ja'far now had far more than they'd bargained for.

"Everyone has their own story," Zady agreed. "How will you pick out the relevant ones?"

"That's the thing," said Babs. "One of the first things *I* noticed was the priority page."

"A system of sorting information in the Guild," Ja'far cut in.

131

He now seemed entirely resigned to telling us everything.

"Right, 'priority' is when someone had a previous arrest, or was really closely involved in one or was a main suspect," Babs said in a rush. "Well, there *is* one in the stuff they sent over, but it's not about Nouronnihar. It's about Bertie."

"Bertie?" Luca looked at me, lost.

"Who is Bertie?" I asked, looking at my mother.

Zady pursed her lips, focused on the two officers. "*That's* why you went to Gene's?"

"Bertie," said Ja'far, gruffly, "is the medical intern at the apothecary. Here for the summer from New West Key University."

I thought back to the day before, the three people behind the counter at the apothecary. Gene had been the one in charge, of course, and Petra had been the busy, chatty assistant who greeted us. But there *had* been another person, at the far end of the counter—knocking things off shelves, if I remembered right. They'd totally ignored us.

"He's a werewolf," Babs informed us.

"I'm certain that's not why he was arrested, or nearly arrested," my mother reprimanded.

"It's not," Ja'far agreed, frowning at his assistant. "He was suspected of meddling with medications in the school lab. Certain compounds were going missing."

"I just thought it was interesting," Babs said, chagrined. "Anyway, he wasn't ever arrested or charged. But that was the most obvious actual *crime* in the stuff they sent over. And when we went to Gene's to check in about it—"

"You came away with a shipment she was preparing?" I prompted.

"*He* was the one packing it," Babs explained.

Well, no wonder Gene was worried—yet again—about it being late, I couldn't help but think.

"Is that really suspicious, though?" Luca asked.

"Maybe not," Ja'far admitted, "but the fact that he tried to hide it from us was."

"And the fact that he keeps a scalpel in his pocket," Babs added.

At last, the pieces of their investigation so far fell into place. Overnight, they'd identified and traced Nouronnihar, and the resulting flood of information had led them to Gene and Bertie, which had escalated into the confrontation we'd witnessed on the street.

Zady, too, had clearly put the pieces together. "You need my daughter to determine if the shipment was altered in some way?"

"Please," Babs confirmed, turning to me with pleading eyes.

Seeing as this was perhaps the most routine and career-appropriate task I'd ever been asked to complete for the police, I saw no reason to turn him down. "If you have the packing slip, or you know what it was supposed to be, that's easy. I can run a few tests to check what's actually in the bottles," I said. "I may need to get some things from home, depending on how much equipment you have here. And the tests will probably take a while."

"That's alright," said Babs. "In the meantime, you can help us sort out everything else."

I hesitated, glancing at Officer Ja'far. For the first time—for just a moment—he looked grateful as he nodded.

17

Tell Me Another

Babs did not stop thanking me as he led the way down the hall. I decided it was nice to be appreciated properly by the local police.

I just hoped the appreciation wasn't premature.

"You can use this room," Babs said, letting me into a small room at the back of the station, bare and unremarkable except for a table and a high window. "It's the second interrogation room, technically, but we never have had to interrogate two people at once."

"Seems like that could change soon," I reminded him. "But this is a good place to set up, so I'll take it. The tests should be done tomorrow morning—I'll clean everything up for you and you can have the room back then."

"Anything you need," Babs agreed, backing out the door. In a moment, he returned with the heavy wooden box of bottles I'd seen him loading into the police cart earlier.

The door swung shut as he left, and I let it stay that way. Dimly, I could hear Luca and Ja'far talking in the hallway, and my mother taking her leave—she'd already mentioned that she planned to head back home, to check on (and update, no doubt) William and Aly. I let the words and footsteps fade away from my sphere of focus. For that quiet moment, it was just me and an alchemical mystery.

I lifted the lid off the box and set it on the table—it could make a handy tray if I needed one later. At first, I surveyed the shipment without my goggles on, just getting a feel for first impressions. The box held thirty-two medium-sized glass bottles, four rows of eight. Shredded newspaper was packed around and in between each and every single bottle— my initial guess was that this, perhaps, could have been the reason the shipment took so long to pack. I, too, had been terrified of breaking glass when I was an apprentice. But to my more seasoned eye now, the box was definitely over-cushioned.

Just like carrying a scalpel purely to shred newspaper is overkill. But I set that thought aside.

The shipment information, a routine form carefully filled out in block letters, was tucked into one end of the box. I pulled my gloves from my bag and put them on before fishing out the paper. When I unfolded it, though, it looked entirely harmless. Gene's address was at the top, followed by—

Jasmin's, I realized, reading the unfamiliar Palace address. *Now it makes even more sense that Gene was so upset. That must be a very valuable account for the apothecary.*

It was a little surprising, too. But perhaps that was because of my own experiences at the Sanctuary, and the suspicion of murder? After all, a massive compound like Jasmin's was bound to need some necessities. Still, though, I would have assumed she ordered everything in, rather than relying on a small local business.

Beneath the addresses, the inventory was listed: thirty-two bottles of a standard cleaning potion. I glanced up from the sheet, looking through the box again. Each bottle was topped off with a cork, but beneath that, I could see the glimmers of a light blue liquid in each one. Based on what I knew and could see so far, it was entirely possible that this shipment was innocent.

And yet—cleaning potions! That was both good and bad news. The good part was that I'd made about a million in my time, and could easily test these with basic equipment. The bad news was it did beg the question, what needed so much cleaning at Palace Jasmin?

Maybe this is a regular delivery, I told myself, glancing over the shipment details again. It didn't say anything about being a repeat order or a standing monthly purchase. Down at the bottom, though, there *was* a note about payment—*refer to Morgiana,* Gene or perhaps Bertie had written. That told me that the apothecary did enough business with the Palace that they knew who to contact. I wondered if they knew about Dean's new role yet—or if they knew *all* about him, and that's why the shipment was not directed to his somewhat incompetent attention?

I set the paper aside. It had told me all it could for now. The next task was to dive in and test the potions.

With a little thrill of relish, I pulled the first one from the upper left corner of the box. It was nice to focus on a task that I had full confidence I could complete. I glanced over the bottle first, checking the labels. The large sticker on the front bore Gene's logo and directions for use, while a smaller sticker on the back identified this specific potion as *product of Halcyon Sea Alchemy, New West Key.* I had expected something like that. Apothecary shops often created their own blends of medicine or made pills to order, but they didn't usually make all their potions from scratch. Potion-making was more alchemy than medicine, after all. Clearly Gene ordered this cleaning potion in bulk and then redistributed it to the citizens of Wellspring—and the Palace.

Of course, that limited the chances that Bertie—or anyone on Kairoi—had tampered with anything. Still, he could have added ingredients, or opened the bottles and replaced the liquid before resealing them. The apothecary shop would have plenty of replacement corks or sealing spells on hand.

I pulled my goggles down into place, grinning at the potion bottle. Somehow, I'd missed this quiet process of experimentation much more than I'd thought.

The first bottle passed my initial sniff test—a highly unscientific and slightly dangerous test, to be sure, but a very useful one nonetheless. Paracelsus had often been known to judge an apprentice's potion purely by its smell. I moved through each bottle in turn, one by one, testing the corks and investigating the potions by sight and smell at first. In short order, all thirty-two were lined up in the box lid, opened and investigated, awaiting further tests.

I paused to consider my options. Funny, how at home I could feel, even in a dusty police interrogation room!

After making a few quick decisions, I stowed my goggles and gloves, then let myself out of the room. I found Luca and the officers in an office across the hallway—surrounded by a sea of envelopes and papers.

"Hello, Red," Luca said cheerfully as I stopped by their open door. There was no safe place in the room to step, so I lingered in the hallway. "How are you getting on? I'm helping them organize everything from the other station. It got pretty jumbled up in transit, I think."

"Or it was always this way," Officer Ja'far grumbled. Despite looking the most at home in the office, seated in the lone chair behind the desk, his expression was downright miserable.

"Or it could have been the transit," Babs said, more optimistically. "The Guild is still working out some issues with our hard-copy sharing system . . . ."

That smacked of magic and teleportation spells gone awry, and I decided not to ask. "I've had good luck so far. Initially, my thoughts are that this is a totally normal shipment—with a few reservations." I told them about the alchemical supplier, Halcyon Sea Alchemy, and the fact that every single bottle seemed to be a cleaning potion. "Granted, Jasmin's Palace is a big place," I added. "But still—to order *only* a crateful of cleaning potions, and a *crate*ful at that—I mean, these are pretty strong. Just one would last a month, I'd think. But that's just me."

"Add it to the list to ask them about," Officer Ja'far sighed.

Babs did just that, scribbling in his Guild-issue notebook.

"And *do* check them, just to be sure," Ja'far added to me.

"I planned on it," I assured him. "And on that note, I need something large and waterproof—preferably a cauldron—and however much salt you have. And some clear glasses. And after I have those all set up, I should be free to join you," I added, casting another glance at Luca on the ground surrounded by growing piles of paper. I wondered if I'd regret my offer to help.

"You'll be just in time," Luca told me, smiling as Babs scurried past him to get me the things I needed from somewhere further down the hall. Waving a handful of accounting sheets,

Luca added, "Most of this stuff *is* about shipping, like Officer Babs said. Remember how Sinbad mentioned something about that first ship he sailed on having five sails? I think they're mentioned in here, too. Take a look at this logo."

I bent to investigate obediently. At the top right corner of each page Luca had picked out, a little ink drawing depicted a ship with a mass of sails and rigging. The image was too small for me to make out clearly, but Luca had more experience looking at printed details than I did. "Hmmm, definitely interesting," I agreed. "Especially since Nouronnihar had that shipping ledger in with her things."

"It shows up a lot in these papers, but I got the impression from the sailors that it's not a normal ship for these waters. I think it's worth asking them about," Luca said, looking toward Officer Ja'far for approval.

The police officer was clearly less suited to paperwork than his assistant. He lifted his head like a starving man offered a feast. "Anything," he said, "to get out of this office."

* * *

Officer Babs was able to get me everything I needed—almost (the cauldron was in fact a banged-up cooking pot from the station's tiny kitchen), and as soon as I set up my makeshift lab, the four of us trooped off.

I had half expected Babs to stay behind, to guard the station and my experiment. But he set the alarm spell on the station and then left it without another word. I soon found out why. When we got to the hotel, it was Babs who dealt with the front staff, while Ja'far added only an authoritative glare to the interaction.

The hotel itself was different than I expected. The lobby was dark, almost overflowing with the colorful tapestries so popular on Kairoi. There were no windows, but a lively water feature babbled in the center of the room, surrounded by low sofas and potted plants. A statue rising above the water depicted Morrigan, an ancient goddess of fate—and war. But other than that, the place was innocuous and welcoming, despite the heavy shadow. The desk itself was set right next to the door—otherwise, in the gloom, I might have missed it. The staff in question seemed to be a young local girl, a badge pinned to her silky sleeve.

"They're some team, huh?" Luca whispered to me as the police officers got what they wanted and the girl led us to a set of stairs.

"And here I thought we were bad," I agreed, joking quietly. William had often accused Luca and I of being joined at the hip, but so far we'd done more separate investigation than Babs and Ja'far had.

"Maybe it's because it's their first case," Luca said sympathetically, his voice muffled by footsteps on thick carpet as we all climbed the stairs. "And what a case!"

What a case, indeed. I didn't have time to say anything. The stairs opened abruptly onto a landing on the second floor. Like the first floor, it was cluttered with sofas and tapestries, but here at least there was a large window facing out over the street. None of the landscape was visible—the window was stained in vivid colors, a random pattern of blues and purples and reds. The hotel management might have meant it to be calming, or inspiring, perhaps, but it struck me as incredibly dramatic. Especially as the light fell around the sailors, who were clustered on one sofa around a faintly shining lamp. They looked up from their work as we came in. Sinbad, sitting in the center, was holding up what appeared to be a spider-web style brainstorming sheet.

"We just wanted to follow up on something with you," Officer Babs began brightly. It was just as well he did, because the hotel employee had disappeared down the stairs again. "Where were you all yesterday evening?"

"Here," said Sinbad.

"Out for a walk," said Jason, at the same time.

"Together," Sinbad added. "We were here, and then we went for a walk. We were in the market getting dinner at twilight—ask the kabob stall merchant, she'll tell you. We always stick together. Fleece almost got run over by the bus when we first got here. What a close call it was, too."

"Thank you!" Officer Babs made careful notes, his face hidden behind his little book.

In the silence, Sinbad's gaze slid to me.

"Nice to see you again," I said, a little self-consciously. "Luca and I were just telling the officers about your story, about all the different ships you've sailed on out of New West Key, and . . . they were very interested in it."

It was hard not to be distracted as I spoke. My eyes roamed the colorful room, noting maps and lists tacked up to the walls. It was almost surreal until I realized: *this* was the sailors' "headquarters," from which they were planning their return to glory.

Luca confirmed my suspicions by flopping down on the nearest sofa comfortably, as though he'd been there before. "I'd like to hear it again, myself. Especially how it started, on such a big ship."

"Oh, *that* tale." Sinbad cleared his throat. "Please, officers, sit."

As they did, rather stiffly, silence reigned.

Luca looked expectantly from Sinbad to Jason, who sat beside him. I noted Fleece in the background, leaning over the sofa. But didn't that leave one missing? *Archer,* I remembered. *The first mate.* She was nowhere in evidence.

"We don't have all day," Officer Ja'far said at last, clearing his throat.

"Of course, of course." Sinbad, too, coughed. "I was just a lad, myself. I had no business being on such a grand ship, but it did take a mighty amount of cleaning. The captain liked things to shine. There we were, as proud a crew as ever I—"

Babs looked up from his notebook, where he was scribbling notes.

Sinbad seemed to get the point. He shifted. "I only sailed with them a few months, myself. These big, grand ships, you get tired of them, see. They seem impressive, but oft as not you find there's something suspicious going on underneath."

"What was it in this case?" Babs asked helpfully. "And can you describe the ship's emblem?

Sinbad described a logo precisely like the one Luca had found, and went on to add, "I was only the cleaning boy, myself. I was never privy to the business. But I learned later that the whole company was notorious in New West Key—hoped to run the whole port. If they hadn't been taken by pirates, they might have done real harm."

Interesting thing for him to say. The entire story felt like it had been tilted several degrees since the last time Sinbad told it.

"What were they *doing?*" Officer Ja'far prompted.

"Shipping," said Sinbad, with the air of a professional. "But word on the docks was, their numbers never added up. Never saw such creative counting until I was aboard *The Portress*, years later. If you ask me, they never offloaded enough of their goods. It was a liability, that's what I told them. Finally I said I wouldn't put up with it any more. They ask me on as clerk, and then they disregard everything I say!"

"That was on a different ship, though?" Babs was writing furiously.

"Wait," said Luca. "They were traders . . . who were just collecting things . . . and never selling anything?"

"They weren't pirates," Sinbad assured us hastily. "They had a good eye for buying things at a cheap price. And they'd been at it for years. By the time they finished, they had enough for a king's ransom!"

"And what," said Ja'far, rather icily, "happened to it?"

"I wouldn't know," said Sinbad, serene. "Heard they stashed it somewhere. I was off the ship myself by then. Told them I wouldn't take no more."

"But didn't you say the other day that the ship wrecked?" Luca asked.

"Are we talking about the five-masted ship or *The Portress*?" I clarified, watching Sinbad skeptically.

He tugged at the collar of his shirt. "I, ah, I wasn't there for when *The Portress* wrecked. I was back in New West Key. But I went down with *Djinni* when it was finally attacked by pirates. That was the five-mast. They say the pirates were sent to take it down, paid by other shippers in New West Key."

"But the *Portress* was the one with treasure?" Babs asked, echoing his fellow officer in a more friendly tone.

"No, no, not that one," said Sinbad. "All that was left of *The Portress* was washed-up planks and an old dagger—that's what I heard. But *Djinni* had enough wealth for palaces upon palaces. The pirates got at that, though, and made quick work of it. Why are you asking me about this? Leave talk of lost treasure beneath the waves."

"Lots of people like to speculate about that kind of thing," Luca pointed out. "It doesn't mean there's anything wrong."

"I know that, of course," said Sinbad. "But don't you know all treasure lost in the Blue Desert Isles is cursed by the soothsayers of Kairoi?"

18

Ill Winds

"He's lying," I hissed, as the four of us found ourselves safely out on the street.

"You thought so too?" Officer Babs beamed obliviously in the hot sunshine.

I shook my head. "No—"

"She means, we *know* he must have lied at some point because a lot of that was not what he told us earlier," Luca said, coming to my rescue.

"Walk and talk," Officer Ja'far demanded. "What exactly did he tell you earlier? And when exactly was it?"

"It was just this morning, and a little bit yesterday," Luca said, obliging as ever. Officer Babs pulled out his trusty notebook to take notes as we walked, headed for the police station again. "He told us his whole life story, at least as relates to shipping, but not with so many details. No mention of the pirates being paid off, or—"

"—Or 'soothsayers' on Kairoi and curses," I put in, still annoyed at the theatrics of it all. "And hardly anything about anyone on New West Key, for that matter. And what was that about Fleece almost getting hit by Bessie?"

"He might've left out details to you, but wanted to be sure he was telling the police everything now?" Babs suggested, looking up from his notes.

I looked at the officer, my head to one side. Sometimes he sounded very naive. Was it an act, somehow? Or was this why he needed Ja'far?

The question was bound to be unanswered. As we returned to the police station, Babs offered to get us a takeout lunch from a nearby sandwich shop, Visions in Bread. Neither Luca nor I could turn him down. We ate with the officers, sorting amiably through more paperwork, for a while before Luca brought up the sailors again.

"I just feel like something's off," he said, crinkling up his paper sandwich wrapper. "Corrupt shipping companies in New West Key makes a kind of sense, but what could he mean about the Springers cursing treasure? Have many ships gone down near here?"

"I never heard of any such thing," I said, looking to the police officers, who shifted uneasily. "Unless you count Sinbad's ship just recently, I suppose."

"We can go to the town council for that kind of thing later," Babs said eventually. "With all these loose ends, it will take time to tie them up."

"That's why we are going to the Palace next," Ja'far decided. "There are too many unanswered questions."

It seemed abrupt, but then, the ship inquiry *had* interrupted the whole potions investigation. I swallowed the last of my sub and said, "On that note, don't forget to ask about—"

"You," Ja'far interrupted, swinging to face me, "are coming too. And so are you," he said to Luca. "Wait out front and we'll pick you up in the cart."

In a matter of moments, we found ourselves lingering in front of the police station. Both officers disappeared around the building, brooking no argument. I glanced at Luca with wide eyes.

"He keeps doing that," Luca chuckled. "Gets you every time, huh?"

"I can't tell if he hates us or likes us," I admitted, shaking my head with my own rueful grin. "Why ask us to come along?"

Was he coming up with an excuse to leave the station? Does he not want us to meet Brooks? The question hung in the air as I met Luca's thoughtful gaze.

"Maybe he wants the backup, and doesn't even care who it is," Luca suggested at last. "Given what you've told me about Jasmin's place, it sounds really intimidating. Especially for just two young officers."

"Intimidating's only the half of it," I assured him. A clatter and a rattle from around the building announced the approach of the police cart. "But I guess you're about to find out for yourself."

* * *

A scant half an hour later, Luca and I did our best to look like official backup as Officer Ja'far went toe-to-toe with Dean.

For his part, Dean seemed more flummoxed than ever. His hair stuck up in all directions. There were bags under his dark eyes. He gestured wildly from behind the safety of his desk, his voice echoing in the massive "office" room beside the courtyard.

"I don't know anything about pirates," Dean protested.

"But do you know about the *Djinni*?" Officer Ja'far pressed.

"You mean those blighters that go about granting wishes?" Dean looked thoroughly confused.

Ja'far was not to be distracted. "How about shipping orders from New West Key?"

"No! Why would I?"

"You can *read,* can't you? Haven't you looked through your employer's records?"

"Why the blazes would I do a thing like that?"

"To *do your job,* maybe?"

"My job isn't to *investigate* Jasmin," Dean concluded, breathless but triumphant. "That's *your* job!"

"And you're not helping us do it," the officer retorted. "One more useless remark and you'll spend a night at the station!"

"Ja'far," Babs interjected, just barely.

"I can't help it if I can't tell you anything of use," Dean said, ignoring the assistant officer. "Maybe you're looking for the wrong things!"

"Are you looking for cleaning potions?" Officer Ja'far asked, in an alarming and yet perfectly-executed pivot.

"What the devil should I know about cleaning potions?" Dean asked, clearly as thrown off by the question as he was supposed to be.

"Ja'far," hissed Babs.

"Not now. Just what *do* you know? What is your job?" Ja'far asked Dean irritably.

Dean drew himself up. "It's very important!"

"But what *is* it?"

"*Ja'ja!*" Babs all but shouted.

The officer turned from glowering across Dean's desk to glare at Babs, then at us, and then over our shoulders. I followed his glance—and saw Jasmin herself bearing down on us.

"We're very sorry to show up uninvited—" Babs began, addressing her in a ramble.

"I will not stand for this treatment of my staff," Jasmin said. She ignored everyone in the room except Officer Ja'far.

The officer turned to face her squarely. "Regardless of your opinion, illegal behavior is subject to punishment."

"If you have evidence my secretary has behaved illegally, you should have brought it to me," Jasmin replied. She stood with her feet planted and her spine straight. Luca nudged me as we looked on, and I nodded. She was undoubtedly the ruler of this palace.

"We have evidence *you* have behaved illegally," Officer Ja'far said, unexpectedly.

The room fell so silent that even the birds chirping outside seemed to listen in. *Did he get too riled up and overstep himself?* I wondered.

The answer came in Jasmin's definitive statement. "I don't believe you have evidence of any kind. This is harassment. You have two seconds to tell me why I shouldn't have my head of security throw you out right now."

All heads swiveled to Officer Ja'far to see how he would respond. I'm half certain Luca was holding his breath.

But it was Officer Babs who leapt in. "If you please, Jasmin, we've got off on the wrong foot altogether. Officer Ja'far and I actually have important business with Raja, and some new information to go over. In the meantime, have you met Luca?"

Poor Luca. Jasmin narrowed her dark eyes as she turned to him.

"Um, hi," said Luca, faintly. "I'm Red's partner. This place is really nice. Do you have a library?"

I couldn't help it. I snorted. Jasmin shifted to consider me, still faintly hostile, and then turned to address Officer Babs. "Dean will call security now, and you will ask your questions. I do not expect to be bothered by you again. You two," she said, singling out Luca and myself just as Ja'far had earlier, "will come with me."

Luca and I exchanged a glance and shrugged. I'd expected to be bombarded by memories of the past when I visited Kairoi. If only I'd known how bossy the present would be!

19

A Thousand Thousand Stories

It turned out that Jasmin *did* have a library.

We followed Jasmin in silence at first. As she walked—now that she wasn't yelling—I was reminded of how short and slight she was. Her footsteps made no noise as she led us out through the courtyard and down a series of covered walkways amid the blooming flowers. *Definitely fairy blood,* I thought, making a mental note to ask William what kind of fairy he thought she might be—and if it mattered.

Her long pink hair glowed faintly in the shadow as we crossed a clear, vibrant pond and approached a round tower. Surrounded as we were by trailing vines and a thick cover of leaves, it was difficult to see where we were headed. But I glimpsed the tower's golden roof stories above us, and saw the excited glint in Luca's eye as we approached a doorway decorated with literary quotes.

An unseen attendant opened the door for us and then left us alone—in a huge, rounded room walled in bookshelves. The walls went up, and up, and up, until they faded into the arched roof high above us. One long, spiral balcony twisted its way up to that height, accompanied by the occasional window. The place was awash in golden light and a nice, fresh breeze. There were even blooming flowers on every reading table.

But clearly, as far as Luca was concerned, the most magical element was the books.

"You can go," Jasmin told him, her defensiveness fading a little. She even went so far as to smile crookedly at the delight in his eyes. "Find anything you like. I wish to talk to your partner for a moment."

My Luca knew a potential trap when he heard one, even if it was dressed up with stories and books. He glanced at me to make sure I'd be okay. I nodded to him. I was interested to hear what Jasmin would say—interested what authority, if any, she thought I had.

Luca smiled and thanked Jasmin, and soon was lost amid the shelves and comfy chairs.

Without saying anything—without even looking at me—Jasmin began slowly making her way up the spiral balcony. I went with her, matching her steps. She'd obviously expected me to. Once we were a story up and still climbing, she said in a low, clear voice, "The police officers are buffoons."

Startled, I laughed at first. She glanced up at me at last, and in that moment I understood that it had been Luca's and my irreverence that had convinced her to let us stay. I relaxed slightly and told her, "They're brand new, and I get the impression they think they have a lot to prove. But their hearts are in the right place."

"I wonder," said Jasmin.

"Luca and William and I come from a small town with a similarly small police force," I said. "I've seen how officers in that situation have to really push themselves when a big crime comes along. I think Babs and Ja'far just aren't used to it yet."

"Or they're hiding something," Jasmin countered. "Maybe they don't want the crime solved at all. Do you really know anything of their background?"

"Not a whole lot," I said carefully, a little surprised at her insistence. *Did she single me out as the gossip?* "But they were with us before and after the body was found, which is a pretty good alibi if you ask me. And either way, they've been training at the police guild for ten years. And before that, they were well known here in town. My mothers remember them well."

"You *are* from here," Jasmin said. "Not from a different small town."

"Well—yes and no," I admitted, shifting my shoulders uncomfortably as we continued walking slowly up. "I was born and raised in Wellspring, yes. But I left twelve years ago to study alchemy, and I've set up my shop elsewhere. I'm only here visiting now."

"In Belville," Jasmin said. "With William. Where you met Luca."

I glanced at her. As we passed a window, sunlight fell across her face, casting shadows from her lowered lashes. *She's obviously looked into me, and maybe the others*, I thought. *So why ask me questions on top of that?* It was odd, but then again, maybe an incredibly rich heiress had to develop her own protocols when it came to meeting new people. I decided to be honest. "Yes. William and I actually met in Brass, and then we traveled for a few years while I was saving up to buy a shop. It's sort of expected of an alchemist, building up your skills before you actually start your own business."

"But you did not come back to set up your shop here." Jasmin looked up at me again as she said it, and I got the feeling this was an important question, somehow.

"Nooo," I answered slowly. "To be honest, it never really occurred to me. I didn't think there'd be a need for an alchemist on Kairoi. Maybe Gene was more enterprising than me," I added, seeing a chance to touch on the apothecary and find out where that got me.

It got me nowhere, though. Jasmin hardly seemed to hear the comment about Gene. Instead, she was nodding, saying, "This makes sense. The people of Wellspring—your *Spring of the Unicorn*—they are not so open to new ideas."

"I hadn't thought of it that way, exactly," I admitted thoughtfully. "But I can't disagree with you. But if you knew that much, why did *you* come here?"

"It was perfect," she said. "The perfect place to build my Palace." She paused by another window, setting her hands on the sill as she looked out. When I joined her, looking down on the maze of gardens and walkways and palatial buildings, she asked almost aggressively, "Isn't it?"

"Perfect?" I clarified, a little bewildered. "Well, it's really impressive, I'll give you that."

Jasmin was now studying me. "You don't like it."

"I don't—that is—it isn't really my place to say anything about it," I hedged. She waited me out, and I added, "It's weird, is all. It's weird to get used to the fact that what we used to call the 'wild side' of the island is now so—manicured."

She turned to look out the window at her domain again. "It makes you sad?"

"In a way, it does make me wonder about the animals and plants that used to live here," I confessed. By lifting my eyes from the opulence and sheer disbelief of it all, I could see out to the horizon, to the sea. The day was so clear that I could see other isles in the distance. "But I think it's also just me being stubborn. That's what William and Luca have told me. Maybe I have a hard time getting used to new ideas sometimes, too."

"You *are* from here." Jasmin turned abruptly from the window and began her ascent again.

Once more, I fell into step beside her. "Does it make you sad, too?"

"Why would you ask that? It's mine," she insisted, tossing her hair back as she glanced up at me and away.

I wasn't so sure myself why I'd asked. She was so solemn, it just seemed like a natural question. I racked my brain, wondering if there was something more clever or relevant I could ask. Finally I gave up and went with the truth. "It's empty," I said. "It feels empty. I know it's full of flowers and amazing things but—"

"Yes," she concluded. "It is empty."

We were high enough now that I didn't care to look down to the ground level. Instead, I focused on Jasmin's delicate face. "Is that what you wanted? When you came here?"

"Yes," she said again. Then, with a laugh that startled me, she added, "Empty! That is what I wanted. That is what I built. Yes. Do you know," she asked abruptly, "what it is to be in charge of this kind of wealth?"

"Not a clue," I answered honestly. "I don't even know how you made the money in the first place."

"*I* did not make it," she said, with some unexpected bitterness. "Not all of it. My family made their money on fishing. There was not a catch that crossed the decks at New West Key which they did not profit from. But when it was passed to me, I sold that business. I wanted to design clothes instead. I thought the fashion world would be a different place, a new world."

"Was it not?"

Jasmin shrugged. "I was successful." She paused, facing an open door. Before venturing outside, she looked back at me and added, "I made everyone look the way I wanted. But *I* never looked the way I wanted."

She walked out into the sunshine. I hesitated, mulling this over. We had, I realized, made it to the top of the tower. Jasmin was now standing on an exterior balcony that wrapped around the entire thing, just below the roof line, like a lighthouse keeper beneath her light. And even though the sun was so strong that I could only make out her shadow, I finally saw what was going on in this conversation. I'd known from the start that she had to be putting on a facade. Every time she was abrupt, it was her inner self peeking out, almost being seen.

I walked out onto the deck with her. Fortunately, the railing was solid and high. Even so, the island fell away underneath us. I wasn't normally too concerned with heights, but this one was certainly breathtaking.

"You don't know anything about fashion," Jasmin commented, as I joined her at the rail.

It wasn't very nice, but now that I was listening more intently, I heard something there—almost a hint of admiration. So I shrugged off the criticism of my clothing and grinned. "Nope. And Luca usually wears the same thing every day. Not the exact same clothes, of course, but—" I laughed. "You know what I mean. We're not exactly high society."

"But you are not empty society." She looked down, straight down at her palace below. "How do you do it?"

"Is that really what you brought me up here to ask?" I settled my back to the rail, watching her.

Her dark eyes were confused, her perfect eyebrows drawn as she looked up at me. She honestly didn't know the answer to my question, I decided.

I sighed. "You might have been better off asking Luca, to tell the truth. He's better at this kind of thing than me. But since he isn't here . . . I guess what comes to my mind is something my old alchemy teacher used to say. 'Perfect is the enemy of good,' he told us. He even had it burned into the wall at one point."

"'Perfect is the enemy . . .'" Jasmin frowned as she mused over the words. "It does not make sense. Perfect is better than good."

"Technically speaking, you're right," I agreed. "But the whole 'better than' is kind of the problem. If you have something good, but you set it aside to chase something *perfect,* thinking the new thing will be better, then you've lost your good thing. And you'll never have the perfect thing. Perfect doesn't really exist," I told her softly. "It's something we talk about a lot in alchemy. The point of alchemy is to make earthly things better than they are."

"To make a stone into gold," she said at once.

I shook my head. "That's just a metaphor. It doesn't actually work that way. Because *perfect,* in this case, *gold,* is not attainable. It's a 'can't get there from here' sort of situation. But you can still get—"

"No," Jasmin interrupted. For a moment, I wondered just how old she actually was.

"I'm not saying dreams aren't real," I ventured, after a minute. "And I'm not saying you haven't done something amazing here. What I'm saying is, sometimes you have to take a good hard look at where you are and why you're doing things. If you're pushing the limits just because you think you aren't enough—"

"Did *I* say I was not good enough?" Jasmin lifted her head, eyes hard. "Did *I* say I was limited, and not free?"

"No," I said, and left it at that. I couldn't help feeling a little sadder than before. Because *I* hadn't said anything about being free, either. And that made me wonder if perhaps Jasmin had built herself a very large and beautiful cage.

20

In a Bottle

We returned to the ground level to find Luca tucked into an armchair, poring over an old illustrated scroll of *The Thousand and One Tales*. Jasmin, who had been coolly telling me all about the fashion line of cropped tops that made her famous, stopped in her tracks when she saw him. Once again, she smiled.

"It was my favorite when I was a child," she said, gesturing to the vivid title.

"We used to tell it a lot around here, too," I admitted. "I think I was even in a play based on one of the stories once."

"It's in excellent condition," Luca said, looking up at us. "It seems very old. Do you remember where you got it, Jasmin? I know a scholar in Brass who would just love to study something like this."

"Take it, if you like it," Jasmin told him. "I have more."

"Are you sure? I mean, of course you do, have more, that is, but—" Luca settled his gaze on me. "You should see her collection, Red. There's some very rare texts in the glass cabinet, and a whole wall of fashion references. It's probably the best collection I've ever seen."

"That makes sense," I said, with a sideways smile at Jasmin. "Artful clothing is her passion, it sounds like."

"Artful. Yes. I like that," she said, looking thoughtfully at me. Her manner still wasn't warm, but I found myself feeling a little fond of her. Especially when she turned back to Luca and added, "I mean it. Take the scroll. My people will package it for you."

My eyes strayed to the fairy tale scroll again. It was easily yards long and would definitely merit careful packaging. I couldn't help but think of Nouronnihar's poster tube, and Gene's delivery—neither had gone as planned. Neither reflected well on Jasmin, either. *Is it ungrateful to accept something from her when we're helping investigate her and her associates?*

"I have many more," Jasmin concluded.

That much was true. And while her library was beautiful, I got the feeling that Luca had used it more than she had. With the kind of wealth she'd alluded to, she could easily purchase herself twelve more rare scrolls at the drop of a hat.

"I'll take it on loan to finish reading it," Luca decided, ending my moral quandary. "How's that? And before we leave Kairoi, I'll come back and we can compare notes about it."

Jasmin paused, almost looked alarmed. But after a few long seconds, she smiled. "Yes. We will have tea."

"In this climate?" I joked gently.

"Dean is very good in the ways of iced tea," Jasmin said, looking quite personable for a moment.

I was glad to hear he was good for *something.* "I don't suppose that's why you hired him?"

Though I'd only meant to tease, the comment immediately

returned Jasmin to her cool, in-charge, unreachable persona. "My reasons are my own."

"Well, whatever your reasons were for assembling this great library, I really owe you for letting me poke around," Luca said, standing and setting the scroll gently to one side. "Did you two talk about everything you needed to?"

"It probably *is* about time to check on the officers," I said, watching Jasmin to get her take on the matter.

It was there, but only briefly. A flash of derision, or maybe impatience—or frustration?

In the next second, she was waving her hand and an attendant appeared from nowhere. Luca's scroll was whisked away for preparation to travel. We were to meet it at the front gates, presumably with Wellspring's two troublesome officers in tow.

Jasmin led us out of the library tower and back into the garden. Though the air was brighter, the Sanctuary spells kept it the same pleasant temperature that we'd felt inside the building. I looked around more carefully this time as we walked along, two paces behind Jasmin. Now that I wasn't preoccupied with *her*, or with the simple grandeur of the place, I started counting up everything else that lived there. Shimmering gold fish in the ponds, brightly colored frogs here and there, a white egret standing still as a statue in one of the streams. Butterflies in the flowers, songbirds nesting in the trees. It wasn't as empty as I'd thought.

But the animals were shy, and that told me that they rarely saw guests. Which just went to support the idea that Jasmin never invited anyone here. It was a showpiece that never got shown off. A retreat from life—and just what was Jasmin retreating from, when by her own account, she was at the height of her career?

I didn't have much time to ponder. Before we'd made it back to the main building, an approaching party met us in a breezeway connecting two courtyards. Babs and Ja'far, and with them, a large woman who could only be the head of security.

She looked like she'd learned her trade in the most dubious of port cities, and half expected to wake up and find herself back there at any moment. Her clothing was tight-fitting and black—*good thing for her this place is climate-controlled*, I thought. Her graying hair was braided tightly against her scalp, pulling her dark forehead taut. Below that, mirrored sunglasses obscured her face. She was as tall as Ja'far and as stocky as Babs. The two faded into her shadow.

And I noticed they hadn't persuaded her to leave behind the collapsible staff strapped to her waist.

"Jasmin," she said, her voice clipped. It was a greeting, an acknowledgment, and a request for immediate attention all in one.

If Jasmin was upset to see the officers again, she didn't show it. Instead, with one sighing breath, she turned to introduce us. "This is Red, and Luca. My head of security, Raja."

I was impressed by her manners, even though I shouldn't have been. She'd been just as cool under tense scrutiny from day one.

"The officers have questions about the system," Raja said, without so much as a glance in our direction. Apparently, she'd already summed us up. "You may want to decide how much to tell them."

Jasmin tensed at first, pursing her lips at Raja. I could understand that—she'd put Jasmin in an awkward position.

To dismiss everyone now and tell us *nothing* would beg the question, why?

So instead, she indicated a set of patio furniture arranged at the edge of the nearest pool.

* * *

Luca had his feet in the water. Of course.

And since he'd done it first, why shouldn't I join him?

We sat side by side in the shade of a magnificent silky willow, our shoes off and our legs up to the knee in a tranquil pool tiled in deep blue dotted with stars. Because of the pool's deeply curved edge, we could watch Jasmin and the two police officers under their umbrella—and Raja, standing resolutely in the sun, could watch us.

So far, the conversation had been nothing I could keep track of: all names of security spells and types of magitech protections. It would have been interesting to William, but as far as I was concerned, most of the details went in one ear and out the other. Clearly, the officers were hoping that someone at Palace Jasmin had picked up some trace of Nouronnihar, her murderer, or other foul play. Apparently Raja had been unyielding about the alibis for everyone in the compound, and so they'd taken this more nitty-gritty, technological approach.

I kicked my feet through the water and wondered what William, Zady, and Aly were up to. A water salamander scooted by along the tiles. Somewhere in the bushes there was a rustling—perhaps a bird coming back to its nest.

"Too bad I don't still have that scroll," Luca whispered in my ear.

I chuckled. "Like you'd risk reading it near the pool."

"I'd find a deck chair. There's a really nice nook over there by—"

"Isn't that right, Red?" Ja'far asked pointedly.

I looked up guiltily. They were only a yard away, across the narrow section of the pool; there'd been no need for him to raise his voice—except that I'd tuned out their conversation completely. "Sorry?"

"We know there is powerful magic here," the officer repeated, giving me his best *cooperate for once, you undisciplined civilian* look.

"Oh. Well." I focused on Jasmin, knowing that the officer was probably trying to intimidate some information out of her, but also acutely aware that I was no magical expert. "William, who was here with me yesterday, said he could sense it. He thought maybe you'd done it all yourself."

Before I could add, *if that's how it works? Can one person enchant an entire palace?*, I noticed the gleam of satisfaction in Jasmin's dark eyes. "He is smart. The patterns and the colors are mine. It is woven throughout my palace."

I was busy thinking *William's sure going to be sad he missed that*, but Luca had his head more in the game. He caught on with a quick intake of breath and said wonderingly, "The tiles everywhere!"

"And the fabrics," Jasmin said, a little smug.

"I understand fabrics and fashion, but I don't understand whatever else you're talking about," I told them, lost.

"That's because it is too obvious," said Jasmin.

"You're a flower fairy," Luca concluded. Under the umbrella across from us, Babs was scribbling fiercely. "That makes total sense. See, Red, flower fairy magic is heavily tied to one *place*, usually where they've chosen to live, and by incorporating arcane symbols into the basic design of the palace, she can strengthen her magic even more."

"The design and color," Jasmin reiterated. "Yes. It was on my mother's side, the magic."

"You've done a wonderful job," Luca enthused. "I can't imagine how much work planning something like that would take."

"But for what purpose?" I asked, still feeling a little lost. "Just to make the palace pleasant to be in?"

"Not pleasant. Safe," said Jasmin. She glanced over her shoulder at Raja, and I realized suddenly why the head of security had referred this conversation to Jasmin herself.

"Why do you feel you need to go to such lengths to be safe?" Officer Ja'far asked. Unlike Luca and me, he did not sound remotely impressed. Instead, he sounded vaguely suspicious.

"Have you ever been responsible for this much wealth, officer?" she asked in return.

Without thinking better of it, I wrinkled my nose. When Jasmin had given me that line earlier, it had sounded more sincere. I had believed then that the wealth could be a burden— but now it sounded more like an excuse.

"Wealth your family made through shipping," Ja'far observed. "Out of New West Key."

"Fishing," Jasmin corrected. But her eyes shifted back to Raja for just a moment.

"Fishing, mainly," Babs agreed. "But you do have a fashion line called *Jinni*, right? I wonder if that's named after a ship your family once owned, the *Djinni?*"

Luca and I exchanged a quick look. *How long has he been sitting on* that *connection?*

Jasmin recovered quickly, however. "My father had a stake

in the company, nothing more, when he first settled in New West Key. He sold his interest in shipping to focus on fishing, as I have said."

A fine story, but I couldn't help but wonder if Nouronnihar had been working for that same company—and if her coming to Kairoi had been no coincidence.

Babs must have felt the same way, because I saw him elbow Ja'far. With this encouragement, the officer pressed another point. "Have you ever received specific threats or been the victim of attempted crimes?"

Jasmin hesitated. "I have learned it is best to be aware of my surroundings. That is all."

"Is it an extension of your spells on the ferry gate?" I blurted out.

She gave me a strange, considering look. "Yes."

"You're making yourself aware of everything on this island, then," Officer Ja'far jumped in. "And remind us, why is it that you know nothing about the murder that happened on your doorstep?"

"Of your own secretary," Babs added helpfully.

"I had never met her," Jasmin protested. "I did not know she was here."

"How could that be the case?" Ja'far was nearly triumphant. "If you're really that vigilant, how could you miss such an obvious breach in security?"

The look on Jasmin's face was striking. I cleared my throat, remembering something William had told me. But before I could speak, the bushes behind Luca and I rustled again, this time reaching a fever pitch of noise and excitement.

"It's not Jasmin's fault," Dean yelled, leaping out behind us with leaves stuck in his wild hair. "It's mine!"

21

The Unexpected

A scuffle ensued. After much yelling and splashing as people ran to and fro through the pool, we caught our breath to find:

Dean in the custody of Ja'far and Babs, where Luca and I had just been sitting

Babs also in the custody of Raja, who was simultaneously eyeing Dean distrustfully

Jasmin alone beneath her umbrella, on her feet

. . . all while Luca and I sprawled on the deck where the officers had once been. Something—maybe wet tile, maybe a guild-issue boot—had tripped me up. I just hoped it hadn't been a salamander.

The silence, when it fell, was thick. Babs stared at Dean and Ja'far stared at Raja. Jasmin and Dean stared at each other. Luca caught my eye and we nearly laughed.

Jasmin recovered herself first. "You fool," she said to Dean. "You don't know anything."

"I do though," he protested. "I bally well know everything, since I'm the blighter who did it. I have a whole stack of razors in my room. I insist upon being arrested."

"Wish granted," Raja said dryly, letting go of Babs so that the officers could focus on their charge.

"Stop!" Jasmin insisted. To Dean, she added, "You weren't even here when the girl went missing."

"Yes I was," he said, drawing himself up—and the two police officers along with him. "I got here early. Had you all fooled, didn't I? Maybe I'm not so foolish after all!"

Luca and I exchanged another glance. Either he really was not at all as foolish as he seemed, or he was even *more* foolish.

"Why aren't you taking me away yet?" Dean demanded, shaking his arms in the officers' grips. "Cart me off and I will tell you all."

"Don't you dare," said Jasmin. I couldn't tell which of them she meant to address.

"I think I *will,*" Officer Ja'far said, teeth tightly clenched, "if nothing else, to see how jail cools your head."

"Do you figure they teach them to talk that way at the Guild?" Luca leaned over to whisper to me.

"You two," Ja'far said, eyes blazing as though he'd heard the comment. "Come along. We're leaving."

They must have cuffed Dean in the mayhem earlier, for Officer Ja'far now marched him off without another word. Raja went with him. In their wake, I saw something sparkling on the ground. Leaning over the narrow strip of pool to investigate, I saw it was a set of keys—keys identical to the ones in the estuary. Identical to Nouronnihar's. But these were obviously Dean's, lost in the fight.

Everyone really has the exact same key ring? The thought made my stomach drop. Even with Dean "confessing," this case seemed impossible. At every turn, some new complication arose.

"You can't arrest my secretary!" Jasmin shouted after them.

"Sorry, but he kind of can," said Babs, who'd lingered to pick up his notebook. He took the keys from my outstretched hand, too, but kept his focus on Jasmin. "You don't have to worry. We'll let him go if it turns out he didn't do anything."

"*If!*" Jasmin stamped her foot as Babs, too, scuttled down the walkway toward the front gates.

Luca helped me up. After hitting the tiled deck hard, we were both moving a little slower than everyone else. "Sorry about that, Jasmin," he said kindly.

"Where even was he?" Jasmin murmured, shaking her hair down over her face.

I looked around. The nook Luca had hoped to read in was nearby and would have been safe from Raja's view. Suddenly, the rustles I'd heard earlier made a lot more sense. "I think he was listening in. Jasmin, I realize this is a delicate subject, but I guess you can't quite 'sense' where people are? That's not part of your safety spells?"

"No. No, that is not how my magic works," Jasmin said, her hands up as if to cover her face. "Why would he say those things?"

She was distraught. I decided I'd interrogate William—or even Luca—about fairy spells later. "No idea, Jasmin. But I'm sure it'll be cleared up."

"He may have been trying to protect you," Luca added softly.

Jasmin looked up, her eyes hard again and her hands clenched. "I don't need protection!"

* * *

The phrase echoed in my mind as we rattled back toward Wellspring. The atmosphere in the back of the police cart was tense, as Dean ignored Babs and Babs ignored the fact that he was being ignored. Luca and I sat beside each other in silence.

Is it because she's already protecting herself so well? That thought didn't ring true, since Jasmin still seemed to be on edge, even in her Sanctuary. Of course, police activity and snooping employees could put anyone on edge. And then, there was the fact that a murder had occurred on or very close to her property, and the added evidence that she could be more closely tied to the victim than she'd let on . . .

Is it because she's afraid something else will come to light? Jasmin certainly wasn't an open book. But I also failed to see what she could worry about Dean, of all people, finding out.

Unless he was lying when he said he hadn't looked into her files earlier. I observed Dean surreptitiously in the afternoon sun. His head was tilted up, nose in the air, jaw set. He had pride, then—he wasn't *only* the bumbling, oblivious secretary we'd first met . . .

. . . But then again, he'd also been running around Jasmin's gardens without any kind of hat, and with his collar half buttoned down. He was absolutely going to get a sunburn before we made it back to the station.

It could be because she doesn't think he's the one to be doing any protecting, I decided. *I wonder if she has some kind of business policy or plan for helping out employees who get in trouble with the law. Assuming they're innocent, of course.*

I nudged Luca and we proceeded to have a short conversation entirely made up of glances and nods. At the end of it, I said aloud, "Hey, Dean. How about you borrow Luca's hat? We can get him a spare at home."

Dean's suspicion quickly melted into surprise as he looked between the two of us. "I say, that's topping of you. I—"

"You can't *give* things to a prisoner!" Babs interrupted, scandalized.

"Okay, fine," Luca said reasonably. "How about you give him your hat, so you know there's nothing hidden in it? And then you can borrow my hat instead."

"He's already getting burned," I added.

As though struck by the reality all at once, Dean squirmed pathetically.

"But it's a police hat," Babs said, looking at his charge uncertainly.

"Aren't the police supposed to look after citizens as well as deliver justice?" Luca asked.

"Yes," Babs admitted. "But he isn't really a citizen, is he?"

The cart hit a rut in the road and in the ensuing bounce, Dean's collar jostled, revealing an even more extensive sunburn.

"For goodness' sake," I said. "Babs, give him your hat right now. It'll only be until we get to town."

After a momentary game of "musical hats," everyone was settled again. Dean looked up at the brim that shaded his nose. "Never had an officer's hat before," he said. "Might get used to it."

"You're not helping your case," I warned him, as Babs bristled.

After that, everyone clammed up again.

Fortunately, we pulled into town shortly afterward. While Officers Ja'far and Babs escorted their prisoner to the main interrogation room, I peeked in at my experiment. Everything was progressing as I'd expected. Early results indicated that the potions truly were, as advertised, cleaning potions.

But did we ever find out why they need so many? I made my way slowly down the hall, hoping to run into Babs.

I found him sitting at the front desk, going over his notes. "There you are," he said, looking up. "Ja'far is doing the preliminary stuff with Dean, so I thought I'd take a moment. Your Luca's outside, by the way."

"Thanks," I said. I no longer tried to correct people who said things like *your Luca.* "I just wanted to tell you that the experiment is looking good—and here, if you let me make a few notes for you, you can check it yourself in the morning."

"You're not coming back? I don't have to tell what color they are, do I?" Officer Babs sounded alarmed, even as he handed me his notebook.

"No, you'll be fine." I scribbled down what to expect if the potions were, indeed, cleaning solutions. As I did, I said, "I think we have a family outing planned, actually. Say, did Raja tell you anything about the potions order?"

"Only the bare minimum." Babs sighed, removing his hat—Luca's hat—and crumpling it against the desk. "It's a lot harder out on your own, isn't it?"

I hesitated. "Well, you're not totally alone. What about Gene herself? Was there anything on her in your files?"

"Studied at New West Key University," Babs recited. "Worked part time as a clerk on the docks. Been here a year. Raja said she's the only supplier in Wellspring they use. But wouldn't say anything about why they needed so much cleaning fluid."

"Yeah, I can see how Raja might not be the forthcoming type," I sympathized, handing the notebook back. "But don't worry just yet. Questions will start resolving themselves soon enough. And speaking of, I *will* still clean up your room and equipment for you, if you like. It just might not be until tomorrow afternoon."

"That's okay," Babs said. "We'll be here. If we're not out getting yelled at by more suspects."

I chuckled at that. "Good luck with Dean. And maybe get some rest, if you can."

As I turned to head out the front door, to join Luca and head home, Officer Babs called out one more time. "Red. Here, take Luca's hat back to him. And—thank you. For going along with all this."

He caught me off-guard, I'll admit. I smiled at him as I took the hat. "Don't worry about it. After all, back when we met on the marina, none of us could have expected how things have gone. Right?"

22

The Open Sea

My parents were incredibly gracious about Luca and I having investigated all day—and of course, incredibly curious. The town had collectively decided to do another divination session that night, this time using kelp as an offering, since Nouronnihar had been merfolk. Aly and William went to it, but I stayed home, happy just to play cards with Zady and Luca. After our whirlwind of a day, I was honestly looking forward to our planned boat trip free from mystery.

I should have known better, of course.

We rose early to head down to the beach launch, where we'd find the boat we'd rented for the day. But Aly had gone on ahead and checked in on the rental shop—not to mention the police station. Even at that early hour, she'd managed to shake down Officer Babs for some information.

"They got Dean's full confession," she informed us, even before we'd managed to launch the boat.

"It was love, wasn't it?" Zady asked, smug.

"Can we please get past the breakers before you start

174

comparing notes about your bets?" I said to them both. I was knee-deep in the surf, just about to pull the shallow-hulled boat out into the water, and *not* in the mood for details.

"You had a bet about who did it?" Luca asked from across the prow.

"Not *who, why,*" Aly told him. She got into position at the boat's stern. "But Cinnabar's right. Out we go!"

Working as a team, we pushed the boat out to deeper water and jumped in. Zady sat at the back, working a magic propeller system that could get the boat past the breaking waves. William, no doubt interested in this latest edition of transportation magic, helped. Meanwhile, Luca and Aly and I worked to unfurl the one large sail, which would take over powering the boat once we were in calmer waters.

Calmer waters came quickly—I'd always found the transition between shallow breakers and rolling ocean waves a little abrupt, myself. On boating trips as a kid, I'd thought of it as passing through a magic border into a new world. Today, though, our "new world" contained some familiar old problems . . .

"The problem," Zady declared, "is that even though they don't really believe him, he keeps ruining his alibi."

"They don't believe him?" Luca sat near the prow, smiling as I came over to sit beside him. Baby Island was visible on the horizon, a smaller, more weathered version of the craggy Kairoi behind us. Aly was our captain, of course.

William still sat with Zady at the back of the boat, his floppy ears waving in the breeze and his tail wagging. "Start at the beginning," he insisted. "What did Dean say?"

Aly kept her eyes on the horizon, but she spoke loud enough that everyone on the small boat could hear. "According to

Babs, Dean's confession boiled down to" I love *Jasmin and I killed Nouronnihar so that I could be Jasmin's secretary."*

"But how could he murder someone and then move the body when he was on the bus with us?" Luca asked.

"And how did he even know about Nouronnihar in the first place?" I added, even more dubiously.

William was similarly skeptical. "If it's alibis the officers are worried about, Dean's seems like the strongest of anyone on the island."

"That's assuming they know the time of death," Zady pointed out primly.

"And that's the thing," Aly agreed. "Babs was saying they got permission from the family to analyze Nouronnihar's remains, and the only new thing they learned was that she could have been killed up to an hour before you all encountered something on the road and stopped to look."

"And Dean was insisting that he was already here on the island," Luca said thoughtfully.

"Yes, but that's obviously silly," I said, tugging my wide sun hat down over my hair. "He was just saying that to incriminate himself. He must have come in on the same catamaran we did. Otherwise, why would he be on the same bus?"

"*I* didn't see him on the boat," William remarked. "Did you?"

Luca and I exchanged a glance. "No," I admitted. "But it's pretty big, and there were so many tourists . . ."

"The catamaran runs on a regular schedule these days, just like Bessie," Aly said. "Babs was thinking he might have come in earlier that same day, but either way, Dean refuses to show any ticket stubs or proof of his itinerary."

"Probably because it would exonerate him," I pointed out.

But Luca was more circumspect. "It *did* seem almost like he fell out of the sky, when he met us at the bus station . . ."

William *woof*ed as an idea struck him. "That arch in the marina. It's magic. Do the locals use it as a focal point for teleportation?"

"Sometimes," Zady answered, as Aly nodded. "I'm sure you've noticed that most of us only have a very little magic, so teleportation is a very big deal. But the arch does have anchor spells meant to help with teleportation, if necessary. It was only meant for small distances—basically, from Wellspring to the marina. If someone needs to get on or off the island very quickly, for example."

"With Jasmin's augmentation, people at the Palace could use it too," William said with confidence.

"Okay, so Dean has provided a motive and effectively erased any alibi for himself—aside from how he moved the body," I summarized. Ahead, the shores of Baby Island were coming into focus.

"Did they say anything about that part?" William asked Aly.

"No, we didn't have that much time," she said, her short hair swinging as she shook her head ruefully. "He did mention that they'd asked Raja for alibis for everyone else in the compound, and basically everyone vouches for everyone else. But none of it's very convincing. Jasmin was on her own reading all afternoon, her assistant Morgiana was busy overseeing preparations for the new secretary's rooms, and even Raja herself was doing a solo round of the walls at the time."

"That sounds as useful as what the sailors said," I commented. "'Out walking,' 'sitting around in our headquarters together,' 'out buying kabobs' . . ."

"None of it very provable," Luca agreed.

"Except the room thing. We saw those rooms, and they were

immaculate," William reminded me.

"And presumably more than one person was involved in the cleaning," I said, nodding. "Did they ask if any of the guards reported anything?"

"No one heard or saw anything, as far as I know," Aly relayed. "Certainly nothing Babs was excited about."

"Those poor boys," Zady commented.

"They'll be fine," I said, unsure if it was confidence or fervent hope that made me speak. "Speaking of cleaning, Aly, did Babs mention anything about the potions?"

"Not to me, but as I was leaving, Gene was just going over," was the answer, as Aly steered us carefully toward a bay where we could beach the boat.

"Was she?" Zady looked interested. "Because she had been told to, or because she wanted to demand her merchandise back?"

"Oh, I don't think she'll get it back," I said, wincing as I thought of my experiment.

"I'd bet it was the latter, but I think Cinnabar is right," Aly added. "It seemed to me Babs was quite short with her as I left."

"Petra was saying that the whole scene caused a lot of tension in town," Zady told Luca and me. "No one's quite sure if they can trust the apothecary shop."

"They've never been sure of that," Aly put in, rather cheerfully. "And last night, the kelp offering brought up some interesting visions of bottles, scales, and an ominous anchor. No one from New West Key is looking good right now. Of course, Gene's shop has been odd from the beginning. And wouldn't it be more odd, if it was *love* that came along and disrupted everything?"

"By causing murder, you mean?" I asked dryly. Bottles and scales—by which I assumed she meant weighing scales, not fish scales—*could* implicate an apothecary, but they also harkened back to Nouronnihar's passion for nautical decorations. None of it seemed to point to Dean. "Love might be the cause of a misguided attempt at 'rescuing,' but I doubt it was the motive for this particular crime."

"But if you think about it, if Dean is so set on confessing, it must mean he thinks Jasmin did it," Luca said brightly.

The four of us looked at him. I hadn't had that thought yet myself, and I was surprised—though I could certainly see the sense in it. Aly, when I looked back, was smiling her wry, crooked grin. Zady looked like the matron presiding over gossip at teatime. William had his head on one side.

"If that was the case," he observed, "maybe jail is the best place for Dean to be."

"The secretary position does seem to be a very short-term one," Zady agreed.

I wondered at that. I knew very little of Jasmin, and what I did know did not preclude her being a murderer. She *was* awfully worried about the safety of her home. And her explanation of "all this wealth" had been just vague enough . . . particularly when you thought that some of that family wealth could have been made in shady shipping deals.

And yet, I couldn't help but think, *why does it seem like everyone here is intent on sticking themselves into prisons of their own design? Are they each just that desperate for a new start?*

Aly's triumphant cry roused me from my thoughts. "Land ho!"

23

A Deserted Isle

Baby Island *was* truly deserted, rumors and potential shipwrecks notwithstanding. Dark volcanic rock formed the bulk of the island, but wind and sea had softened it a great deal over time, turning what had once been a jagged volcano into a little cluster of rounded hills. As kids, we'd always said that the island looked like the humped back of a sea monster.

All that erosion had been good for the island's plant life, though. The "sea monster" now had a generous coating of palm trees, vines, and spiky yuccas. In the bay where we landed, black sand stretched in a wide, luxurious crescent between the waves and the trees, bounded by low cliffs. Tradition had it that once, all the Blue Desert Isles had had similarly black sand, and that's where the name "Blue Desert" had come from. I had my reservations, not least because of the clear difference between "black" and "blue." The black sand on Baby Island's beaches was simply a product of the minerals present on the island; it just so happened that the rocks which had made this island were more basaltic than the rocks which

180

helped to form the neighboring isles. So my alchemist's brain told me, in any case.

My companions were much more interested in playing on the beach than analyzing its chemical contents. We'd barely finished securing the boat before a water fight began.

Once we were all ready to dry off, Zady and William picked a particularly nice spot under a large palm tree at the edge of the beach to be "ours." They began unpacking Zady's hamper, which turned out to include a large picnic blanket and, of course, multiple sunshades, in true magical fashion. While William helped Zady unpack and set up our camp for the day, Aly came over to Luca and me and put her arm around my shoulder.

"They'll be awhile," she said, confidently. "Just wait until you see how much food your mother made us bring."

"I won't complain about a large lunch," Luca said cheerfully as he wrung seawater out of his hat.

"I doubt you will either," I said to Aly, grinning.

"I won't," she admitted. "But how about we leave them to it for a bit? Want to find the tallest spot on the island?"

I looked up at the forested rocks appraisingly. If Aly was going to insist on dragging us on a hike, it would be better to go earlier than later in the day, when the sun was high. I doubted we'd actually *get* to the tallest point on the island—surely a hike like that would take a few hours—but it might be fun to get a better vantage point, at least.

"I'm game if you are," Luca told me.

"Alright," I agreed. "Someone ought to look after you two."

"That's the spirit." Aly clapped me on the back and went over to the picnic operation to inform Zady of our plans—and to nab a few water bottles. Luca and I accepted ours gratefully as she returned to us. "We got the all-clear," she said. "How about we start back by the boat? I think I saw a trail over there."

"Do people come here often to picnic and hike?" Luca asked, as the three of us fell into line.

"Every once in a while," Aly told him from the front. "Anyone who's not afraid of the rumors, that is."

"Speaking of," I piped up, "my friend Officer Thorn back in Belville had heard stories that Officer Brooks was mixed up with an ifrit somehow."

With unerring ease, Aly led us past the boat and turned onto what was, indeed, a trail. Dark, sandy soil led us between the tree trunks, and we were soon in mottled shade, much to my relief.

"Do you think the ifrit in that story and the ifrit that's supposed to live on this island are the same?" Luca asked from the back.

Though she kept her gaze on the ground, avoiding roots or rocks, Aly shook her head. "I've lived in these islands all my life, and I've never seen any *proof* of an ifrit."

"But what did happen, with Officer Brooks?" I pressed. "Did the town do any kind of investigation, or—?"

"Or divination?" For a brief second, Aly looked over her shoulder at me and grinned. "Sure, everyone *tried*. But no one could corroborate anything."

"It must have been hard," Luca added, "when the person you wanted to investigate was the person who would usually be doing the investigating. Was he really in trouble?"

"It *was* hard on the town. But if you ask me, that was because no one could find an answer," Aly said, with humor. "After Officer Brooks saw the effects of his report, he clammed up pretty quick."

We followed the trail into a ravine between two rocky cliffs, the air around us filtered through palm fronds and heavy with the smell of earth. I glanced back at Luca, who beamed at me.

Aly kept a steady pace up front, but she seemed momentarily distracted. I prompted again, "What was his actual report, though?"

"Zady would remember better than I would," she said. "I didn't pay as much attention at the time as you might think. You were pretty little then, and we had our hands full just getting you to stay still long enough to eat and cleaning up after your 'mud potions.'"

"Was Red an alchemist even then?" The delight was apparent in Luca's voice.

"Can we *please* focus?" I insisted, laughing despite myself.

"Alright, alright." Aly paused for a moment, and as she thought, a bird called overhead. As the trail turned and began making long switchbacks up over the rocks, she finally said, "It was a lost child story. That's why I blocked so much of it out. The one time I *did* try to help out with one of the town's divination fires, all I could see in the flames was you, Cinnabar.

"It didn't start on Kairoi—I remember that much. The little girl was from one of the big name families in Oasis. Actually, I think they were *the* big name family, back in the day. That's partly why there was so much fuss."

"The Dragon clan?" Luca asked as we rounded another corner.

Aly nodded. "Exactly. They knew how to pull strings. And I'm not saying I blame them. I would have tried everything, too, if it had been my child. But the whole thing was confusing from the start. It was the family that reported her missing, but . . . the more everyone looked into it, the more it seemed like she could only have been spirited away by someone *in* the family."

"They meant to abandon her?" I asked, pained even though I had no memory of this at all.

"Something about prophecies and successions, no doubt," Aly said, a bitter edge to her voice. "That was what we all thought, in Wellspring. But of course that only meant we tried harder to help find her. There had been a terrible storm when she went missing. Early divination efforts seemed to suggest she was on a boat, or a raft, lost in the waves."

"And the divination led you here?" Luca concluded.

We emerged onto a little outcrop, a spur off the trail. The tops of the palm trees that grew up from the beach waved at our feet. The sun's glint off of the ocean was almost unbearable, and in the distance, there was the volcano, Wellspring, Kairoi.

"Officer Brooks led the team that came over here to look," Aly said. She stood with her hands on her hips, gazing across at her home island like she was looking back in time. "That's about the last thing everyone can agree on, looking back."

So he did come out here, I thought. *So much for the first strike against him. But why didn't he tell the Guild that?*

A sound, like a rock clattering down the cliff face, made me turn back to look at the trail. There was a flash of blue bird feathers, but that was all. Luca poked me, reminding me to drink some water, and I set the distraction aside.

"I guess they didn't find anything?" I asked, quietly. Seeing as Officer Brooks had not, so far, been discussed as a hero, it seemed an unfortunate but safe bet.

"Some people swore they *did* find something," Aly said. She turned, leading us back to the trail. Apparently, the sightseeing break was over. "And some people swore it must have been the girl. But others insisted there was nothing at all. And since they came back empty-handed, it was hard to believe the first group."

"That's awful," Luca said. "How did they explain it?"

"That's the thing," Aly replied, taking the next switchback with even more gusto. "No one really could. None of their stories made sense. Officer Brooks was the most coherent. He had to write a report, after all. But his story was that he'd spotted a lost child, followed it, and it had then turned into a huge magical being that promised to tell him the secrets to all the islands' secrets if we all promised to give it whatever it wanted in return."

"*What?*" I exclaimed. However I had expected the story to end, it had not been like that!

"Ifrits *are* known for occasionally making deals for magical favors," Luca said thoughtfully, behind me. "So in that way, I could see the story almost making sense. But even so, most research suggests it's very dangerous to make open-ended deals like that. Each ifrit is different, but overall, they can be very . . . ruthless."

"That's certainly what we thought," Aly said dryly. "Besides, imagine telling several islands full of diviners that in one fell swoop, you're going to eliminate all their secrets. No one was too excited about the idea, let me tell you."

"I imagine the Police Guild would not be pleased with the idea, either, no matter how much they wanted to solve the case," Luca added.

"Not to mention the fact that he thought the lost child *was* an ifrit?" I shook my head, panting as the trail inclined yet more steeply upward. To our left, further up the hill, the bushes rustled in the breeze.

Luca, too, latched on to this point. "Did they ever find her? Anywhere?"

"Not that I know of," Aly answered. "For a while, every year on the anniversary of the storm, we'd hold a vigil at the bonfire and try to do some more Seeing. But nothing ever came out of it that made any sense."

So Brooks failed to solve the case, and *wanted to make a terrible deal with an unknown magical force that would have affected the entire region,* I thought. *Those must be the true "two strikes" the Guild has on his record. I bet the only reason it took them so long to replace him is that no one wanted to come all the way out here to work at such a tiny police station.*

While we mulled over our separate thoughts, the trail turned its final switchback and took us to the top of the hill. The foliage was much more sparse up here, the air bright and fresh. Low bushes and reedy grass grew in patches on the rocky soil, but actual rocks were visible too, cropping up everywhere across the uneven hilltop. I knew it was all due to tricks of erosion, but the effect was somehow more eerie; it was almost as if someone had started making a rock maze, but had given up before they got the walls more than a few feet high.

Probably just the story making me paranoid, I thought, shrugging off the impression.

Aly hopped up onto a nearby rock to scout out the rest of the trail. "Not bad so far!" she declared.

"This is really interesting," Luca agreed. As he wandered past her to inspect some tiny white flowers, he added, "I've never been anywhere like this. The terrain is so different from home. It almost feels like—"

"Luca!" Aly and I cried in unison, as he tumbled out of sight.

In no more than a second, we stood where Luca had just been admiring flowers. It was clear what had happened: the rocks and brush had concealed a jagged hole in the ground—a long gash, whose lip we now stood on. Luca had slipped into the darkness below—a darkness inside the hill we had just climbed up.

A cave?

"Luca! Are you okay?" I called, searching the shadows for any signs.

"Um, thank you," he said, his voice muffled. Louder, he added, "I'm fine! And . . . there's someone else here."

Turns out, Baby Island was not as deserted as I'd thought.

24

Running Water

Aly and I followed the gash in the top of the hill until it ran down to a little ledge obscured in brush, where we could enter more safely than Luca had. What was a ledge on the outside of the hill turned out to be a ledge inside the cave, too. As we paused, letting our eyes adjust to the dark, Luca came over and reached up.

I accepted his hand and hopped down to the cave floor with him. We helped Aly lower herself down carefully afterward. Whoever Luca had found was waiting very patiently . . .

And yet, I didn't find it odd. The cave itself felt like a place where time stood still. Sunlight filtered in through the crack above us, where Luca had fallen. It illuminated mossy boulders and a bare basalt floor, polished smooth by age. Somewhere along the edges, there must have been a channel for a stream— I could hear the water running against the rocks. The place was as big as a house, as big as the whole hillside, even. The crack that served as skylight was a good few yards overhead, too far to reach, and I had to wonder how Luca had made the fall without being hurt.

When I finally caught sight of our new friend, however, I stopped wondering.

The vision was human-shaped but slightly too large—not large and muscular in the way Officer Thorn was, nor stretched and tall the way an elf like Gene might be, but simply *larger than life,* somehow. A white robe hung from its straight shoulders and skimmed over a rounded chest and belly, all the way down to the ground, obscured in shadow. The robe was open in front, revealing a long strip of deep red skin. Fortunately, some sort of loincloth completed the costume. Its face, too, was rounded, a wide smile fixed upon us, under golden eyes that seemed to glow faintly. The outlandish creature seemed to have black hair gathered into a top knot . . . but from there, the hair floated upward and seemed to fade away, defying gravity and corporeality both.

I'd never met an ifrit before, but I couldn't help but be reminded of Officer Brooks' tale.

"What interesting visitors you are," the being said. Its voice was melodic, moving from high to low and back again. "Only the cursed one can float, then?"

Aly and I both looked at Luca, who looked a little perturbed. "My first thought when I was falling was to shift," he explained quietly. "I'm not sure if it would have worked, but I didn't have to find out—I was caught."

Though Aly and Zady had made it clear that they could sense the ancient curse on Luca, I wasn't sure if Aly understood this point—that Luca could sometimes 'shift' into shadow, almost like a ghost. But now was clearly not the time for explanations.

"You nearly landed on my head," said the being, chuckling.

I glanced at Luca and then at Aly, who shifted from foot to foot as though she, too, was unsettled. She cleared her throat and spoke up. "And who, may we ask, are you?"

The being laughed louder this time, the sound filling the cavern around us. "I could ask you the same thing, little friends. How brave of you to come straight into my home."

"We didn't mean to intrude," I said.

"Of course you did. You always do," our host said, waving one wide, red hand. "Isn't that the nature of looking for something?"

"We were only looking for our friend," Aly said, her voice hard. "We'll leave you to your peace now."

"Oh, don't be in such a rush." The being moved closer, though I could not tell if it was walking or floating. "Since you're here, why don't you tell me your heart's desire?"

"There's really no need," I said, wondering how fast we might be able to jump back onto the ledge. I could make it, definitely, but Aly and Luca both would have more trouble.

"There really is," said the magical creature, its smile growing. "Unless you want me to take offense for this intrusion into my home."

We glanced at each other. The silence was thick and foreboding. *Should we play along, or not?*

Luca made his decision first. "I already have my heart's desire," he said, putting his arm around me.

"Companionship and acceptance," the being purred. "How nice for you. And as for the others?"

"I could say the same," I declared.

"Come, come," was the answer. "An alchemist never wants something simple."

"A true alchemist understands that the search for simplicity and truth is its own reward," I retorted.

"Oh, very good," the being said. It turned to focus on Aly,

standing at my left. "And you? Give me something new, won't you? Tell me your wish."

"I . . ." Aly shifted again, and looked at me before saying, "I've already had my share of dreams. I could say I wanted my strength back, but it would only be partly true."

Her injury again. Zady had downplayed it in her letters, I realized. And in that moment, I did earnestly regret that I hadn't come back to visit sooner.

"Your intrusion is forgiven," the being decided. "But are you certain you don't want what is only partly true? I am very good at partial truths."

"You're an ifrit," Luca said softly, confirming my suspicions.

"And does it matter?" the ifrit moved toward us again, a sweeping, graceful motion. Still that same wide smile. "All that means is that I can *do* things for you. And you can do things for me."

"We've already done what we came here to do," I said, my hand snaking around Luca's waist.

But Luca seemed to be considering something. Cautiously, he said, "I suppose you've done things for many of the people on the nearby islands already."

"Many," agreed the ifrit. "But then again, not so many as you might think. People are narrow-minded, I find. So rarely do they truly dream *big* . . ."

"Riches and power seem big enough to me," Luca said with a shrug.

I had never in my life heard Luca mention money that way. In that moment, I realized what he was doing. He was using half-truths to lure the ifrit into telling us more of its own accord.

And it worked. "True wealth and power is *land*, little scholar.

What do possessions and titles get you, if you don't have your slice of safety?"

"That's what you've been up to all these years," Aly said, her teeth gritted. She might have caught on to Luca's trick, but it was clear she was going to be more confrontational with it—she'd never been one to pull her punches. "You've been trying to scare people away from Baby Island so you can have it for yourself."

"I'm so uninterested in *years*," said the ifrit, with an expansive shrug of the shoulders and that same amused smile. "Such a little measure of time. How could you know what I wish? Would you like me to tell you?"

"We don't need you to," Luca cut in.

"That's right," I added, when the ifrit looked like it might disagree. My mind raced. "We already know you stole a child because you wanted to keep your island safe."

"*Stole? A child?*" the ifrit seemed to puff up in indignation. It may have been a trick of the mind, but for a moment I could have sworn it filled the entire cave. "I have no need to steal," it said haughtily. "Mortals *give* me everything I desire, of their own free will."

"How nice for you," Aly said, rather snappily. "But sometimes not helping is as bad as stealing."

"What determined little friends you all are," the ifrit observed. "How very disagreeable. You could use that determination to dream, rather than to annoy me."

"I think we've all made our positions clear," I said, doing my best to remain level-headed. "If you've had enough conversation, then we'll take our leave."

"We answered your questions," Luca reminded the ifrit hastily.

"But you've been no fun at all," the ifrit said. "I will not help you out."

With another wave of its large hand, the ledge behind us crumbled.

Panic shot through my chest. Confined spaces were already not my strong suit, and a confined space with no way out . . .

Luca moved to hold my hand, and squeezed it. I took a deep breath, doing my best to stay calm. And in that moment of silence, I heard the running water again.

"You couldn't do anything directly if you tried," Aly challenged, her voice angry. She probably knew how upset I was.

But her challenge sounded foolhardy and dangerous, and it didn't make me any less upset.

The ifrit stared her down. And then, with a swirling flick of the wrist, it laughed again. "Maybe you *are* fun. Not everyone sees so well. The things we could do—"

"Not today," Luca interrupted, his voice firm.

My feet were itching to run.

"We see exactly what you are," Aly added.

The ifrit gave her that same hard stare, lifted its hand once more. And then, with an insolent twist to its smile, it said, "Not any more."

And with that, the ifrit winked out. Only a puff of smoke remained.

I caught my breath. The ifrit appeared to be gone, but other than that, the cave and ourselves were unscathed.

Luca winked at me, his light eyes bright in the darkness. *Touchy,* he mouthed.

Aly nudged my shoulder, and nodded.

I swallowed, trusting their judgment. Hopefully, the ifrit *had* simply thrown a tantrum and decided to leave us alone.

But at this point, Luca and Aly's faces shifted into concern and contemplation. It was clear neither of them had an idea of how to get ourselves out.

I followed their example of being nonverbal, in case the ifrit was listening in. I nudged them both, and then led the way toward the sound of running water.

Of course, it was at the far side of the cave, in the deepest shadow. Though I was confident that running water meant some way in and out, I did falter at the darkness. But Luca was right behind me, with Aly beside him. I took one more slow breath and reached down for the water running past my feet, trying to ascertain how much was there and how deep the channel was.

It felt no bigger than a stormwater drain at home, and the water was deliciously cold and fast. I edged along the stream carefully, following it deeper into the shadow. Normally I had good vision in the dark, but this was so complete that even my goggles would have done me little good. I simply had to feel my way, stay vigilant, and hope.

The stream dipped downward and ran close to the wall. I bumped my head and scraped my right shoulder several times, but what I was most afraid of—a sudden fall, the stream bed giving way underneath us—never happened. Instead, the stream ran us straight into another wall.

I paused as my nose hit the rock and Luca hit my back. I wanted to curse aloud.

Instead, in the pause, I realized that the water was now running *over* my toes.

The stream apparently ran into the wall and curved past it, heading sharply right. I waved my hand out in the right direction, testing this idea. Where before there had been a solid wall, I found a slim opening, just big enough to slide through.

Nothing for it, I decided. With another deep breath, I stepped through.

Luca and Aly followed close. This time, we were more ready for the stream's twists. We went around one more corner, and began to see a glow ahead. After slipping carefully down another incline and ducking under a low overhang, we found ourselves abruptly in the sunlight.

25

Oases

The little stream poured over my sandals and plunged into a clear pool below. Dark cliffs extended on either side, circling around the pool and some mossy boulders. At the far end of the grotto, there was a break in the rocks and a few palm fronds that I hoped indicated a trail back to the beach.

After the uncertainty of the cave, this little place was an oasis indeed.

"Wow," Luca said, shuffling onto the ledge beside me. "We should move our picnic here!"

"Is that really a good idea?" I asked, looking over my shoulder where we'd just emerged.

Aly, bringing up the rear, caught my glance. "If you ask me, it *is* a good idea. At the very least, to bring William up here. I think the ifrit is bound to its cave, but William could say for sure."

"I agree," Luca added more seriously. "Despite Officer Brooks' story of being led to the ifrit, we stumbled across it entirely by accident. It didn't even seem to know we were on the island. If it was able to reach people on the beach, I think it would have tried harder with us."

"You two are the experts," I conceded. We helped each other clamber down the hillside, and then decided that as I was the fastest, I would run back down to the beach. I left Luca and Aly with their toes in the pool, and followed the trail I'd spotted earlier. In moments, it took me to the sand.

I wonder if this is how people are supposed *to come across the ifrit,* I thought, as I emerged at a clear trail head that we'd missed earlier only by chance. *It did say people have come to see it. Maybe someone's spread stories about the cave behind the waterfall, and that's how people come to make deals.*

It didn't explain Brooks, but then again, a lot of that particular event was still unexplained. I tucked the thought aside for later and sprinted over to Zady and William, to fill them in on our misadventure.

At first, they were not excited about the idea of packing up their freshly-made camp. But once we'd made our way back to the grove, they understood.

"I will confess, this is very charming," Zady said, shaking her picnic blanket out over a large, reasonably flat boulder.

"As long as it isn't magical," said Aly. From her perch beside Luca on another of the rocks, she looked at William. "What do you think?"

William glowed blue, his nose in the air, considering the steep hillside and the little cave opening from whence we'd come. "I can sense the magic on the cave itself, but it doesn't come down as far as the pool and the grotto. Looks like a pretty strong containment spell, if I had to guess."

"Often the case with ifrits," Luca said, kicking his feet through the water. "There's some debate about whether they *choose* their specific location, perhaps in order to enhance their magic, or if they get bound there by someone else. But in general they are found inhabiting a very small space, sometimes even as small as—"

"We get it," I teased, tossing a spare flask of water to him. He caught it with a grin.

"Aly realized it first," he concluded, generously.

"Did you?" Zady was still setting out picnic goods, but she paused to raise an eyebrow at her partner. *Do we need to talk about this later?* was the general implication, I thought.

"We'd just been talking about Officer Brooks," Aly said with a shrug. "It's something that's always bothered me about his story. If he ran into some magical creature that could reveal all these secrets, then why hasn't it ever done so? Why was it waiting for some human to *ask* it to do so?"

"That's how it goes when you start dabbling in *really* strong magic," William said, from his spot on the picnic blanket. "If you're doing it just for your own gain, the spell tends to collapse in on itself. Having someone else ask makes the magic more stable. That's where a lot of sorcerers get tripped up."

"The more boundaries are in place, the more powerful the force," Luca agreed. "I've read that. It's why ifrits choose such small places. And if you ask me, it brings up some really fascinating points about the theory of magic . . ."

And with that, we settled in for a very delicious—and philosophical—lunch.

* * *

The rest of our day trip was pure vacation, not a mystery in sight. After exploring the grotto a little more, we returned to the beach to swim and lounge. It was one of those lovely, endless afternoons, and by the time we needed to head home, everyone was much more relaxed.

Including me—although, as we landed back on Kairoi, I could have sworn I saw a shadow on the beach.

Assuring myself that it was just a local out for a walk, I helped the others secure the boat and then told them I was going to run into town for a moment. I had promised Babs to clean up his investigation room, after all. But I was positive it would only take a few moments, so I sent everyone else home ahead of me.

It was twilight by then, and the beach was deserted but the town was not. The market was still going strong, and many people had gathered for a third try at fire-gazing to help the investigation. According to Aly, the results of the kelp offering the night before had been dubious at best; tonight, it smelled like they were using jasmine. The scent was lovely, but it also gave me a sense of foreboding. Much like the fact that I still had an itchy feeling at the back of my neck, like somehow something had followed us from Baby Island.

But that is impossible, I reminded myself firmly. *And if you need to hear* why *it's impossible again, you can set William and Luca philosophizing again when you get back.*

For now, though, there was work to do. I jogged lightly up the steps to the police station and knocked at the door.

Light was spilling from the windows, so I didn't expect to wait long. In fact it was only a moment before I heard Babs' voice shouting, "Come in!"

"I would have just let myself in," I explained, as I did just that and found him behind the front desk, "but I figured visiting hours are over."

"You aren't here to see Dean, are you?" Babs looked up wearily from a pile of papers on his desk. It was a well-stacked pile—Luca had taught the police officers that much, at least—but nonetheless it was huge, and it was clear that Babs was *not* entirely grateful for New West Key's determination to share information.

"No, I meant you two, or really, your interrogation room," I said. "I came by to clean up. Is Officer Ja'far in his office? He didn't leave you to do all this on your own, did he?"

"We split the piles," Babs said by way of answer, looking down at his own with the air of a marooned first mate.

"Anything good?" I asked sympathetically.

"I don't know what's good any more," Babs said, rather pathetically. "Did you know Oasis and New West Key control the fish trade in these waters? Because I do. Now. It's all here in these ledgers. Though why they sent us stuff about *Oasis* when we're in *Kairoi* is something I'll never—"

"Yes, it sounds very thorough," I said, heading him off. Many people in our clan felt a bit, well, *touchy* about the apparent superiority of Oasis. I recognized it as a rant that could go on for ages. "Maybe I'd better leave you to it?"

Babs nodded miserably. "Your potions are still back there. I didn't touch them. It looked to me like they *were* just cleaning potions after all, but who knows, maybe they all turned out the wrong color and I couldn't tell."

I'd been about to pass his desk, eager to get to work, but that made me pause. "Officer Babs, maybe you—and Ja'far— should take a break. Come back at it in the morning with a fresh start."

"But there's a *murderer* loose," said Babs.

I bit my lip. He sounded young and petulant, but that wasn't what surprised me: it was his determination. In that moment, I really felt for both police officers. Especially now that I knew what they'd meant by their superior officer wanting to "consult a powerful being" instead of investigate.

"Yes," I said, gently. "There *is* a murderer loose. And from what we can tell, they're pretty crafty. But if I've learned anything from the police officer back home, it's that small stations like this have to rely on their community. And I don't just mean asking some of us to do things," I said, as Babs lifted his head to protest. "I mean you also have to trust that the vast majority of the town wants this to be solved, too. So they're keeping an eye on one another, and racking their brains for clues. And they'll keep each other safe as much as they can. Do you see what I mean? It's not helpful for you two to hole up in here and push yourselves so hard that even if you *do* catch the murder, you'll be just as likely to keel over from exhaustion as you are to cuff them."

"Harsh," said a new voice from the hall. Officer Ja'far. He'd emerged, but was literally leaning on his office door.

"But . . . maybe true," Babs admitted from his desk.

"Definitely true," I insisted. "Sorry to go all 'big sister' on you, but trust me, I've seen my share of investigations by this point. So how about I go check the experiment and clean it up, while you two put away your papers and get ready to close the station for the night?"

I marched down the hall before either could argue.

Despite Babs' uncharacteristic self-doubt, the potions were indeed just cleaning potions. The results were unequivocal. Fortunately, that made cleaning up quite simple, since the potions had been designed to leave no trace in the first place.

The shopkeeper in me did feel a twinge of regret about

the fact that we'd destroyed an entire crate of perfectly fine, sellable potions. *Sold* potions, in fact. It wasn't a loss that was anywhere near as important as the loss of a life, though. And even a dead end could end up being helpful in putting the case together.

Mysteries are about people, I told myself, much as I'd lectured Babs and Ja'far. *Not about papers and potions.*

Though I *did* wonder if any of the officers' papers said anything about a little missing girl . . .

. . . . But I certainly wasn't going to bring it up now, not when they'd finally agreed to take a break. I emerged from the station's little kitchen to find both officers waiting by the front door.

"Alright, then," I said, smiling faintly at them. "Let's all go get some rest, shall we?"

26

False Starts

We didn't rest for very long.

It was morning, but only barely, when I and all my companions were awoken by a furious pounding at the front door. And when we opened it . . .

Who could it be, but Officers Babs and Ja'far?

"All hands on deck," they insisted, bleary-eyed. "There's an intruder at the Palace."

* * *

"This'd better not be some false alarm," William grumped, as the five of us rattled along in the back of the police cart, racing for the western side of the island.

"I'm sure Jasmin's anti-intruder spells are very good," yawned Luca.

"Then why should they need *us?*" Aly was not a fan of interrupted sleep. Neither was Zady, who was actually still sleeping on Aly's shoulder.

I decided not to mention that I'd just recently given the

officers the "you must trust in your community" talk.

"I bet you," said William, only too glad to have company in his gloomy mood, "that it was just another new secretary that set off the alarm."

"You'd better keep your smart opinions to yourself," I warned him, as we turned onto the palace drive. "We're nearly there. And I don't think Raja's much of one to put up with commentary."

* * *

Naturally, Jasmin—or Raja—had already organized the Palace employees before we'd arrived. There was probably a plan in place, I realized. Our little party of seven barreled straight into what was already an ongoing search.

Raja was at the front gate, barking orders. From her directions, it was clear that there were at least four teams of armed guards, sweeping the grounds in every direction. Attendants and guards filled the grounds around the entryway, too, some talking in low whispers, some peering into the bushes, and—most worryingly—some receiving minor first aid from Morgiana, whose white hair stood out like a beacon in the early morning shadow.

"Was there some kind of fight?" I asked the officers, watching as a young guard had his ankle wrapped.

"Not that we heard of," Babs said. He sounded just as concerned as I was.

"All we were told was that the security spell was tripped," Officer Ja'far said, grimly. Leaving the rest of us beside the cart, he strode directly for Jasmin—who stood illuminated by the light from the double front doors.

"I don't see what we can do that they can't," Aly murmured, as we huddled and waited for direction.

Officer Babs, lingering nearby, overheard. "It's really more about procedure," he said, a bit nervously. "Outside investigators to confirm that there really *was* a security breach, to make sure everyone is treated fairly, that sort of thing . . ."

"Bit late for that," William observed. "If they already have teams of people out looking for someone, they might have found what they're looking for."

"It can't have been *that* long since the alarm went off," Luca said more optimistically.

"Less than half an hour," Officer Babs supplied. "But . . . most intruders either get away in the first few minutes or not at all."

It was difficult to tell which outcome he thought was worse.

* * *

In the end, the officers asked us to station ourselves around the entryway, where most of the action was taking place. Zady and Aly went to help with any remaining first aid emergencies—purely accidental trips and falls while searching, we were assured—while Luca assigned himself to Raja, much to her evident disdain. William lingered by the gate, glowing as he interacted with the Palace security spells. The pair of officers roamed back and forth as needed, wherever some new action sprang up or new report came in. Amid the bustle, I decided to go sit beside Jasmin.

She'd claimed a gilded wooden bench beneath a healthy, flowering vine. I doubted the luxury was very comforting to her now, though. In the growing light, her face looked more pale and wan than ever, and she fiddled anxiously with the tie string on her plush pink robe, continuously tightening it and then picking at its ends.

"Is this the first time something like this has happened?"

"In a while," she said, her low voice strained. "There were a few times when we first came here. But the spells were still new then."

"You mean, it was just kinks in the system being worked out?"

"Something like that," she said, waving one delicate hand before returning to picking at her belt.

William, whose specialty happened to be protection spells, never allowed any of his creations to have *kinks*. But I decided that wasn't a helpful thing to mention. Maybe fairy magic was a little more trial-and-error than William's variety.

"Did anyone actually see or hear anything?" I asked, more to the point.

Jasmin shook her head impatiently. "No. No. It may well have been a ghost."

May as *well have been,* I thought she meant to say. But in the shock, it was understandable that she would skip a word here or there. "Do you think you know who it was?"

"That is what the officers said. Why? Why would I know? If I knew, why would I need to search?" She tossed back her long, bright hair.

"That's fair," I said. "I just—"

"What about Dean," she interrupted.

I hesitated. "What about him?"

"Is he alright? Have they done something to him?"

"Well," I said slowly, "I didn't see him yesterday. But from what I hear, he's perfectly fine. Just, ah . . . sticking to his story."

For a moment we sat in silence, side by side on the bench. From our vantage point, we could see everyone in the front plaza, running back and forth in front of the big palace gates. All this activity, and Jasmin had asked me about Dean—and *not,* it seemed, because she thought he had been the one to trip the alarm.

Briefly, William's secretary joke came back to me. This time, though, I felt bad for Jasmin. A business person had to place a lot of trust in their secretary, effectively making them their second-in-command. And it did not seem like trust came easily to Jasmin.

"He's a fool," she said abruptly. And then, "They won't charge him?"

"I doubt they have enough evidence, at least, not yet," I said, wryly. "And tonight's break-in may complicate matters."

"Why?" For the first time, Jasmin met my eyes.

"Because he *definitely* wasn't the one to set off your alarm, if he's safe in the station," I said, watching her carefully.

"Oh, yes. That." Jasmin waved her hand dismissively again, then sat hunched over herself, staring out at the hustle and bustle. "But then—what if?"

What if what, I was about to ask. At that moment, though, William bounded up.

"Have you been to Baby Island?" he demanded, of Jasmin.

Jasmin sat up straight as a rod, her eyes hardening. "I know no Baby Island."

"You can see it from your tower," I said mildly, intrigued by both the question and the reaction. "And probably most of the rooms in your palace."

"You never went there?" William pressed.

"No," Jasmin declared. "Why should I?"

William glowed a little, then settled down beside my feet. He looked up at me with his head tilted, as though trying to figure out how much to say.

"If that is all," Jasmin said stiffly. She then solved William's dilemma for him by getting up and stalking over to Raja and Luca.

"What's up?" I asked William quietly.

"I'm not sure," he admitted, with a whine. "I thought for a moment I sensed the ifrit's magic. Now that we've been there and I've seen it, something here reminded me of it. But I'm not sure what. There's too many other traces."

"There must be about a million spells on this place," I agreed. "But you think the ifrit thing is important?"

"It's not enough to be definite," William admitted. "But I think that this palace and the ifrit have more to do with each other than Jasmin says."

27

Dead Ends

William might not have been definite, but I persuaded him to report his findings, at least. By mid morning, everyone had given up the search at Palace Jasmin. The officers gave us a lift back to Wellspring, and then William I lingered at the police station to make a report.

Officer Babs sat at the front desk talking it over with us, but his heart clearly wasn't in it. He seemed more dismayed than curious to hear William mention the ifrit. And behind him, through the wall, we could all hear muffled yelling as Officer Ja'far interviewed Dean once again.

"We thought he might have an accomplice who set off the alarm spell," Babs told us, glumly.

"Sounds like not," William commented.

I had to agree that it did not sound like the interview was going well.

Just then, the door behind us opened. Yet another unhappy face met us as we turned to see the newcomer. It was the apothecary assistant, Bertie, and he was in tears.

I hadn't been this close to Bertie before. He was very pale and slightly overweight, with shaggy brown hair and brown eyes that were currently red-rimmed and puffy. A scraggly beard was vying for position along his jawline. Like Gene, he wore a white lab coat, but beneath that he was clearly in khaki shorts and leather sandals.

"If this is about the potions shipment," Babs sighed, "I already told Petra that—"

"It's not!" Bertie wailed. William and I made room, and he crashed against the front desk between us. "Gene said I have to tell you everything. She said either I tell you, or she will."

"You have a second interview room," I reminded Officer Babs. "I got everything out of it."

"I've been dosing myself at nights when I'm supposed to be restocking, okay?" Bertie cried.

Around the distraught medical student, William caught my eye, panting. I knew exactly what he wanted to say: *well, there's not much need for a lengthy interview after all, is there?*

"Uh," said Babs, scrambling to find a clean page in his notebook. "Come again?"

"You really don't have to get into it out here," I said, this time addressing Bertie. It was for his own sake I was trying to get him to be discreet.

"What does it matter," he said, rubbing at his eyes. "Everyone knows. That's why the police in 'Key knew me, okay? Only I left for my internship. But I didn't stop. I've been doing it here too."

I caught William's eye again, wondering, *should we leave?*

William clearly wasn't going to let gossip this good go to waste.

Officer Babs was scribbling as fast as his fingers could go, on the backside of one of his pages of notes. "Wait—dosing yourself with what?"

"Wolfsmallow," said Bertie, despondent.

That made a whole lot of sense—to me, at least. Recalling that Bertie was a werewolf, and looking at him now, I could piece things together. Many werewolves did look simply like humans, of course, but some wanted more wolfish features, like pointed teeth or thicker hair. Some resorted to taking wolfsmallow, as an opposite to wolfsbane, as a solution . . . not a medically or alchemically *recommended* solution, but nevertheless, a home remedy that could become an addiction.

However, Officer Babs had none of my experience. He stopped writing and wrinkled his nose. It was obvious he was going to ask why Bertie was bothering him with this when wolfsmallow had nothing to do with cleaning potions.

I intervened, clearing my throat. "Officer, wolfsmallow dosing is a recognized problem in . . . in apothecaries, and other circles. I can attest to that. It's also the kind of thing that does cast a long shadow on a practitioner's reputation. It brings all their decisions into question."

"That's what Gene said!" Bertie wailed again.

"And that's effectively what happened here," I reminded Officer Babs.

"And now you've admitted to it," Babs said, not unkindly, looking at his notes. "But not to murder?"

"I don't even *know* the person who was murdered," Bertie protested, before another sob erupted. "I don't know *everyone* in New West Key, okay?"

"How about I see you home," William said. Apparently, his better nature had kicked in. "The officers can come find you if they have more questions. You coming, Red?" he added, as he began shepherding Bertie toward the door.

"You go on ahead," I said. "I have one more thing to talk about here."

I waited until we were alone again. As the door closed behind William and a still-sobbing Bertie, another door opened and Officer Ja'far joined us in the front room. He looked every bit as beleaguered as he had the day before. And Officer Babs, still scribbling in his notebook, had made no protest at any of this.

"What's going on?" Ja'far asked. "You were saying you have something to say?"

"I do," I said. "But you might prefer somewhere a little more private . . ."

* * *

I slammed the door to Ja'far's office behind me and turned to lean against it, staring down at Babs and Ja'far, who sat at the edge of the big desk like children.

"What is going on out there?" I demanded. "Is *this* the result of ten years' training at the Guild?"

Officer Ja'far looked genuinely taken aback. But Officer Babs, sneaking a glance at his friend, looked a little guilty.

"It's not your fault that none of us got the rest we needed," I conceded, beginning to pace back and forth in front of them, "but consider what you've been doing just in the past half hour. Berating suspects so loudly the whole station can hear you? Letting witnesses confess to serious crimes out in the open, while *crying*, no less? This is basically the *opposite* of what I meant when I said you should try trusting the community! Bertie was seriously upset, Babs! And Ja'far, I know Dean is annoying, but really—you were *shouting* at him!"

"You're shouting," Babs said, not looking at me.

"I am," I agreed, taking a deep breath. "But *I'm* just an alchemist, and a community member to boot. You both have had special training. You're expected to be professional. What would your mentors at the Guild say if they could see you now?"

To my surprise, it was Ja'far who broke. He put his head in his hands, leaning down to rest his elbows on his knees.

Seeing that, I softened a little. "Listen, I'm not saying you are bad investigators. I know you can do better than badgering witnesses this way. So . . . why *aren't* you?"

"Maybe we can't," said Babs, sniffling.

"You can," I insisted. "Remember how excited you were, when we first met back at the marina? You were picture-perfect new officers."

"But we *aren't*," said Ja'far, without looking up.

"We're failures," Babs agreed. "We're just *hooligans!*"

It was very serious in that little office, but I almost had to laugh at that. Thinking it over, I tugged a chair toward me and sat down facing them. "Did Officer Brooks tell you that?"

Babs nodded.

"Let me guess," I went on. "Fifteen years ago, because you had vandalized the bonfire?"

At that, Ja'far did finally look up, though he didn't lift his head. "You remember that?"

"I didn't at first, but I had a few suspicions," I admitted, smiling now. "But surely you can see what a huge difference there is between that infraction years ago, and what you have both become now?"

"There isn't a difference to Officer Brooks," Ja'far said

darkly.

"Yeah, well, I literally have not seen him help with this investigation *once*," I replied. "I don't even know where he is, ever. At least you two are trying."

"But we'll *never* fit in," Babs burst, his own tears catching up to him. "We never have. Like you. You know what it's like, growing up here and not wanting to end up like everyone else."

"Sure," I said, "but—"

Babs wasn't listening; he kept rambling. "That's why I said we should—that's why—it's all my fault—"

"It isn't," Ja'far interrupted sternly. "I never would have got this far without you."

"But we never even practiced divination—I said it was just for chumps—I was just jealous—"

"There's no point trying to be like everyone else," Ja'far insisted, presumably in an attempt to comfort his friend.

I followed this, more or less. It seemed that Babs was the one who truly felt out of place, and he worried he'd dragged Ja'far along with him. But I doubted Ja'far could be dragged anywhere he didn't already want to go. In fact, he seemed poignantly afraid of admitting how much he relied on his friend.

I knew that some people, notably Jasmin, had had their doubts about these two from the beginning. But I really did believe in them.

"Listen," I said to them, once more. "You're right, and you're wrong. I think you don't have to try to be someone you're not, be that a diviner or some kind of hard-core investigator. Just be yourselves—and I do think you will fit in. Your Guild sent you here for a reason."

"Yeah, that no one else would take the position," Babs snuffled.

"Well, I'm not *too* surprised." I smiled. "But still. You'll get there. Just not by being so unkind to everyone—including yourselves."

Ja'far sat up straight, at last. "I can't believe you are lecturing us."

"I only meant to reprimand a little, but it got out of hand," I agreed lightly.

"Red always knows best," Babs said. I was fairly certain he was teasing me, but in the next moment, he reached to one side of the desk and pulled out a familiar-looking diary.

"What—" I started to protest. My stomach was rumbling, and I wanted to meet my family for brunch. It was hardly the time for more reading . . .

"You know what it's like, growing up here and being different," Babs repeated, ignoring me. "*You* know. You were the most different of everyone. You went away and didn't even come back. So, here. You look through this one. See if you find what we can't."

He thrust Nouronnihar's diary into my hands, and Ja'far did not protest. Words failed me.

You didn't even come back . . .

28

The Darkest Night

> *Sometimes I wonder if I will ever break free from them.*
> *Maybe I should have never left home in the first place.*
> *But I just wanted to settle down—is that so wrong? I*
> *thought I was following my star. Oh, Atargatis!*
> *I've started applying for other work. Maybe just by*
> *getting away, if I am smart, I can escape. There was a*
> *play troupe in Oasis, but that one's a long shot, I think. I*
> *have a better chance for secretarial work on one of the*
> *smaller islands—I just had the first interview for that one*
> *today. I had to go to the cafe to do it so that they wouldn't*
> *notice. I don't know if I made a good impression, but*
> *honestly, the interview itself was*

A ball went whizzing past my nose.

I dropped Nouronnihar's diary in alarm. But it wasn't a mysterious *they*—it was just Luca, running after the stray volleyball. Apparently, while I'd sat down and

216

started reading, he had started up a game with Sinbad, Jason, and Fleece.

Luca smiled before he ran back to the waiting teams, but I didn't say anything. I did consider joining them, even just to talk to the sailors. But after my confrontation with Babs and Ja'far, I wasn't too keen on talking to more people—especially people I was only vaguely acquainted with, who were also tied up in mystery.

I wasn't even making good progress with my reading.

Even though I retrieved it from the sand and shook it clean, I hesitated before reading again. Somehow, my heart wasn't in it.

The trouble was, it was so hard to focus when my mind wasn't at peace. I knew that well enough. "The worst alchemist is a distracted alchemist," another of Paracelsus' immortal quotes. Normally, thinking of my old mentor made me feel a little better.

At that moment, though, I frowned at Nouronnihar's diary in my lap. It wasn't her fault. No; I'd never met her, and so far, even with the aspersions cast by the New West Key police force and her own desperation, she didn't seem to have done anything tangibly wrong. From her writings so far, I gathered that her unbalanced ledger *was* from the company that owned *Djinni*, a company she never named but did speak of as having dealings with pirates and massive, grandiose ships. It was all there, but my brain was failing to put the pieces together. *I'm just tired,* I thought.

Tired—that was exactly it, and recognizing it didn't make it any easier. I wasn't *take a nap in the shade of the beach umbrella* tired.

I was *running around cleaning up other people's messes* tired.

Sweet Luca. He was making good friends with the sailors, and privately, I worried a little that they seemed like prime suspects in a murder. Whatever the true facts of the story, Sinbad had been involved with the *Djinni*—and piracy, by his own admission. Could I keep him from getting too close to Luca? No, of course not. And besides, it wasn't like Luca was going to sign on with them and sail away . . .

. . . Despite what William might say. And even William, dripping saltwater on the sand as he dozed beside Zady, calmly writing her letters, made me worry. He was more at home on Kairoi than I was. And sure, that wasn't something I *ought* to worry about, but—for years, William and I had been a united front in unfamiliar territory. Now, watching him so comfortable made me feel vaguely uneasy.

Not to mention watching Aly go walking and Zady keep up her correspondence like nothing in the world had changed.

And that's just it. I crossed my arms around my knees, diary and all, and stared out at the sea. I had changed while I was away. And coming back was changing me, too—I could feel it. The whole time Babs and Ja'far had been pouring out their hearts, had I treated them rationally and distantly? No, I'd eaten the whole thing up. I'd felt bad for them. I'd even tried to comfort them—as if I was some kind of sage, or at the very least, an older sister. Never mind the fact that *I* was the stranger here.

Abruptly, I got up and walked to the water's edge, standing with my hands on my hips.

What was it Babs had said?

You know what it's like, growing up here and not wanting to end up like everyone else . . .

Sure, I'd told him.

A cold wave hit my ankles, and I started walking in. And then I dove.

I came up tossing my head, to get the water out of my eyes. Just off shore, I treaded water, turning to face the shore. All was idyllic. Luca scored a point in his volleyball game. I could just barely see the diary and chair that I'd abandoned, the work I *should* be doing, to help solve a crime . . .

No. That was what I should have said.

Truthfully, I had no idea what it was like to grow up in Wellspring and not want to be a diviner. Babs and Ja'far both had the skill. They could have fit in and they chose not to, feeling out their paths each in their own way.

I had never had the option.

I had never been a rebel and I had never gotten away with being sullen, not for long. I had never *not* wanted to be just like everyone else. To have the skill, to be good enough. To be like my parents, like the rest of my family. To be perfect.

The waves rolled under me, and I let them carry me just a little further in, to a sand bar. I knew instinctively when I was getting too deep. Because it was no good to tell myself that *perfect is the enemy of good,* and it was no use reminding myself that obviously, no one on Kairoi was perfect. Those weren't the reasons for my tears.

This was something new, and at the same time, I had a feeling it was exactly why I hadn't wanted to come back.

Because alchemy is not for telling the future. Work for the police aside, it rarely comes with more answers than questions. I knew this inside and out, because I had worked hard to master my chosen field. I was the best alchemist I could be— hopefully getting better, bit by bit, all the time. I was the best *everything* I could manage. I did my best for William and for

Luca and for all my friends back in Belville, and even for this pair of too-young, too-short-tempered police officers I barely knew.

Just so that they could turn around and tell me that they knew exactly how I felt, and take over my holiday and interrupt my breakfasts and pour out all their woes, and then say *oh we can't do this any more, it's too hard and we don't want to try or do what we're supposed to, how about you take the responsibility from here?*

No. I'm sick and tired of doing my best.

A wave tumbled over my head and pulled me forward, into the shallows. I landed on my knees and turned around immediately to yell into the roar of the ocean. "I didn't come back here to be pushed around!"

But you did, said a voice in my head. *Of course you did. To spend time here, you must apologize for the years that you were gone. You must face the child that you were here, and all the ways you tried to make yourself fit into a shape you were never meant to have.*

"I don't have to apologize," I murmured, head above water. Aly had told me that. I had not believed her.

Because it was around every corner. *You've been gone for so long.* With it came a sense of obligation. *Was it worth it? What is your excuse for having been away?*

I dove underwater again to wash the tears away. When I came up, I stood on that sandbar and yelled at the sky, "When I'm at home, I don't want to be *someone else!*"

And when I stay at home, I don't have to think about the fact that me, *the person I always was and have become, doesn't actually fit in the place where I grew up.*

Home. So far from these waves, and from the desert-hot

sun I'd once thought I couldn't live without.

Suddenly I was so angry, and at last I understood why. It wasn't the case or the police or the otherwise-idyllic family visit. I was mad at myself. I wanted to take that misfit child and shake sense into her. I wanted to confront that lonely adult and force her to look at herself honestly. I wanted to go back and redo every conversation where I had been too self-disparaging and too accommodating in hopes of *finding* a place for myself, rather than just *making* one.

I wanted to take all my feelings of self-doubt and comparison and judgment and fear and pour them out into the sea.

Frustrated and unable to do any of those, I let myself fall backward to float on the waves, slowly drifting to shore.

"Hey, there." I knew Luca's voice without opening my eyes, just like I knew the warm sand under my shoulders. "Look what washed up."

"I *feel* washed up," I told him. After a moment, I pulled myself into a sitting position next to him. The waves surged around our feet.

Luca was looking at me steadily. One of the sailors had loaned him another hat. When I met his eyes, he put an arm around my shoulder and leaned in, sharing his shade.

"How was your game?" I asked quietly.

"Sinbad and I won," he told me. "No contest. . . . Red, I think you might like Sinbad. He hasn't been home in a long time either. You're not the only one."

"Point taken." I wiped at some sand on my cheek. "But I'd rather save the getting-to-know-you stuff until he's not a murder suspect."

"Getting reserved in your old age?" Luca teased. He had once been a murder suspect himself, and I hadn't believed it for a minute.

"Getting tired," I said more seriously, sighing.

"You certainly have a right to do that." Luca was silent for a moment before he looked back at me. "But you know, Red, I wonder if you're really looking at things."

I frowned at him. "It feels like that's *all* I've done."

"True, but *really*, I mean. Honestly. That's what you're good at," he added, his voice soft. When I said nothing, he went on. "You always saw me, remember. Maybe it's not so bad."

"You're different." I scrunched up my nose. It did not escape my notice that Luca was praising me for something I'd just been furious at myself over. But I knew to listen to him when it came to this kind of thing. I knew he meant his point sincerely, and that it must be worth thinking over. "Do you *really* think that was because of my heritage? Now that you've been here and you see how it works, I mean."

"I do," Luca said firmly. "I absolutely do, Red. I think the best stories are about outliers."

"Luca," I protested. "I was *just* feeling bad about that!"

He held me tighter, sympathetic, but then smiled. "Now that we've come here, I think I understand why. But I also think there's a strength there, Red. Think of me and that curse. If I wasn't cursed, there are ways I wouldn't have been able to help you."

"I get that, but I don't see how it applies here. Aside from the usual helping the police sort of way, and I've got mixed feelings about that at the moment, let me tell you."

"That's fair." Luca chuckled. "But I actually meant it regarding *you*. If you look at yourself the way you look at everything else, objectively, like an alchemist—or a storyteller, what do you see?"

I hesitated. "Honestly? I . . . see someone who's still struggling with broken dreams from childhood. But also someone who's made a good career and home for herself, even so." I glanced at Luca as I said it, and saw his eyes warm. Struck by another inspiration, I added, "Also someone who *does* try for objectivity, while knowing a lot about subjectivity . . . and divination."

Luca's smile widened. "I'd definitely say you know more about being objective and rational than Brooks."

"And Babs and Ja'far. Though hopefully they get there in time," I added, shaking my head. "No, I'm sure they will. On their own. But in the meantime . . .

"In the meantime," I decided, with a growing sense of purpose, "there *is* something here that only I can do."

29

Rubbing the Lamp

I don't know if I made a good impression, but honestly, the interview itself was odd. She seemed more like she was looking for a typist than a true secretary. I almost wanted to offer to ship her one of the new automatic magitech typewriters from the university.

But I was nice, of course, and I do have a good feeling about it. This could really be my new start. I could leave shipping and sailing behind. Maybe not completely, but . . . I could have a home, a real home, and not one where I have to falsify books and reports just to get by.

Here's hoping.

I finished the rest of the diary while I lay in the sun, drying off and musing over my new idea. *A new start. Here's hoping.* Nouronnihar's words, though it was clear she'd been conflicted and frightened, only strengthened my resolve. When I looked up, Zady had set down her letters and was observing me.

"William and Aly just went for ice cream," she said. "You seemed a little too . . . absorbed."

"And Luca is asleep." I looked over to where he dozed in a beach chair and smiled. "All for the best, probably. There's something I need to talk to you about."

"Come over here and sit, then," Zady said, patting the empty chair beside her in the shade. "You mountain folk are bound to all get terrible sunburns if you insist on spending much more time at the beach."

I did as she suggested—and rolled my eyes, too. But I also noticed how she'd said *you mountain folk*. It felt natural.

"Your Luca has certainly thrown himself into the traveling life," she added.

Traveling, not *vacationing.* I looked at her askance. "What do you mean?"

"Just that I think it's a good sign of how much he'd like to be part of your life," Zady said innocently. "You ought to have such a devoted partner."

"You and Aly set a good example," I said, thinking.

"In that way, at least." Zady sighed. "To other things, perhaps we were *too* devoted. This island, for instance."

"I wouldn't say that exactly, but it *is* kind of related to what I wanted to bring up," I admitted, now that I'd settled in. "The thing is, growing up here and never being able to See anything—I know it's kind of obvious, but . . . I don't think I ever told you how angry that made me. And how afraid."

"No, I don't think you ever did," Zady said gently. And then, more sadly, "I don't think you should have had to."

"What do you mean?" I asked.

"Aly and I, we were always so excited for you. We knew you'd do something great and that the divination didn't matter. But, looking back now, I think we let our own hopes for you get in the way of our seeing how *you* felt, in the moment."

For a moment, I gaped. Then, swallowing, I finally found words—a question I'd always wondered about. "Did you know I would become an alchemist?"

"We can't *know* anything about the future for certain," Zady reminded me. "We just knew you would find your own way."

"Honestly, that does sound like something Aly would say."

My mother smiled at me gently. "But it is my own fault, too, for thinking too much in the long term."

"It is hard," I admitted. "It's hard doing something completely new all the time. Sometimes it felt like we were on two completely different levels. Like, you and everyone else, you were all getting messages from the gods in the flames . . . and I was just a kid rubbing sticks together."

"I am so sorry," Zady said, reaching out to take my hand.

"It's okay. I didn't really come here for an apology. I actually thought I might owe you one. I know I . . . well, I got so fed up with myself not being what I wanted, that I stopped really looking at myself at all, I think."

I could not make me look how I wanted. Jasmin had said it, too.

"And yet," said my mother, "you have come a very long way from rubbing sticks together, Cinnabar. I wonder," she added, her voice more light, "if we ever told you about your name?"

"Well, we never really got to do the initiation thing," I reminded her—but my voice, too, came lightly. In the distance, the waves crashed. "You told me the whole thing about 'Red,' of course."

"Little Red Riding Hood. Aly was so proud of that—so proud thinking of you going out into the world on your own, just as you have," Zady said fondly. "But Cinnabar had a purpose too. I suppose I assumed you'd figure it out in time."

"There's been a lot to figure out," I said mildly.

"Yes." Zady turned fully to me, and took my other hand as well. "I was the one who chose 'Cinnabar.' Because the mineral cinnabar is beloved of the old god Hermes . . . in fact, it becomes mercury in liquid form, as I'm sure you know now."

"I do," I agreed. "But why Hermes?"

"Because the god of messages also watches over those who travel—and those who seek to make old things new."

I pondered this for a full minute. It was, in a way, the best good luck wish my mother could have given me. And at the same time, it was confirmation that I was not precisely meant to stay here—that I was an 'outlier,' as Luca had said. More than ever, I could see the power in that now. "On that note," I told Zady, "I have an idea I'd like to try."

* * *

That evening, we gathered with most of the rest of the town around the sacred bonfire in the plaza. Aly and Zady had spread the word, and now were about to take part in the divination session. Luca and William sat looking on, the solemn atmosphere only partially obscuring their excitement.

"Welcome, everyone," Zady said, standing beside the fire to begin the proceedings. "We have a very special request tonight. We're going to try something a little different."

Through the clear twilight, I nodded at Babs and Ja'far. They'd released Dean earlier that evening, and now stood to guard—or take part in?—the proceedings. I glanced around at the rest of the circle, and then I stepped forward . . .

And threw Nouronnihar's diary into the flames.

"Let us see," declared Zady, "what a story of troubles, escapes, and hopes can show us."

There was a gasp and a rustle at first, but slowly, everyone settled down and stared into the fire, looking for signs. In the background, a rattle and tambourine played.

I stood for a moment to make sure my work was complete before withdrawing to sit beside Luca on one of the benches.

"Very theatrical," he whispered. "Even knowing what to expect, it was a shock."

I winked at him with a confidence mostly born of surprise. I was, honestly, shocked that my plan had worked so far.

When I'd outlined my plans to Zady earlier, she'd been intrigued but also worried. Amongst Springers, it was tradition to use plants—like the reeds, kelp, and flowers the town had tried so far—as both a focus for their divination, and a sacrifice to whatever force or deity might be involved. The clan was open to suggestions on that front. However, no one had ever tried burning anything *other* than plant material before, not with the blessing of the family. And burning evidence was surely a bad idea . . .

. . . . But that was where *I* could shine. Using a few commonplace ingredients from the apothecary, I'd treated Nouronnihar's diary to be fireproof. Gene had had her own reservations about selling anything to me, but as it had been Bertie's troubles that helped me come up with the idea, I'd thought it was only fair to involve them somehow.

The thing was, all the plants the town had tried so far were about *where* or *who* the crime concerned. But crimes, I'd found, were usually about wanting something different. Like Bertie's dosing, for example—he was motivated by a desire to be *more* wolfish. And whoever had killed Nouronnihar must have wanted a reality other than the status quo. They wanted a dangerous secret to be undone.

Nouronnihar herself had been desperate for change, and that was the second idea on which my plan hinged. I was hoping that, rather than the physical diary itself, the longing and desperation in Nouronnihar's words would serve as a "sacrifice" for the divination. I had no idea if it could work—no idea how it *would* work, exactly—but my mothers had been willing to give it a go, and they had convinced the rest of the clan.

Luca and I watched the Springers at work, the firelight reflected in their eyes. Some swayed, even hummed a little as they searched the flames for inspiration. Beside us, William was glowing, too.

"I really hope it works," I confided in Luca in the barest whisper.

"I think it's the best shot anyone's come up with so far," he whispered back.

"Her story was just so emotional. I couldn't help but think, even if something in here isn't exactly *why* she was killed, the murderer probably felt just as desperate for a new chance."

"That kind of symmetry definitely seems plausible to me," Luca murmured. "And no matter what, Red, it's really cool that you got them to come together like this."

I glanced across the circle to where Officer Ja'far and Officer Babs stood at the edge of the plaza, watching the proceedings. Was it just the bonfire, or did they both seem to have a new light of hope and understanding in their eyes?

The tambourine faded, and then the rattle, too, came to a

decisive stop.

This time, Aly stood, her eyes bright. "With thanks to the higher powers, we end our first search. Who would like to share what they have Seen?"

I waited anxiously for someone to speak. This was the part of the plan I had no control over. Since I could not See the way the others could, I had no idea where this experiment had led. Had it worked at all? Had anyone found any new clues?

"A ship," someone called. I nearly leapt from my seat. *A good sign!*

"Gold," said another. Petra, from the apothecary.

"A map," added the girl from the hotel.

"A treasure lost," said Zady.

Luca and I looked at each other. *A lost treasure?* That sounded more up Sinbad's alley than Nouronnihar's. *Although, she did have all that maritime stuff in her luggage . . . And she was mixed up with the* Djinni . . .

Across the circle, Officer Ja'far cleared his throat. "A family."

Family? Like the lost child, maybe? I hadn't expected that. In an automatic gesture, I glanced at the fire, as though to confirm his idea.

I didn't see any signs or symbols, of course. But for just a moment I could have sworn that through the smoke, there was a faintly glowing unicorn racing down the road out of town.

And that's when I got my second bright idea of the day.

30

Making a Wish

The next morning dawned bright and clear on a crowd of people waiting for the bus.

I'd asked Babs and Ja'far to come through, and they certainly had. They'd managed to round up all four sailors, even Archer, whom I'd only really seen once. Gene, Bertie, and Petra lingered nearby as well. Combined with Zady, Aly, William, Luca, and myself, that made fourteen of us. *If thirteen's unlucky,* I thought, *let's hope fourteen is especially* good *luck.*

We piled onto the bus. If Suzy thought anything about this unusual morning crew, she kept her opinions to herself.

Please, I added silently. *Let this go more smoothly than the last time some of us were here . . .*

Officer Ja'far and Babs sat up front with William and me. William was focused on the road—I'd given him a special task to do. I knew I'd have my hands full with everyone else on the bus. No one seemed to have caught on yet, and I expected a little bit of trouble.

True enough, under his breath, Ja'far said, "I still say we

could have taken the police cart and gone the short way."

"There's a reason I want to go the long way," I assured him. From the second row, sitting with my parents, Luca caught my eye and nodded.

"Besides," Babs added, "there's no way we could cram this many people into the back of the cart."

I glanced back at our coerced crew. Luca and Aly, naturally, looked like they were having the time of their lives. Zady was thoughtful. Everyone else looked vaguely reproachful. In the very last row, Gene had actually covered her face with her scarf and refused to look at anyone. Jason and Fleece had gone back to sleep, leaning on each other. When my eye caught Sinbad's, nearer the middle of the bus, he cleared his throat and announced, "This reminds me of the time the pirates came and abducted me to make me serve as their cook!"

Another few details that don't fit the previous story he told me. I rolled my eyes and grinned, shrugging the little lies off. "*Pirates* isn't too far off, Sinbad. You'll see."

"But why *are* we here?" Bertie piped up, his voice wavering.

"Don't worry," I told him. "We just need all hands on deck, that's all."

I turned back to sit rightways in my seat, smiling. After all those times Officer Thorn had used that line on me, I hadn't realized how satisfying it could be.

The bus continued its path around the island, same as ever. Luca and William were pressed to the windows. They hadn't seen this landscape yet, except in glimpses from Wellspring. The sand glimmered as we skirted the volcano. No one lived south of Wellspring, between the town and the ferry dock. No one even bothered to run or walk here, or to build their compound here, or to murder and be found here . . .

And just why *was* everyone so interested in the estuary side of Kairoi, anyway? Was it simple geography—or was there something else, hidden in plain sight?

I thought of the divination session last night and was more certain than ever that we were on the right track.

The bus screeched to a halt at the marina. Fortunately, no one was waiting to board—there would barely have been room! Sailors bustled to and fro amid the boats, but no one even glanced our way. I looked back at *our* sailors, grounded and reduced to bus travel instead of sailing the seas. Sinbad looked wistful. Archer looked downright upset. Jason and Fleece were still sleeping, Jason's head pillowed on Fleece's curly hair.

As the bus lurched back into its route, however, I knew it was time to take charge. We didn't have much longer now before we hit Jasmin's driveway—the scene of the crime.

I turned backward in my seat again, bracing myself to rise up on my knees. "Everyone, I think it's time to start getting ready."

"Ready for what?" Zady called, obligingly. For her dislike of crowds, she was doing well now, holding on to Aly's hand.

"I told you earlier we need help," I said, looking around at attentive, wary faces. "If you were at the divination last night, you might understand why. This side of the island has become a dangerous place to be. Or even to sail near," I said, looking at Sinbad and his first mate.

Sinbad looked resigned—if his stories were even half true, he was used to danger. Archer, on the other hand, looked anything but.

And Gene had yet to look up from her scarf.

"Officer Ja'far and Officer Babs have conducted their investigations," I went on, "and they've come to a conclusion."

This resulted in surprised looks from *everyone* on the bus. I only hoped Babs and Ja'far's looks weren't as obvious to everyone else as they were to me.

We'd come to the hard part, the storytelling part. *Everything else is downhill from here,* I reminded myself. And, technically, nothing I planned to say was a lie—it was all just partial truths. Partial truths which, hopefully, our passengers would help fill in.

"We know why a woman was murdered and abandoned here," I said, starting off generally. "This side of the island used to be just as deserted as the other. But now, there's a veritable palace here. And each of you have come through here, for one reason or another, haven't you? Each of you knows something about Palace Jasmin."

I glanced around the bus again. All the newcomers and returners to Wellspring, here in one small space. Officer Ja'far had caught on, and he looked resolute. Jason was elbowing Fleece, even though they'd both woken up when I'd begun talking. Sailors shipwrecked here; a small business in town, tied to this place; even Aly had met with some danger here— her injury from running, just a few years ago.

Aside from my own friends, Petra was the only one who met my gaze directly. Her eyes sparkled.

"I knew it," she said, piping up from the back of the bus. "I knew this place was dangerous! Didn't I try to tell you, Gene? Nobody likes it being here."

"No one from town," I agreed. "Even Jasmin herself knows that. But Gene only just recently got here herself."

I glanced out the windows as I waited for Gene to say something. Halfway there. Timing—that had been one of my big reminders, when I'd reflected on the divination last night. *Everything takes time.*

"I was here long before Jasmin," Gene said finally, lifting her head.

"Hardly, dear," said Zady, looking back over her shoulder. "To be a local in Wellspring, you have to stick around for *years.*"

"That's true," I said, grinning crookedly at my mother before focusing on Gene. "And it's also true that building a place like Jasmin's 'Palace' takes time. Not to mention the negotiations that must have taken place to sell the land."

"Did you find out who *did* sell the land?" Aly asked, looking curiously between myself and the police officers.

Babs shook his head, remembered himself, and looked up at me.

I bit my cheek. "There's one person I can think of who would have, yes. And even though they might have moved fast, Jasmin's people still had a lot of work to do to make the palace happen. It would have taken months . . . Right, Gene?"

The apothecary looked like she might be sick.

"I was there right at the beginning," Petra said helpfully, looking speculatively at her boss. "I was the shop's very first hire. Come to think of it, you *did* have an awful lot of business to take care of those days, didn't you, Gene? You always said it was the marina you were going to, but you ought to know better than to lie to someone like us."

Like us. It made me wince a little to hear it—I felt sorry for Gene. But Petra had a point, and it was Petra's lie-detecting, gossiping tendencies that both made her fit into Wellspring's community *and* effective in this moment for ferreting out the truth.

"You've all known this *whole time?*" Gene had dropped her

scarf. She was looking at me like a drowning woman. "All along, you *knew?*"

I hear you, friend, I thought, sympathetically. But needs must—we had to get to the bottom of this before we pulled up in front of the Palace driveway.

"Just because we know a thing doesn't mean we say it," Zady told her, primly.

"For better or worse, sometimes," Aly added, with a cautioning look at her wife.

"You were the coordinator on the ground," I said, refocusing on Gene. "You've been here a year. Just long enough to get the lay of the land and set things in motion."

"There's nothing wrong with that," Gene said defiantly, though her voice wavered.

"It does make one wonder," Petra said, this time unhelpfully.

I was hoping we wouldn't have to go in that direction. I felt for Gene. I was hoping she wasn't the one who'd done the really dirty work . . .

"I'm not a *miracle worker*," Gene burst. "It's not like I'm some super villain. All I could do was keep an eye on things and make reports. It was nothing!"

"There was a vision for the Palace," I pressed. "You helped make it come true."

"And all that time you got mad at *me*," Bertie scoffed.

This set Gene off, and once again, I had trouble blaming her. "*You* got in trouble for tampering with medicines. That is *completely* different. I studied medicine—I want to *help* people. That's the only reason I'm here—because I wanted to *help!* All the rest of you think about is yourselves and your cursed creepy town!"

Officer Ja'far, I noticed, had his handcuffs halfway out. The sailors were looking on with wide eyes.

"I was trying to do a good thing," Gene continued, her voice breaking. "She needed help. She needed me to look after things."

"Why?" I asked. "Why couldn't she just come here herself?"

"She needed someone in town," Gene went on, tearfully. I wasn't sure she'd even heard me. "She asked me to set up there. I thought, sure, why not? People in Wellspring deserve medicines like anyone else. If only I'd known how *petty* and *shortsighted* you all are, then—"

"Whoa, let's not go down that road," I protested.

Petra looked aghast, but it didn't last more than a second before she was talking. "I knew it! I knew you were up to something no good all along! Helping people, ha! You hardly even noticed when anyone needed—"

"*I'm* not the petty one, they are!" Bertie was yelling.

Even Aly had lost her temper. "If it was such a trial being here, why stay?" she was shouting.

"Everyone, please!" Officer Ja'far demanded, to no avail.

At that moment, William *woofed*. The bus ground to a halt, throwing us all forward and then back against our seats. Now *everyone* was yelling.

With a sense of silent foreboding within myself, I glanced out the bus's door to see who was waiting for us at the end of the road from Palace Jasmin.

31

Singing a Song

Dean and Jasmin were nowhere in sight. Instead, the assistant, Morgiana, stood alone beside the road. Her white hair gleamed in the sun.

I let Babs and Ja'far take over calming everyone down and herding them off the bus in an orderly fashion. William and I stepped down ahead of the crowd.

Morgiana's eyes were blank as she looked up at me. "Your note said the police needed to see Jasmin here? Why are all these people on the bus? Those sailors are not allowed here!"

"It's a surprise party," said William sarcastically.

"All of these people have been involved in the mystery here," I said, more diplomatically, "and they want to help solve it. We're looking for something. Where's Jasmin, or Dean?"

Even Raja would have more authority, right? I thought, glancing the assistant up and down.

She wore long white sleeves and a black jumper that went down to the tops of her black boots. Out here, far from Jasmin's temperature-control spells, I could see her sweating. And yet she hadn't pulled back her hair, or even brought along a hat or parasol.

"Raja said it was a security risk," Morgiana said.

"What is? Leaving the palace grounds?" William snorted.

"One of our employees *did* just get arrested," Morgiana pointed out.

"And then released," I added, looking at her more carefully. "What do you have to fear from the police?"

"Nothing," she said.

Her answer seemed personal, and genuine. In fact, it sounded almost sanctimonious. For just a brief flash, it made me wonder how she felt about working for Dean. She was so clearly much more competent than he was.

A question came to mind, and with it, the spark of inspiration I'd been looking for.

Officer Ja'far led a string of quiet, rather resentful sailors from the bus, followed by the townsfolk. Last to alight were Officer Babs and Luca, who looked at me with his head tilted to one side.

I smiled back at him.

Suzy stayed on the bus, but with the flick of a switch, she activated an awning. It popped out over Bessie's windows, shading everyone who stood in the road—everyone except William, Morgiana, and me.

Gene was staring at the ground again. I began to pace, slowly, until I was standing near her. "There's a lot of people mixed up in this case," I said as I went, "and a lot of them *are* just trying to do the right thing. Even so, we've heard a lot of lies—from everyone. And a lot of details have been left out. Funny, don't you think, for an island renowned for its truth-seeking?"

I came to a halt and looked from Gene to Morgiana, then back again. "Gene, who was it who asked you to move to

Wellspring?"

Gene examined her sandals.

"Who asked you for reports about Kairoi and the Palace?" I pressed.

"I wasn't aware this was going to be a lengthy meeting," Morgiana protested. Next to her, William glowed faintly against the backdrop of reeds.

"It's not," I promised. "I think I know exactly what Gene hasn't told us, so I'll cut to the chase. On the bus, Gene insisted that she studied medicine in order to help people. I believe that. I think, in medical school, she met the person who would get her mixed up in this mess. She met *you*, Morgiana."

The assistant said scornfully, "I don't have a medical degree."

"Neither does Bertie," Babs piped up.

"Hey!" Bertie hissed.

"The point there is," I said firmly, "that just because you go to a school doesn't mean you'll wind up with a degree."

"*Honestly!*" Bertie protested.

"But you could still pick up skills. Like patching up fellow employees. Or even," I said, a thought occurring suddenly, "a penchant for cleanliness."

That order had *been directed to Morgiana . . . not to Jasmin, and not to Dean.* It made me feel even more certain.

And for the first time, Morgiana wavered. "I don't see what that has to do with anything."

"It means you and Gene have to do with each other," I replied, looking back at Gene. "Isn't that right? You came here to help your friend . . . to help her set up a magnificent palace, despite the locals' resistance."

Gene glanced to her left, to Petra, biting her lip. She gave the smallest of affirmative nods.

"I still don't see what this has to do with anything," Morgiana said, her voice becoming slightly shrill. "Why did you want to see Jasmin? Why bring us all out here in this heat?"

"It really *doesn't* have much to do with Jasmin so far, and that's what's interesting about it," I told her. "We know how you're related to Gene, now, and we know why Gene's tied up in Jasmin's business. But how exactly are *you* related to Jasmin herself?"

"I'm not," Morgiana protested. "That is, I'm not part of her plan. This is all *her* project and *her* land."

Babs coughed, and spoke up again. "But she *is* part of the plan, Red! Raja told me during our initial interview," he said, flipping excitedly through his notebook before adding, "Morgiana was the second secretary, after the one who left suddenly, and before Nouronnihar!"

I was stunned. I'd had an inkling, but I had *not* expected that much to be forthcoming.

"Why didn't you *say* anything?" Officer Ja'far asked, astounded, as everyone else reeled and I raced to think through this development.

"I thought everyone knew," Babs said innocently. "You were right there when we were talking."

Right there, probably having a staring contest with Raja, I thought, momentarily distracted.

"And anyway," Babs went on, "it was in the binder. But it's not like she went on to become the secretary again after Nouronnihar's death, right? So there's not really any motive there, is there?"

"I don't think this was about career advancement. If it was, she would have turned Dean away at the gates," I said, as I turned back to Morgiana.

"I haven't done anything," she said haughtily. "I would know much better than to try. That *Dean* has had Jasmin wrapped around his little finger ever since he got here!"

I doubted that, but I also saw it for the vague attempt at distraction that it was. So I focused until I could see clearly. "No—it's you, Morgiana, who have had Jasmin all wrapped up this entire time. That's the only way it makes sense. Jasmin's busy with her fashion line and her trade empire; it's highly unlikely she was the one who oversaw the building here. In fact, she told me that this was the *perfect* place for her Palace. I doubt anyone standing here right now thinks it's a great place to be. So why would Jasmin think it was ideal . . . unless someone's reports had convinced her it was?"

"I don't know what you're talking about," Morgiana insisted. "I was busy preparing the suite for Nouronnihar when she didn't turn up. Ask the staff."

Behind her, the long grasses of the estuary stirred. Something glinted, like the barest hint of a horn. I thought of the omens others had seen in the fire last night, and the whisper in the smoke. I decided to trust it. "You do seem to have an alibi, it's true. But let's set that story aside for a moment, and consider another. You were in New West Key, at school with Gene. Jasmin and her empire were right there, looking for advice. Somehow, you became her right hand, her advisor . . . and when the time came, you had your friend help you set up this place. When Jasmin moved here, maybe you found that the other secretary got in your way. So you convinced them to leave, and then took over the job yourself. But then something went wrong, and you left the position—you even helped hire your replacements—both of them. Why was that?"

"None of this makes any sense," Morgiana scoffed.

"But it does! It bally well does!"

From the reeds, a disheveled Dean leapt onto the road beside William. Picture-perfect as ever, Jasmin followed.

Amid the gasps of surprise—over Morgiana's own protest—Dean went on proudly, "I asked around! These blighters said I was silly for not looking into my employer, but I didn't need to. I looked into the *employees.* Wanted to know what the last bloke in my position had done, you know, and when I asked the staff they told me it was *Morgiana,* 'pon my soul, only she resigned the post because she said it was *too much work!"*

"Too much work?" I echoed, confused. From what I'd seen during visits to the Sanctuary, Morgiana had always been doing *all* the work, and Dean had been literally creeping around in bushes, presumably doing *none.*

"I should have known you were never cut out for it," Morgiana hissed at Dean. "You're just some society boy who was reading his father's secretary's newsletter!"

"Is any of that true?" Officer Ja'far, perhaps one of the "blighters" Dean had referred to, asked Jasmin.

"It—it is, actually," she said, shifting to look between Morgiana and Dean. For the first time, she looked uncertain. "She said she needed a position with more personal time. She was very professional and kind about it."

"Even interviewed *me,"* said Dean. "And I happened to need this job, I'll have you know. But I've known since I got here she was reading the mail."

"Excuse me?" Apparently this was news to Officer Ja'far.

As one, everyone in the road turned back to Dean. This was starting to feel like a tennis match. "Everyone's mail, don't you know," he said. "Not just her own. I don't know how it's done around New West Key, but back in Argen, we're all on to the wheeze. Used to do it as a schoolkid back in the day. Steam the letters open, iron them back shut. Only you have to be careful about it or the iron leaves a mark. I've ironed enough bally letters—and clothes—in my time to know."

"Of course you have," William muttered.

It was a silly little interjection, but it was right, and I grinned as another piece fell into place. Dean, with his decidedly Argen manner of speaking and his very practical types of experience. He'd said himself how much he needed the work at Palace Jasmin. Everyone took him for a 'society boy,' but the opposite was probably true. He was just the sort of person to catch out a highly orderly, rather snobbish busybody like Morgiana.

But why was she acting such a busybody, and what did it have to do with Nouronnihar? That was the lingering question. And all eyes, now, were on her.

"It's all nonsense," was her declaration. "Just silly stories."

"Then tell me what we're all doing here out on the road," Dean said promptly. "*You* read Red's letter and thought you'd just keep it to yourself, that's what."

"Earlier, when we came up," I realized, "you said you knew we'd *asked* to see Jasmin out here—but not that you'd actually *told* her and been sent in her place."

"She never said anything," Jasmin put in, still looking faintly puzzled. "It was Dean who came to find me. He said something was going on down by the road."

"I found it hidden," said Dean triumphantly. "The note. Tried to feed it to the heron, she did. Too bad there weren't any active fireplaces to burn it in, what, Morgiana? All this bally heat, eh?"

Morgiana was the darkness to his sunny cheerfulness. "I should. Have sent. You far. Away." The words barely escaped through her teeth, coming out higher and higher, almost a screech.

"You *have* been orchestrating this whole place, manipulating Jasmin and everyone else, from behind the scenes all along, then," I interpreted. "But why? And *what happened with Nouronnihar?*"

"You want to know what happened?" Morgiana's eyes were pitch black now, and the question was nearly a scream.

"Red," someone said. Someone from back by the bus—Zady, I thought, without looking behind me to confirm.

"Watch out!" cried another voice. Sinbad? I'd almost forgotten the sailors were there. *"Banshee!"*

"Why? What's going on?" That one was easy to identify: Officer Babs.

"Don't you dare!" Luca.

In the next second, William flared bright blue like an exploding star, Aly threw herself onto the road in front of me, Morgiana shrieked an impossible note, and I fell backwards into shadow.

A Wild Ride

For a moment there was nothing but the running of hooves in my mind.

Then I opened my eyes. Luca had caught me, the shadow and mist receding to leave only sunlight as he smiled down at me. "Are you okay?"

"Just a little stunned." I struggled into an upright position. The world fell into place around us. Aly was sitting next to me, her face relieved. Officer Ja'far and Babs had run up on Luca's side. In front of us, Dean was holding Jasmin tightly, shielding her with his embrace . . . and William was sitting smugly beneath a large blue bubble.

Inside the bubble, Morgiana was still shrieking.

It was obvious, but we couldn't hear it. She hung suspended in midair within the bubble, her white hair fanned out around her like the rays of a lifeless sun. Her eyes were equally void, fixed on all of us, her mouth wide open in an impotent wail.

I shook my head, trying to think of what to do next. "Someone said . . ."

"Banshee," Officer Ja'far finished grimly. Looking over his

shoulder, he beckoned the sailors forward. "You, Sinbad. You knew about this?"

Followed loyally by Archer, Sinbad stepped up, albeit reluctantly. "I didn't—I wouldn't—"

"We all knew," Petra interjected. When I glanced to where she stood in the shade, I saw that despite everything that had happened on the bus, she had one arm around Gene . . . and a steadying hand on Jason. She looked from the officers to Zady beside her. "Didn't you feel something?"

"I wouldn't have been able to say 'banshee,' but there was definitely something off," Aly said. She was nursing her leg, I realized. But of course she gave me a brave smile.

Officer Babs looked up at Ja'far. "Looks like we have more training to do."

"It was only in that last moment," Zady said, clearly still worried. "William, love, how long can you keep that up?"

"Not forever," he replied, panting. "So spill, sailors. The *truth* this time, Sinbad, if you don't mind."

"Leave him alone." It wasn't Sinbad, but Archer who spoke up. She stepped in front of her captain, focused stubbornly on the officers. "It wasn't his fault, it was mine."

Luca shifted behind me. He hadn't let go of my shoulders yet. I reached up to hold his hand, worried about what we were going to hear for his sake.

"Explain," Ja'far demanded.

"The captain knows about banshees on account of him sailing with them," Archer said, with one quick glance of apology over her shoulder at Sinbad. "*The Portress.* That's how he knows 'em when he sees 'em. That's all. It was *my* fault we got mixed up in this Palace business. I'm the one who wrecked the ship."

Sinbad looked like a caricature of amazement. He'd clearly had no inkling of this. I couldn't help but notice that Jason, on the other hand, looked quite calm . . .

"I knew about the treasure, see," Archer said, with a heavy sigh. "*The Portress*'s lost treasure. An' I thought as how, shipping wasn't working out. Too many eyes on everything you do. But if we got a little capital, got a good headwind in our sails, then we could make it work."

"You mean, pay off the import agents?" Aly suggested dryly.

Archer shrugged. "I been looking for it this whole time. Only me."

"You and Jason," I said, glancing back at the shaded group again.

"He never!" Petra protested.

"Gotta stick together," was Jason's dubious defense of himself.

"That makes sense now," Luca said beside me. "All this time, Archer, you've been going off alone—and Jason's been going after you. He's been worried."

"Worried sick," Sinbad agreed with a cough. "Like we all were."

"I didn't want to tell you til I *knew*," Archer said.

I thought back to the first time I'd seen Archer—with a garden spade in tow. *To think we* didn't *know,* I mused wryly. *A sailor determined to dig for treasure. Not half as surprising as murder.*

And seeing them now, I highly doubted the sailors had been involved with *that*.

Instead, something else stuck out to me. *She wanted not the* Djinni*'s treasure, but* The Portress*'s . . .*

William clearly thought the sailors had had their time. He

barked to regain attention. "That's nice, but does anyone have something *relevant* to say? Any suggestions about what to do here?"

"*The Portress*," Sinbad said slowly. If William hadn't been occupied, I half thought he might've bitten the distracted sailor. That was, until he added, "I never thought about it til now. The captains—they had a daughter."

"In New West Key?" I asked, seeing light.

"Must've been," Sinbad said thoughtfully. "That was where we'd sailed from."

"So you've been looking for the ship's treasure," I said to Archer before turning to the officers. "What if Morgiana has, as well?"

"All this time," Jasmin said faintly. "The times the security spells went off—"

Dean, still holding on to her, agreed. "Those dratted cleaning potions—"

"The need for more personal time after she didn't find the treasure right away," Babs added. Then, eyes wide, he looked down at me. "Nouronnihar's shipping documents?"

"No—not directly," I said, thinking it through. "Nouronnihar was mixed up with a different shipping agency. But she *did* have a lot of nautical knick knacks and—and even a book about lost treasures! Practically every page was bookmarked. She surely knew about the treasure on Kairoi, and if she happened to mention it to Morgiana, about how it might be fun to look for in her spare time—"

I looked up at Sinbad as another thought struck. "After it wrecked, all that was left from the ship was a dagger? Was that true?"

"Of course it was true," he said, though he did look abashed.

"I have it on good authority it was all sent on to the daughter."

"A daughter with a score to settle and an inheritance to claim," Officer Babs mused.

Officer Ja'far, meanwhile, turned to Jasmin. For the first time since I'd talked to them yesterday, he stood completely straight. "Alibi or no, it's enough to take seriously. We'll need to search Morgiana's rooms—with your permission. We could also use Raja's help to secure the suspect."

"Here," said Raja, stepping from the opposite bushes.

"*Finally,*" William said.

"Has she been there this *whole time?*" Luca whispered to me. I chuckled, and felt relief wash through me at last.

Even Officer Ja'far briefly smiled down at us before adding to Jasmin, "Might I suggest that you consider giving these people a bit of breakfast, and respite from the sun?"

* * *

While the others *ooh*ed and *ahh*ed over Palace Jasmin, and lounged under a shady gazebo stuffing their faces with breakfast bites and iced tea, Jasmin walked out along a nearby stream. Leaving Luca to try to soften my parents toward the opulent palace by himself, I followed her.

She nodded at me as I came up, and continued walking along the tiled path. Once we were screened from the others by leaves and vines, she said quietly, "It's still hard to believe."

"I can understand how it would be," I assured her. "How long had you known Morgiana?"

"Two years ago," said Jasmin. "She was introduced to me as the authority in the Blue Desert Isles. She worked for the best real estate company in New West Key. That is what I do not understand. How did she accomplish that? Was it all a lie?"

"I don't think it was a lie, exactly," I said, pushing aside a spray of fragrant flowers as we paced. "I think she had a goal and she worked really hard to achieve it. And—I think she had some magical help."

Jasmin looked at me with deep, uncertain eyes. "Go on."

"There's an ifrit that lives on an island nearby," I said. "She probably never told you, or wanted you to find out about it. It's kind of a local legend. Well, a few days ago, my family and I literally stumbled across it. And—it tried to offer us wishes—but the wishes came with catches."

"She said she could not run such a palace," Jasmin said, catching on with a quick intake of breath.

"Exactly." I nodded. "And I was thinking, who *would* have sold you the land? No one in Wellspring—and no one else has the authority. No one would even try, except a ridiculously powerful—and tricky—local magical being."

"I always dealt through Morgiana." Jasmin sounded like she regretted the fact.

"Well, ostensibly, that's what you'd hired her for—at least at the start," I said reasonably. "My guess is, she wanted the ifrit to tell her where the treasure was, and he *did*, but he told her so vaguely that all she really knew was that it was somewhere on this side of Kairoi. Then she asked for dominion over the land, so that she could search freely, but the ifrit gave her a deed that she couldn't own herself. So, with *that*, she probably used her third bargain to give herself a leg up in the world of elite island paradise-buyers. No offense," I said, and Jasmin nodded companionably. I concluded, "I think she was very resourceful—but desperate, too. Especially after months of looking."

For a moment, we walked in silence, startling a jewel-toned frog before it leapt into the stream.

"She did tell me once she had lost her parents," Jasmin said quietly. "She told me of her heritage. Banshees are sometimes thought unlucky, like ghosts, she said. But she promised to bring me luck, because I had given her a chance. And I—I believed in her. Though I *had* asked her to meet Nouronnihar, and thought it strange that she did not, I said nothing. I shielded her from the police. I told the cleaners they needn't tell the police anything . . . When the truth was, Morgiana could easily have changed the story and covered her tracks."

"It's not a mistake to trust others," I said, answering the anguish in her voice.

"But if I had not—if *I* had perhaps gone to meet Nouronnihar—if I had simply *done my business myself*—"

"Things probably would have ended in just the same way, just at a later date," I told her sadly. "Nouronnihar seemed like she was really excited about all things nautical. She probably brought it up the first chance she got . . . And Morgiana couldn't stand someone else here knowing."

"Lucky for Archer she simply campaigned to have the sailors banned from the grounds," Jasmin said with a shudder.

"And lucky for Dean you didn't expect him or send a welcome party," I teased, a little grimly. "Not that he knew anything about it."

"Him! No, he knew nothing about it," Jasmin said, with her first genuine smile. "I *was* worried for him when he was released by the police. But even then, I did not know why. I still did not suspect Morgiana."

This admission encouraged me, and I smiled back. "What are you going to do now, Jasmin? Morgiana will hopefully admit everything to the police soon, and you know what Wellspring's like—everyone will know, one way or the other. But I don't think anyone will challenge a deed the ifrit made. In fact, they might respect it all the more."

"It is unorthodox," said Jasmin, "but also, it is now my home."

She seemed to have more to say, so I waited, while we walked around a bend in the path. Atop a little curved bridge, Jasmin paused. She met my eyes directly. "I want to stay."

"So, figure out how to, then," I told her, smiling. "Will you just keep ignoring what everyone else thinks?"

"Ignoring what they think!" Jasmin lingered, glancing down at the pool below, before meeting my gaze again. "Do you think I was ever able to ignore what they think?"

"I think, based on what you were saying in the library, that you built this whole place because you cared too much about what other people think . . . and wanted to run away from that feeling. But I don't think it worked."

"No. It did not." Jasmin nodded. "Seeing Morgiana now, the way she was able to lie to me . . . It makes me see. I came to a new place and made all my old mistakes."

"I came to an old place and made some new ones," I told her, ruefully. "I still say nobody's perfect."

"Yes." Jasmin mused on this for a minute, then asked abruptly, "Did you know, Dean does not mind?"

"About you not being perfect?" I chuckled. "That's because he already thinks you *are* perfect, flaws and all. He basically told us as much before he even met you." Seeing how this made her flush, I added kindly, "It's pretty neat, the way some people are like that."

"Yes," Jasmin said again. "People you do not have to hide from." She glanced ahead; the path curved again, and the faint sound of laughter told me that it would soon lead us back to where we'd started. "I will invite more people in," Jasmin decided.

"I think that's an excellent idea," I told her.

She smiled once more, and we walked down the rest of the path together.

33

Palaces and Homes

The next morning, as we savored our last breakfast of the trip with Aly and Zady, another knock came at the front door.

William whined. "What could it possibly be *this* time?"

"One way to find out," Aly said, rising from her chair to answer the door.

Rather than official summonses and shouts, though, friendly chatter filled the front hall. In another moment Aly returned, leading Dean and Jasmin.

"Find a seat anywhere," Aly was saying, pulling a few stools over from the kitchen island. "We were just eating. Do you want a cinnamon roll? Orange juice? Tea?"

While Dean asked Aly for two cups of tea and handily speared a cinnamon roll with a fork, Jasmin nodded to Zady and the rest of us. "Thank you for your welcome. The officers told us you leave today, Red. We thought we'd come to say goodbye."

"And share the gossip, don't you know," Dean said cheerfully. "We've just come from the station, see. Final reports and whatnot."

"Did Morgiana say anything new?" Luca asked, with interest.

"Did she explain her alibi?" I added, swallowing a bite of egg casserole.

Jasmin accepted tea from Aly via Dean, and paused to stir honey into it. "She did not, but she did not need to."

"Fellow at the Palace came forward," Dean added helpfully. He was cutting the cinnamon roll into two pieces, leaning precariously over his little slice of the table. "One of Raja's security minions. Admitted to having basically the biggest crush on Morgiana known to star-crossed lovers, and gave that as his reason for forgetting to mention that she *did*, in fact, go out to meet Nouronnihar that day. He was the one to let her out. Says he did it all the time. But she told him once she didn't trust Suzy, so she would always teleport from the driveway to the arch. The police figure she picked up Nouronnihar that evening from the catamaran before ours, and then had to walk back with her . . . giving them time to talk along the way. By the time they got back to the Palace road, Nouronnihar must've let something slip, and we weren't too far behind in the bus."

"He also let her use his set of keys the past several days," Jasmin murmured.

"Thought she lost hers while out on one of her moonlit walks," Dean agreed. "He thought they were romantic, but no doubt she was out there plotting where to dig, and all that."

"So she was definitely there—and she lost her keys, then had to use his," I realized, thinking it over. "Can they prove that?"

"They believe they can," said Jasmin. "With the new witness. He admits to everything. To realize that he was helpful in a murder is very distasteful to him."

"Not to mention, they found the dagger and a bunch of bally old maps in her room. And we all saw that she does have magic, maybe enough to hide or move a body, in a pinch. And the fact that they traced her back to New West Key," Dean added. "Got her employment records, family tree, the whole bit."

"I'm sure the officers are looking forward to yet more paperwork," Luca said, winking at me across the table.

"They seemed in pretty high spirits if you ask me," Dean said. He waved a bite of cinnamon roll for emphasis. "Trial's not til next month, of course, but they consider it a done deal, all told. The old blighter there's retiring and everything, I gather. Making it official."

"Officer Brooks is not a 'blighter,'" Zady said, with some amusement. "He has done good for this town. But I am glad to see a new generation take over."

"And speaking of him, there was one more thing I was wondering about. So I'm glad to see you, Jasmin," I said, thinking especially of her vow yesterday to let more people in. First coming *out* seemed like a very good start.

"I am glad to be seen," she said. And for once, she really did look it. Her dark eyes shone as she separated her half of cinnamon roll from Dean's grasp. "What did you wish to ask?"

"Baby Island," I said. Beside me, William pricked up his ears. I focused on Jasmin, adding, "You *did* know about it, didn't you?"

Jasmin glanced at Dean, hesitating for just a moment. Then she sighed. "You are kind people. There is no reason I should not tell you."

"We'll see it goes no further than this room, if that's what you want," Aly promised. Pretty generously, I thought. She retook her seat beside Zady, both all ears.

"It seems an unfortunate name to me," Jasmin said. "Baby Island. But I must explain from the beginning.

"My father was very unusual in his family. He married my mother against their wishes. At first, he and my mother still lived with them, trying to make peace. But when their firstborn child disappeared . . ."

There was a collective inhale as we all caught on.

"The lost girl was your older sister," Zady guessed, her voice full of sympathy.

"When she was not found, my parents decided to move. To start over," Jasmin said. "They took over the branch of family business in New West Key, leaving Oasis behind. I myself was born in New West Key. We did not visit Oasis, but I did know the story, of Baby Island and how the town of Wellspring tried to find my sister. My parents never stopped looking. And I . . . I find some comfort, strange as it is, in seeing the island every day now."

"You favor your mother pretty strongly," Aly observed, giving Jasmin an appraising look. "But based on your story, you're not such a stranger here as everyone thinks."

"I do not mind being the stranger here," Jasmin said. "At least, I did not at first. Everyone expected it, in a way. They did not expect me to fit in."

"You can fit wherever you want to," Dean said, loyally.

"Hear, hear," said Luca, raising his glass. "Do what feels best to you. And who knows—you may yet find your older sister. Stranger things have happened."

"We may," Jasmin agreed, looking at Dean.

Watching them both, I smiled. It struck me as interesting

how family legacy had played out over the past few days—for Jasmin, for Morgiana, even for me. Clearly, *legacy* could be a heavy burden, but meant little compared to what one decided to do with it.

"If you want our help, I'm sure we Springers would be glad to provide it," Zady offered. "Especially now that Red has shown us new possibilities for feeding the fire."

"You'd better hope Gene can help you with the fire-proofing," I said, smiling. "If she decides to stay."

"Time will tell," said Aly. "The real question now is, will you keep looking for the buried treasure?"

***

"Next time you visit," Aly reiterated several hours later, as she hugged me at the marina, "*that's* when we'll find the treasure."

"This is becoming an obsession," Zady warned. She was both smiling and wiping tears from her eyes.

"You probably already found it. It was probably the treasure that you tripped over on that fateful run," I teased.

Aly's face light with the possibility. "I think I remember just where it was . . ."

"No," Zady said firmly, though she was laughing, too.

"Hey," I added, more seriously. "I'm sorry I didn't come back sooner."

"I told you, you don't have to be sorry," Aly insisted. "Everything happens in its own time, right, Red?"

The nickname warmed my heart. "Yeah, I think it does."

And just in their own time, Luca and William joined us. They'd hauled all our bags off the bus—now there was nothing for it but to walk out under the archway, and on to the catamaran, and begin the long journey home.

On the road behind us, Bessie roared to life and rumbled away. I turned to look, distracted by the noise. As the bus cleared the station, it revealed a lineup of familiar faces.

"How in Beyond did you manage that?" I asked, turning to grin at officers, sailors, and Seers alike.

"Stowed in the luggage hold," Sinbad declared. "Not my first voyage as a stowaway!"

"There must have been a lot more room in there than I thought," I said, looking to my mothers for an explanation of this impromptu goodbye party.

"Bessie has her secrets," Zady said, with a smile. "I just told a few people which ship you happened to be leaving on, Red. I hope you don't mind."

"Not a bit," I said, grinning at our new and old friends as they crossed the road to join us. "As long as the sailors don't steal Luca away."

"We could use another mate," Archer said, rather ruefully.

"Not happening," William said, with a growl.

Amid much laughter, we shook hands and exchanged hugs with the people of Wellspring. It was strange to think how their lives would continue to change after we left. And yet, I felt contented, knowing we'd been part of their story for this chapter, at least.

I paused when Officer Babs and Officer Ja'far came up, though.

"We owe you a lot," said Ja'far, stiff as ever in his khaki uniform.

"Like, a *lot* a lot," Babs explained. "We wouldn't have got it if it wasn't for you. But we'll get the next one, promise."

"I'm sure you will," I told them. "And hey, if you ever need a third officer, Dean seemed pretty fond of the hat . . ."

Officer Ja'far blanched, and Babs patted him on the back. "I think we have things covered."

"Good. Keep an eye on Aly and Zady for me, won't you?" I gave each officer a hug and added, more quietly, "I'm worried Aly is going to become an incorrigible treasure hunter."

"I heard that!" Aly called across the crowd.

"Time to go, then," I grinned at the officers.

After one last round of hugs, I shouldered my bag and ushered William and Luca onto the waiting catamaran. Fortunately, we were the only passengers to be picked up at Kairoi, so we had our choice of spots along the rail. Letting our luggage rest at our feet, we stood and waved until the little crowd of well-wishers had faded from view.

"You know, I never did ask," Luca said thoughtfully as the catamaran sped into open water. "If nicknames are so important amongst the Springers, what did Zady and Aly's signify?"

"You didn't notice from the scroll Jasmin so generously gave you?" I grinned at him. "Don't think we didn't notice that in your luggage."

"She insisted, when they stopped by this morning," Luca said, looking sheepish. "And since she turned out not to be a murderer—"

"I'm just glad you didn't decide to be a pirate," William told him.

"I'd miss the mountains too much," Luca assured us both. "Though, I *could* get used to these sunhats . . ."

As he turned his head to show off his look one last time, the wind caught the edge of the hat and nearly whipped it off. We laughed as Luca scrambled to hold on to his beloved accessory.

"Alright, since you asked," I said, once the distraction had died down. "Aly's full name is Alexandrina. And as for Zady . . . couldn't you guess?"

"Not a clue," Luca said, cheerfully.

"I figured all the writing and sage commentary would have been a dead giveaway," I teased him. "But I guess not every story is as clear as you think."

"And not every alibi as strong," William interjected.

"Thank goodness," said Luca, devoutly, before turning back to me. "So? What is it?"

I grinned at them both. "Scheherazade."

Epilogue

My dearest Red,

I am glad to hear you made it back to Belville safe and sound. You are all welcome here any time. Though Aly and I may have to take you up on your offer of a mountain tour—that cafe does sound especially worth a visit!

You'll be glad to hear, I think, that our Babs and Ja'far are doing quite well. Officer Brooks has officially retired; we had a nice ceremony for him with the full moon just after you left. Our two new officers helped present their case admirably at the trial in Oasis, I hear, and the result was a resounding guilty verdict. The criminal herself never once deigned to speak, but fortunately, we had the evidence we needed to piece the story together. Evidence we gathered in large part due to your efforts, my daughter.

And to Sinbad as well—he did have his role, telling his tales about *The Portress*. Much of it, I would have thought, was idle gossip and exaggeration; but it turns out he was right about one thing: banshees, it turns out, do have the power to make things disappear—if only for a short time. And naturally, it *was* Morgiana's family who ran that ship. What a twisted legacy it became.

Nevertheless, I'm sure you will not be surprised to hear that Aly and the sailors are now scouring the estuary for signs of treasure. Fortunately, they have Jasmin's blessing this time.

Jasmin herself has become a common sight in Wellspring, often in the company of her young man. If the fire signs are to be believed, they will be wed before the year is out. Aly and I have placed our bets . . .

But really, the more interesting question is: when will *you* get married, daughter of mine?

All my love,

Zady

Recipes

The recipes included here have been submitted by the residents of Belville, collected (and at times translated) by the author. Mistakes might have been made at any part of the process, but with any luck, these will bring a bit of fun and inspiration to you, our readers! Always feel free to experiment with the recipes included. And if you do, reach out to info@ellehartford.com to let us know how it went!

That said, without further ado . . .

Red and Luca's Easy Flatbread

This adaptation of Aly's recipe is easy to throw together and makes a nice, soft dough. Luca confirms it's doable even for the bread novice!

Makes 6 breads

Ingredients:
    2 C flour (plus a little more for kneading)
    1/2 tsp salt
    3 1/2 Tbsp unsalted butter
    3/4 C milk

1. Combine the butter and milk in a heat-proof bowl and heat until the butter is melted (you could use a stove, double boiler, or—for the more technologically inclined—a microwave).
2. Add the flour and salt to the bowl and mix well.
3. Sprinkle a counter or cutting board with flour and turn out the dough on top. Knead the dough for a few moments until it is smooth. If it is sticky, add a little more flour.
4. Let it rest: wrap the dough in cling wrap or store in a covered bowl. Keep at room temperature for half an hour.
5. Cut the dough into six pieces and roll each piece into a ball, then flatten it out (easiest to do with a rolling pin on a floured surface).
6. Heat a nonstick pan over high heat. Cook the breads one at a time, for about one and a half minutes on the first side—until puffed, with golden spots—and then less than a minute on the other side.
7. Wrap the cooked breads in a tea towel until ready to eat. You can also brush them with olive oil or butter for extra flavor!

* * *

Dean's Iced Sun Tea

Charm your friends—or perhaps your employer—with this flavorful black tea. This basic recipe is unsweetened, but feel free to add honey, sugar, mint, or milk to taste!

Makes 6 Cups

Ingredients:
  6 C filtered water, room temperature
  2 Tbsp loose leaf tea

1. Put the tea leaves into a large glass pitcher and pour the water over top of them.
2. Place pitcher in direct sunlight, perhaps on a sunny windowsill. Let sit for 30 minutes to an hour, depending on preference (a longer time will mean the tea is stronger).
3. Strain the tea into a new pitcher for cooling and serving.
4. Store tea in fridge or enjoy over ice right away!

* * *

Zady's Perfect Picnic Tips

Hosting the perfect picnic is an art, as Zady knows well. Here are her top five tips for planning a luxurious outing with your loved ones and friends.

1. **Pick the right basket.** You'll want something sturdy and easy to carry, of course, but also consider if you need your food or drinks to be kept cold. If so, make sure you have fresh ice packs (or handy spells!).

2. **Know what to do about pests.** This may mean food covers, bug sprays, citronella, or just a watchful eye at all times. Don't let interlopers ruin your carefully-planned outing.

3. **Plan for foods that taste good at room temperature.** Unless you have cold storage—and even if you do—focus your menu on things that are easy and pleasant to eat without heating or cooling. Sandwiches and wraps are classic choices, as well as a variety of salads, sliced veggies, rice balls, or pastries.

4. **Pack your items thoughtfully.** Place the foods you will eat last—for example, desserts—at the bottom of the basket, and the foods you'll want first at the top. This way, you don't have to dig around to find what you need. Also consider using squish-proof containers and small bottles for sauces.

5. **Always include extra utensils, napkins, and a cutting board!** You can't plan for *everything* that will come up, but you can at least be prepared for the basics. Having extra tools handy will make your party feel effortless!

* * *

William's Recipe for Peace of Mind: The Summer Triangle

"This is a good one," says our favorite familiar, "if you want to really impress your friends. It's not a constellation; it's actually a group of three stars, each in a constellation of its own. A group of stars like this is called an asterism. The three particular stars we're interested in are Deneb (in the constellation Cygnus, the Swan), Vega (in the constellation Lyra, the Harp), and Altair (in the constellation Aquila, the Eagle). Cygnus, Lyra, and Aquila all have their own stories, largely based in Greek mythology. How's that for tying together multiple narratives?

"The Summer Triangle is visible in the eastern sky during summer in the Northern Hemisphere. In June and July, it's near the horizon, but by the time August comes around, it'll be high overhead. Just look for the very big triangle with bright shiny points. You can't miss it."

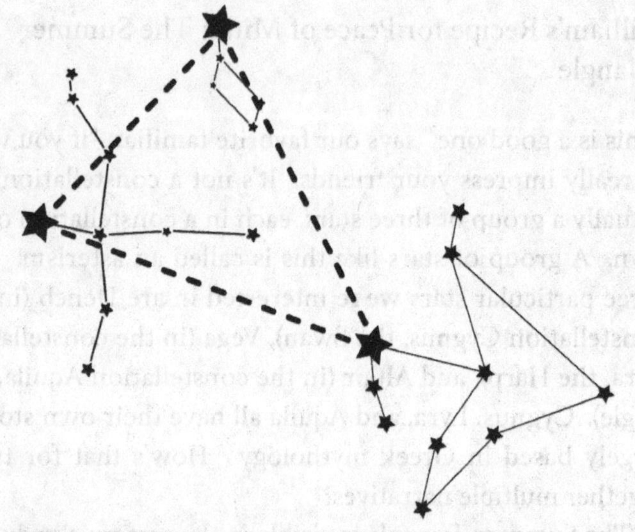

The Summer Triangle
the swan, the harp, and the eagle

Acknowledgments

This has been a homecoming for Red, and likewise it was a labor of love for me! I'm indebted not only to the people who helped me with this book, but to everyone who has helped The Alchemical Tales grow and thrive. You *all* have had a part in Red's adventures, and therefore a part in Red's future, too.

But for this particular book, I am most grateful to my supportive family and my unfailingly encouraging fiance. He always wonders if he is "one of the characters" in the book . . . And my answer is, as always, "not exactly." But our shared love of early twentieth century comedy did inspire one of the new faces in these pages; and I can honestly say that I am lucky to have someone as insightful and thoughtful as Luca in my life.

And finally, as always, I am eternally grateful to the other authors who encouraged me, to Sisters in Crime and Mystery Writers of America, the wonderful book community on Instagram, the Cozy Mystery Tribe, and my amazing ARC readers!

On top of that, I'm thankful to *you*. That means you, reading this! And if you've enjoyed the stories in these pages, I hope you'll take a moment to tell someone or write a review.

About the Author

Elle adores cozy mysteries, fairy tales, and above all, learning new things. As a historian and educator, she believes in the value of stories as a mirror for complicated realities. She currently lives in New Jersey with a grumpy tortoise and a three-legged cat.

Find more stories of Red and her friends at **ellehartford.com**. And while you're there, sign up for Elle's newsletter to get bonus material, behind-the-scenes sneak peeks, and terrible jokes!

Also by Elle Hartford

The Alchemical Tales, a cozy mystery-meets-cozy fantasy series, includes:
Beauty and the Alchemist (book one)
Cold as Snow (book two)
Mermaid for Danger (book three)
Cry Big Bad Wolf (book four)
Cinders to Dust (book five)
Death Pulls the Strings (book six)

A spin-off series of cozy fantasy romance, Pomegranate Cafe Romance, includes:
Worthy in Love (book one)
A Tale of Rowan and Daisy (extra novella)
Strong in Love (book two)
Steady in Love (book three)

And keep an eye out for the upcoming cozy fantasy series, Marine Magic, starting off with *How to Care for Cursed Fish!*